# SLASHED

# SLASHED

## BOOK 2

JO LIGHT

Names: Light, Jo, author

Title: Slashed / Jo Light

Cover design by Teressa J. Martin

ISBN: 978-1-7348823-0-8

FOR MY MOTHER –

Thank you for teaching me to be a strong woman and the value of a little hard work.

SPECIAL THANKS TO THE FOLLOWING PEOPLE:

Miletti for your amazing editing and advice; Teresa for fixing the run-ons; my two beautiful children, Veronica and Christian, whom I love with all my heart; Heni for being my catalyst and muse; Cheryl for being my absolute #1 fan; my Three musketeers: Kimmy, Na, and My; and of course last, but very certainly not least, my family, my friends, and (hopefully) my growing number of readers… You have all made a significant impact in my life- so much so, that it has, and continues to, shape me into the person that was able to have the tenacity to work tirelessly to create this (and more to come)…

THANK YOU!!

# JOHN DOE

# CHAPTER ONE

THE HOTEL ROOM WAS DANK and smelled of stale air, like an old bar room in the early morning hours before its patrons began to arrive to once again fill it with the smell of new smoke, liquor and testosterone filled sweat. Sparse light snuck past the room darkening shades that were purposely drawn in an effort to keep out the already growing number of news station vans littering the small parking lot of the Riverdale Inn.

Detective Emmanuel Castillo, Manny to everyone who knew him, stood in room eleven waiting for Mike Dickerson and his C.S.I. team to conclude their business. As he waited, he watched his partner of six years now, Deshawn Freeman, chat with a uniform nearby. Deshawn's large, linebacker frame towered over the uniformed officer, but his friendly demeanor softened his looming presence. Manny could see them speaking to one another but was not close enough to hear the conversation.

"All set, Manny." Mike Dickerson announced, interrupting Manny's thoughts.

"Yeah, ok." Manny said as his eyes rolled from Deshawn to

Dickerson. "What do you have for me?"

"You've got a John Doe, Caucasian male, mid to late twenties to early thirties. M.E. is putting unofficial time of death within the last thirty-six hours due to the early stages of flaccid rigor. We didn't find any identification; no wallet or belongings of any kind other than the guy's clothes. Hotel clerk says he checked in under a probable fake as Joe Smith and paid cash. Clerk says he was alone when he checked in, but judging by the looks of things, he didn't end up alone. The vic appears to have been deep into some sexual fantasy gone very wrong. His right hand was bound with a zip tie above his head to the bedpost. The left was also zip tied at one point, but the zip tie was cut. At this time, it is unclear as to why. The sliced zip tie was found on the floor near the bed. There are multiple stab wounds to the victim's trunk, arms and legs. There are no apparent defensive wounds which are conducive to him being bound prior to the attack. Blood spatter patterns are indicative of premortem attack. The official report will be given to you guys by Dr. Leavy as soon as she can get one to you." Dickerson finished.

Manny sighed.

*We just got a killer off the streets, and here we are with another one so soon*, he thought.

Manny couldn't help but think of Alex, who he had almost lost to a serial killer. He and Deshawn had barely managed to reach her in time. Manny shot and killed the perpetrator, Robert Benson, Jr.— a psychopath who had become obsessed with Alex.

Dr. Alexandra Aguilar, Manny's closest friend whom he had met in college, was a prominent psychologist in the area. Alex had been helping Manny and Deshawn consult on Benson's case by profiling his behavioral, personality and biographical characteristics as they became available. What they hadn't known was that as they were searching for Benson, Benson had been stalking Alex. Then he kidnapped her, raped her and nearly killed her. Manny shuddered at the memory, so fresh he could almost smell the gunpowder residue on his hands.

"Hey man, you ok?" Deshawn asked, concern on his face.

"Yeah, yeah… You know…. That poor guy." Manny said, gesturing towards the bed where the victim lay.

"Hmm, yeah." Deshawn scoffed.

Manny could tell Deshawn didn't believe him, but that was the least of his worries at that moment.

"Alright, Dickerson, thanks for your help. We will take over from here." Manny ordered.

"You got it. Ok team, let's pack it up and head out." Dickerson ordered.

The room hummed once again with bodies moving about gathering equipment, packing away cameras, brushes, baggies containing evidence, and the sounds of cases snapping shut. The team of crime scene investigators moved quickly, but methodically, like little worker ants each doing their duties—until they were finished and heading out the door. Manny could hear the swarm of reporters attacking the C.S.I. team as they exited the hotel room door, firing questions and demanding answers, to which none were given. Only silence followed, then the turn of the C.S.I. van's engine and doors slamming. Manny smiled.

*Serves them right! News trolls*, he thought.

"You coming?" Deshawn asked, standing next to the bed.

"Hold your horses, Freeman." Manny turned and looked for the M.E.'s assistant.

Manny held up a finger towards the assistant, silently

requesting a few more minutes. The assistant, who was patiently waiting to take the body back to the morgue, nodded in quiet agreement and turned towards the hotel room door. Manny walked over to the bed in no particular hurry to see another corpse.  After so many years on the Homicide Unit, the victims had started to look the same. Manny hated that he was beginning to feel that way, but he was. He thought of Alex again. She was so different than he was in that regard. She always looked at each person, each individual, and tried to find the good in them. Alex kept trying to save everyone. She thought everyone *could* be saved. That was one of the things Manny loved about her. Her faith that good still existed. Manny knew there was very little of it left in the world.

"You are somewhere else today." Deshawn observed.

"Huh?" Manny asked, looking up from the bed.

"Exactly!" Deshawn exclaimed. "You… you are not here are you?"

"I am. I am." Manny protested weakly. "I have a lot on my mind is all."

"Okay, I get it, but remember I am your partner and we are supposed to be able to talk to one another, right?" Deshawn offered gently.

Manny looked away from Deshawn and back to the victim. *Talk? Man, talk about this?  About what kind of sick person could do something like this?  It doesn't compute anymore my friend,* Manny thought as he shook his head back and forth.

"I know, I know. Again, right?  But this is what we do, Manny. We keep the people safe from the bad guys that do sick shit like this." Deshawn answered Manny's silence.

"Do we?" Manny retorted, sounding defeated. "Did we do that here, D?  This guy doesn't look very safe, does he?"

"Nah man, he doesn't. So, we couldn't save this one, but we can get our asses crackin' and catch this crazy motherfucker!" Deshawn beamed his optimistic, big toothed grin at Manny. Manny managed a half smile for his partner. Deshawn always had a way of making things a little less tense, but this go around Manny was having a hard time bouncing back. The heavy weight of another dead victim settled upon his shoulders like the overwhelming guilt a parent feels after not being able to keep the same promise repeatedly to their child. He knew almost losing Alex had a lot to do with his fear of losing more victims, but he wasn't sure how to handle it. He had always been able to push down his emotions and fight through things to solve a case and move to the next. But the inability to shove his feelings aside this time was unnerving.

"You gonna do the honors or can I?" Deshawn asked, his big, goofy smile still plastered on his face.

"Oh please, be my guest." Manny offered, dramatically waving his hand over the body's blanketed form, like a Circus Master introducing the first act.

Deshawn pulled back the white sheet that cloaked the body, revealing a pale, rigid corpse. The zip ties had been removed exposing ligature marks on the man's wrists. A deep, horizontal cut ran the length of his throat approximately three inches below his chin. On his ghost-colored chest, black candle wax had been melted and left to harden, in a sadistic, satanical act.

"Wow, would you look at that!" Deshawn exclaimed. "That's kinky."

"Yeah, a wax and a whack." Manny chuckled, only semi joking.

Dried reddish-brown blood caked around the plethora of stab wounds that marked the victim's colorless body like ancient tribal tattoo art.

"Ha, yeah, guess you could say that." Deshawn snorted.
"Alright, let's let the fella do his job and get this guy to Leavy.
She's gonna want to get going on this one fast." Manny
draped the sheet back over the victim's body.

"Yeah, I'm surprised she ain't blowing up your phone yet."
Deshawn laughed.

"Me too, Pal." Manny agreed.

Manny and Deshawn headed towards the door, peeling
off their vinyl gloves as they went.  Once his gloves were
completely removed, Deshawn clapped Manny on the back.
Manny could feel the tension in his muscles when Deshawn's
hand connected.

"You know I got your back, Manny, right?" Deshawn
giggled.

"Wow, D, you are full of them today, aren't you?"

This time it was Manny's turn to snort.

"Uh huh! I can keep 'em comin' all day long." Deshawn
smiled.

Manny finally smiled his first real smile all day.

"That's a good thing, my friend, because I think I'm gonna
need it."

# CHAPTER TWO

Alexandra Aguilar sat in the unmarked black sedan
with its overly darkened windows, watching the chaos unfold
around her. Two uniformed police officers were posted next
to her vehicle, courtesy of Manny. They flanked the sedan
like two members of England's Royal Guard, stoic and
unmoving. All the while, news reporters and their camera
crew scuttled about the hotel's parking lot as if the ground
was on fire— each scouting for a cool spot to rest their
burning feet. Every reporter wanted the perfect angle, the
sweet spot, from which to film their report on the body
found in room eleven at the Riverdale Inn.

Alex sighed and shook her head. Her anger with Manny had
mostly faded, but it was still present. *How could he make
me stay in the car?* When he had said "let's go get the bad
guys" she thought he meant both of them; as in, he and her.
Not just him!  When they reached the hotel, Manny told
her to remain in the vehicle and he would be back as soon
as he could. She tried to put up a stink, which he quickly
snuffed. Alex sighed again, feeling agitated and a bit sorry

for herself. She knew Manny was only trying to protect her, but it infuriated her that he wouldn't let her make her own decision as to whether she was ready to view a crime scene or not. She could say when she was able to face things again. Unfortunately, this was Manny's arena and he was the referee; if he suggested she wasn't ready for the fight then she wasn't ready.

Alex laid her head back against the seat and closed her eyes. It had been close to four months since she survived Bobby Benson, Jr.'s attack on her, and her body had completely healed. It was her mind that still needed time. Somehow Manny knew this and that is what frustrated her and softened her towards him all at once.  Manny saved her life. He had given her CPR to revive her after she stopped breathing at the scene. Alex had spent a few days in the hospital, and Manny never left her side. Whenever she would wake from whatever drug-induced sleep they were keeping her in, she would see him hunched over in the chair next to her hospital bed, keeping vigil over her. Once she left the hospital, Alex asked Manny to come stay with her for a while. She was unable to return home alone. Since that time, Manny hadn't left her side.

Alex's mind shifted back to the night she finally invited Manny into her bed. He had looked so uncomfortable on the couch.  It was around a month of him staying with her. She got up in the middle of the night to get a glass of water and found him nearly falling off the couch. Alex felt so guilty seeing him like that.  She remembered how he woke with a start, wrinkles of concern fighting for space with the pillow imprints on his face.

"What?  What is it?" he asked startled.

"It's okay. Shh. It's okay. Just come with me." Alex assured him, taking his hand.

Manny did what he was told. He blinked his eyes and squinted them a few times, trying to banish the Sandman's leftovers.

"Alex, where are we going?" he asked, his voice gravelly with sleep.

"To bed." Alex whispered.

"Huh?' Manny asked, confused.

"Manny, hush. Come to bed with me. You were falling off the couch." Alex smirked.

Manny followed Alex into her room. She pulled down the covers on the side of the bed she didn't sleep on and patted the mattress, beckoning him over. Mija meowed in protest from the foot of the bed. Manny had gotten Mija for Alex after Bobby Benson Jr. had murdered her first cat, Elefantito.

"Shh, Mija, it's okay." Alex calmed her.

Manny looked at Alex for reassurance. She nodded and smiled. Still looking a little unsure, like a young boy with his messy bedhead and sleepy face, Manny climbed into bed. Alex covered him with the blankets and tucked them up under his chin, then kissed him gently on the forehead.

"Goodnight, Manny." she whispered.

"Goodnight, sweetie." he whispered back.

Alex smiled, eyes closed, head still back against the seat of the Sedan. After that night, Manny slept every night in her bed with her. Alex was comforted by him being there next to her. He would fold her in his arms so she could lay her head on his chest— her anxiety settled by the beat of his heart against her ear. She felt so safe like that. They never discussed their "relationship" and he never tried anything with her. They hadn't even touched each other in any way other than to cuddle. Manny was kind and respectful, especially after what

Alex had gone through. She wasn't sure she could even try anything close to resembling sex anytime soon. She inhaled deeply and smelled Manny all around her.  It brought her instantly to the night a few weeks ago when he told her he loved her.

They were lying in bed getting ready for sleep, her head on his chest, his arms around her.  Manny kissed her gently on the head. Alex heard him inhale deeply, his nostrils touching her hair, and she giggled. She knew he was smelling her; feeling pieces of her hair lifting as they were being sniffed up into his nose. She tried hard to stifle a laugh.

"What?" he asked, sheepishly.

"You're so weird." Alex snickered again.

"I am not!" he argued. "Why, because I love the smell of your hair?  The smell of you?"

"Um, yeah!" Alex scoffed.

"I don't think that is weird." He laughed.

"Oh no." Alex teased. "Not weird at all."

"Listen, I love the way you smell, okay?" Manny defended himself.

"Mhm." Alex smiled against Manny's chest.

"I do. I love the way you smell. I love the way you laugh. I love your spirit. I love…"

Alex heard Manny take another deep breath in and felt his body tense a bit. He let his breath out slowly, then he spoke.

"I love you, Alex," Manny's voice dropped—deep and full of an emotion she had never heard before— as it caught in his throat.

"Manny…" Alex started, caught off guard.

"I… I'm sorry Alex," Manny cut her off. "It slipped out.  I know it's not a good time. I'm sorry, I shouldn't have…" he trailed off, embarrassed.

"No, Manny, don't do that.  Stop it. It is okay, please.  I, I am, you caught me off guard that's all." Alex stumbled over her words; her stomach tumbling as much as her words.

"No, it isn't the right time." Manny insisted.

Alex could tell by the way his body stiffened that he was upset with himself. She tried to look up at him, but he turned his face away, averting his eyes. Alex sat up on one elbow to face him so that she could gently pull his face towards hers.

"Manny, look at me please."

He did as he was asked. His hazel eyes gazed upon her, searching her face and her eyes. Alex held his gaze for a long moment, carefully choosing her words in her head before replying. Seconds passed before she could muster up the courage to speak them.

"Manny, you are my best friend. I don't know what I would do without you. I would have literally died without you. I would be lost without you…" She paused to look at him and gauge his response.

Manny watched her intently, his eyes still fixed on her face. Alex's body was so close to his that she could feel his heart pounding in his chest. The blood pulsed through her veins, making her own heart pound and her body hot.

"We have been through so much together. Manny, I am so in—"

Alex jumped as the door to the Sedan opened up.

"Hey, sorry. Did I scare you?" Manny asked with concern.

"No, I was dozing off, I guess." she replied, feeling her heart still pounding in her chest and the heat of the memory on her skin. Manny looked at her for a moment longer, then turned to start the engine.  Alex sighed with relief that no more questions followed.

"So?" she asked.

"Well, we have ourselves a John Doe. No identification. Multiple stab wounds. Looks like it started out as consensual sex. He was bound to the bed and his neck was slit. He had some black candle wax melted in a few areas on his chest. They looked like inverted crosses. So, maybe some kind of satanic sex ritual? The vic is in his mid to late twenties to early thirties. Clerk says he paid cash and checked in alone." Manny repeated back the details that Dickerson had given him.

"Multiple stab wounds?" Alex asked.

"Yes." Deshawn, who was sitting next to Manny, replied.

"How many would you guesstimate is multiple in this case?" Alex asked.

"Upwards of thirty?" Deshawn answered.

Alex blew out a whistle from her lips. She sat for a few moments considering the implications of thirty plus stab wounds.

*Interesting*, she thought.

"Hmm." she wondered out loud.

"What?" Manny asked.

"Did you notice a wedding ring on the vic's hand?" Alex asked.

"No, actually I didn't." Manny replied.

"Me either." Deshawn agreed.

"Alex?" Manny questioned.

"A jilted lover maybe? That's a lot of wounds for a typical stabbing. It seems more like a crime of passion, don't you think?" Alex asked Manny and Deshawn.

"Definitely could be." Manny concurred, before changing the subject. "Alex, do you want me to take you home or to the office?" He asked, peering at her through the rear-view mirror.

Alex felt as if she had been punched in the gut. She didn't have time to hide the look of shock from her face before looking up at Manny in the rear-view mirror. She felt the swell of frustration heating her neck and face. Alex turned and looked out the window so that Manny could no longer see her face. She knew that he would recognize her anger at him immediately and did not want to fight with him. It wasn't the time to discuss the matter.  She inhaled deeply and steadied herself before she answered him.

"I guess I will go home for now."

She barely recognized her own voice. The tone was thin, almost flat, and sounded forced to her own ears.  She was sure Manny would notice, but it was all she could manage for the moment.

Manny either didn't notice or chose to ignore her for some reason— he smiled and replied, "as you wish", then steered the sedan towards the highway that led to Alex's, and now his, home. Alex became furious.  She was supposed to be a part of the team. She had always been, since Manny and Deshawn had become partners. She was there with them, consulting on their murder cases from the beginning. She had gone for continuing education so that she had more Criminal Justice background and knowledge make her more qualified to consult on such cases.

*What is he doing?*

She knew he was trying to protect her but enough was enough. She was going to have to talk to him. There was no way she could let this continue. She watched the cars and counted them one by one, taking a deep breath and blowing it out as each one passed. It was one of many great coping mechanisms she had in her arsenal to calm herself. After a while, the angst subsided, but she would not forget the anger and how it made her feel. As Manny drove, Alex silently vowed to speak to him when he returned home that evening.

# CHAPTER THREE

THE SUN WAS BEAMING AS IT SMILED down the warmth of ending summer from its blue celestial backdrop. The temperatures had gradually risen to the low eighties during the day in the last few weeks— comfortably single for now from their usual summer partner of humidity. Manny wished for a brief moment he could enjoy the beauty of the day rather than return to the precinct and dive into another murder case.

*I'm losing my drive,* he thought.

Manny watched Alex get into the house safely before pulling away from the sidewalk.  She was quiet on the ride home. The tension coming from her had been thick. Manny thought it better to pretend he didn't notice. He made small talk with Deshawn until they arrived at the house. Alex hadn't joined in.

Deshawn fiddled with his house keys while Manny drove. They jingled, breaking the monotonous silence between the small talk. The silence didn't bother Manny, though. It was never uncomfortable around Deshawn.

"Hey, you and Alex wanna come over for dinner? Muriel

is whipping up pulled pork. Man, oh man, I cannot wait." Deshawn whistled his excitement for his wife's cooking. Normally, Manny would jump at the chance to have Muriel's home cooking. She was an extraordinary cook, and pulled pork was one of her specialties. But Manny had a sinking feeling that he might be in for a bit of a "chat" when he got home that evening. Before heading to the crime scene, he had tried to get Alex to stay home, but she had insisted on going with him. He was able to get her to stay in the car, but just barely. He knew he was going to hear about that and about him not asking her to return to the precinct with them to go over the case.

"I don't know, D, let me see how she is when I get home." Manny sighed.

"Oh, yeah. Alright brother, no pressure. I know she was pissed." Deshawn whistled again, but this time it was the "boy are you in trouble" kind of whistle.

"Ha!" Manny laughed out loud. "Yeah, you could say that again."

"You know, she kinda has a right to be mad." Deshawn challenged Manny tentatively.

"Hey, what?"

Manny was slightly taken aback that his partner— his friend— was siding with Alex on this one. Deshawn should understand that all he was trying to do was protect her. He almost lost her.

*Why doesn't anyone get that? Does everyone forget that Alex almost died?*

"Listen, Manny. She is a big girl."

"Yeah, yeah, I get that. Thanks for the reminder, but I think I know that already." Manny laid his head back and looked at the ceiling.

"Well, what is she saying about it? I mean, you have asked her about it, right?" Deshawn asked.

"Of course I have, D. She says she is fine." Manny looked at Deshawn again, then rolled his eyes.

"Well, then if she says she is fine then she is fine." Deshawn confirmed as if he had a front row seat in Alex's head.

"No, it's not fine. She's not fine. It's not fine." Manny argued. "Alex is stubborn. She says she is fine. And yes, her body is fine, thankfully fully healed. It's her mind, her memories, *her* that I am concerned with. Do you see what I'm getting at here?" Manny spoke with urgency.

Deshawn sat quietly for a moment. Manny took in a deep breath hoping to bring oxygen to the constricted blood vessels that felt as if they were being squeezed to near popping capacity. Manny reflected on what Alex had endured...the torture her body and mind had gone through. His stomach lurched when images of what that animal had done to her pushed their way into his thoughts. Manny had been lying next to her every night since she brought him into her bed. He had to resist many times the desire to touch her and kiss her. Her smell and the feeling of her body so close to him nearly drove him crazy at times. He knew her mind was so fragile, and it may be for some time to come. He wasn't sure how he could help her, but he knew what he couldn't do and that was to force himself on her in any way. Alex was going to have to be the one to make all the moves. He just had to be patient, no matter how much it killed him.

"I get it, buddy, I do. I don't know what I would do if anything like that ever happened to Muriel. I would definitely flip my shit." Deshawn paused, contemplating his next words carefully. "I know Alex a little too though, and even though I know she is stubborn, I know she is strong.

Like you. Maybe wait and see. Give her the benefit of the doubt, you know. Give her a chance and if it seems like it's getting to be too much for her, pull the plug."

Manny considered what Deshawn said for a few moments. Manny pulled into the parking garage and parked the sedan in one of the designated squad car spots. He turned the key in the lock cylinder to kill the engine then looked at Deshawn.

"I don't want to, you know that." Manny sighed.

"I know." Deshawn nodded.

"It goes against every single protective fiber in my being." Manny protested again.

"I know." Deshawn nodded, again.

"I wanna lock her up in the house and never let her out in this shitty, evil world again." Manny growled.

"I know." Deshawn agreed again, his tone matching Manny's. Manny sighed, resigned.

"You stuck on repeat or something?" Manny asked with a sad attempt at a laugh.

"I *don't* know." Deshawn chuckled.

"Hmm, I am not sure if you are actually kidding or serious on that one." Manny observed. "But getting back to Alex and keeping her hidden."

"Yup?"

"I can't do that though, can I?" Manny asked in a joking manner, but in reality, he was serious.

"No. You can't." Deshawn agreed.

"Shit." Manny moaned.

"She has us, bro." Deshawn reminded him.

"I thought that before, too, D. In fact, I was super confident in that very thought, and look what happened."

"Manny, you gotta find a way to let that shit go. There wasn't much we could have done with that, and you know it. We will tighten up the ranks. So maybe, just maybe, it is better if she is with us more than not."

Manny considered this for a moment. He hadn't thought of it like that.

*Leave it to Deshawn to put it into perspective,* he thought. Manny was almost convinced to buy what Deshawn was selling when his cell phone rang.

"Castillo here."

"Hey, Manny, it's Leavy. I am heading down to the morgue to perform the autopsy. I didn't know if you and Freeman wanted to come join to get a sort of prelim." Dr. Leavy's sounded breathless.

*She must be walking down now,* Manny thought.

"Wow, yeah sure that would be great!" Manny's curiosity piqued.

"Okay, see you when you get here!" Dr. Leavy hung up the phone clogging Manny's ear with silence.

"That was Leavy. She is about to start the autopsy and asked if we wanted to go in to watch to get a heads up on the prelim."

Deshawn looked like he chugged a glass of sour milk. Manny laughed. He knew Deshawn was not a fan of the morgue. Manny couldn't help but wonder how a big tough guy like Freeman, who worked in the Homicide Unit and saw dead bodies frequently, turned into a squeamish schoolgirl when it came to the morgue and autopsies.

"Come on Freeman, it will be fun." Manny teased.

"Oh yeah," Deshawn whined "I can't wait."

# CHAPTER FOUR

THE REAR ENTRANCE OF NEWBURY HOSPITAL was a formidable barrier at which Manny and Deshawn waited to gain access. A matching gray call box hung on the concrete wall next to the gray, unmarked door. Manny opened its lid to call the security officer in charge of who could enter and who could not.

"Security." the voice on the other end answered.

"Hi, this is Detective Castillo here to see Dr. Leavy in the morgue."

"Hold."

Manny returned the receiver back to its cradle and placed the cover back over its box. Within the next minute a buzzing sound emanated from the door announcing their admittance. Deshawn pushed on the bar that draped the middle of the metal door, like a steel belt worn for function rather than fashion. The door closed quietly behind them with a click. Manny looked at Deshawn to gauge his mood. He appeared to be holding up well, so Manny turned and headed down the hall of concrete walls and overhead fluorescent lights with Deshawn closely on his tail.

The first door on the right was the security office. They stopped there first to check in and secure their weapons. They could not take their firearms into the morgue. The security officer scrutinized their badges and wrote down the serial numbers to each of their handguns. He carefully placed the safety on both weapons and unloaded them. A safety lock box was opened, the weapons were placed in, and the safety box was again locked. Once Manny and Deshawn were done at the morgue they would come back and have their firearms returned to them. The security guard nodded the "okay" to go.

At the end of the hall on the left was a door marked "morgue" painted on frosted glass. Manny pushed the button to the right of the door, and a muddled voice came over the loudspeaker.

"Morgue. State your business." the voice insisted.

"Detective Castillo here to see Dr. Leavy." Manny announced, once again.

"Hold." The voice demanded.

Manny looked at Deshawn in time to see him roll his eyes. A few seconds later another buzz, similar to the first one on the loading docks, projected itself seemingly from the frosted glass door. Manny turned the handle and let himself and Deshawn into the entrance to the morgue. A small front office was the first room they entered. A robust woman looked up at them from behind the desk, unenthusiastic about their arrival.

"I need to see some I.D. and you will both need to sign in on the visitors' log."

The monotone voice belonged to a woman that was definitely bored with her job.

Manny and Deshawn both displayed their badges and signed

the log sheet as directed. Without looking up at them a second time, the woman began whatever paperwork she had been previously working on and addressed them one last time.

"She is in the Autopsy Suite. Go into the locker room and change into scrubs and booties then you can join her. You can leave your clothes in one of the lockers. Don't worry, no one will bother them as there isn't anyone else scheduled to drop in."

The woman pointed a chubby finger towards the only other door, (besides the door from which they had entered), in the room. Manny and Deshawn had been here before, but they had never met this woman, and she had never met them. So, she assumed they didn't know what they were doing or where they were going. Manny played along.

"Okay, thank you." he responded.

The plump woman huffed an inaudible blurp.

Manny looked at Deshawn. Deshawn looked back at him and shrugged. They turned and walked through the unmarked door. The door led them into a short hallway that contained three more doors; one on each side and one dead center at the end of the hall. The door on the left was labeled "locker room", the door on the right was labeled "office", and the door straight ahead was labeled "autopsy suite". Manny knew there were two more rooms off the Autopsy Suite; the positive temperature room, nicknamed the "Decomp room", and the negative temperature room, nicknamed "the Froze Zone".

The Decomp room was usually kept around 39 degrees Fahrenheit to slow the rate of decomposition until the body could be autopsied. The "Froze Zone" room was typically kept around negative 58 degrees Fahrenheit, which would completely freeze the body. That room was mainly used for bodies that had not been, or could not be, identified.  Manny could hear Deshawn suck in a breath and knew he had locked eyes on the door. Manny had to stop himself from laughing.

"Ready to change up?" he asked Deshawn.

"Nope." Deshawn shook his head vehemently.

"Well, ready or not, here we go." Manny walked through the "locker room" door.

"Damn it." Deshawn uttered, and followed.

The locker room glowed from the fluorescent lights that hummed quietly above them. A wall of empty lockers stood patiently waiting to be used, their numbers either faded, or completely missing. Some of them had chipped paint, revealing the metal underneath, like the exposed bone of a corpse. Against the wall adjacent to the lockers was a shelf that held four stacks of neatly folded blue scrubs labeled in different sizes. Next to the piles of scrubs stood a bucket of plastic packages that held overshoe booties. Manny walked to where the scrubs sat and grabbed an XL and an XXL.  They changed and threw their street clothes into the lockers, not worrying about the fact that they didn't have a lock to secure their belongings. The cranky gate keeper out front had given them the unsolicited information that no one else would be let in during the autopsy unless Dr. Leavy allowed it— and as far as Manny knew, Leavy hadn't invited anyone else. Once they donned their scrubs and overshoe booties, they walked down the hall to the Autopsy Suite. Manny could hear faint murmurings through the door. He looked at Deshawn and this time even Manny had to prepare himself for the smells he knew were about to assault his nostrils.

"Okay, buddy, I'm ready, are you ready?"

"Let's do this!" Deshawn's shaky, false bravado was unconvincing.

Manny opened the door and the smell of disinfectant and Formalin smacked them in the face. The astringent was strong, but still not enough to completely disguise the smell of decaying flesh. Tears formed at the corners of Manny's eyes as they began to sting from the chemicals. He had to concentrate hard not to reach up and rub them. He heard Deshawn clearing his throat behind him. Once his eyes adjusted, he looked around. Manny had been here before, but for some reason each time was like the first. He never quite got used to it. The bright lights, the smells, the harshness of the light reflecting of the stainless-steel things—from the sinks to the surgical tools used to slice and dice. The bright red biohazard buckets for blood-soaked materials, sharps needles and razor blades were positioned, like strange stop signs, in various places around the autopsy suite. The whole idea that the tile floors had drains built into them to wash the blood off the floors, and the autopsy tables had "troughs" built into them to also wash the blood down, still gave Manny the creeps.

"Oh, there you are boys." Dr. Leavy looked up from the cadaver, ripping Manny from his morbid thoughts.

A mousy girl with large rimmed black glasses and thick lenses that rivaled her boss's, peeked from behind Dr. Leavy and looked up at them as they entered the room. Her white lab coat was embroidered with her name, Sara, and her title, M.E. Assistant. Manny nodded at her. Timid Sara, M.E. Assistant, looked away.

"Yes, sorry we took so long." Manny gave Dr. Leavy an apologetic smile.

"No worries." Leavy didn't look up again. She continued

examining the corpse as she spoke. "The victim has been photographed, weighed and fingerprinted. We charted his dental restorations and missing teeth. He is a Caucasian male, mid to late thirties. Weight is one hundred and forty pounds. Dark brown hair with brown eyes. Fingerprints were not found in AFIS. Nothing significant in his dental charting other than one tooth— his central incisor number nine— does have an existing root canal and a porcelain fused to metal crown. He also had his wisdom teeth extracted. Most likely in his late teens. Only one other restoration in his head on tooth number two. It is an older amalgam filling on the occlusal surface only.  Hopefully, if no one comes forward, his lack of dental work will actually help us find out who he is. We can start with local dental offices, then spread out the search from there, if need be."

Leavy took a breath and looked up to make sure Manny and Deshawn were paying attention. When she was satisfied that they were sufficiently intrigued, she continued.

"He has been completely x-rayed from head to toe. No breaks or fractures were noted other than a very old hairline fracture visualized in his fifth metatarsal. As you can see, I have already completed the Y incision and removed the breast plate along with all the organs. They have been weighed, sampled and tagged. Toxicology and serology reports will be here in a few days, hopefully. I just peeled the scalp and removed the front part of the skull. I was about to examine the brain in situ and take samples. So far though, there has been no evidence of blunt force trauma. I didn't expect any as there were no visible external contusions to the head area." Dr. Leavy continued giving Manny and Deshawn her unofficial preliminary report. As she spoke, she pointed to parts of the victim's body, like Vanna White directing the audience's attention to the next letter on the board.

The victim was laid out on the stainless-steel autopsy table stark naked, the pallor of death exponential under the bright lights of the exam room. The body cavity was empty and clean, the spine and skeletal bones visible with all the organs removed. Manny glanced at it briefly, then at Deshawn to check on him. His brow shined under the lights, but he seemed steady enough on his feet. Manny turned his gaze to the exposed brain. The scalp had been peeled back and the front portion of the bony skull removed with a small saw, to expose the shiny gray peaks and valleys of brain matter. Dr. Leavy examined the brain for a few moments; then with petite, gloved hands she removed the brain with gentle precision, placing it in the metal scale that hung from the ceiling, to weigh it.

"Sara, grab this weight." Leavy ordered.

Timid Sara scrambled over to the white board that hung on the wall and retrieved the black marker to write down the weight.

"Ready, Dr. Leavy." Sara squeaked.

"We have 1,334 grams." Leavy announced. "Pretty darn average." she scoffed.

"Typical man brain huh, Dr. Leavy?" Deshawn chuckled.

"I'd say so." Leavy giggled.

The sound reverberated off the cold tile walls of the autopsy suite. They all looked at each other briefly, then burst out laughing. Even Timid Sara allowed herself a small chuckle. Dr. Leavy removed the brain from the scale and placed it on the shelf that coupled one of the many stainless-steel sinks. She removed samples using a small instrument that allowed her to take punch biopsies of the brain tissue. She placed each sample in a small plastic cassette with stain and a label so each one could be sent to the lab. Manny watched with fascination. After a few moments, Dr. Leavy returned the brain and all the other organs to their owner.  She ordered Sara to begin stitching up the incisions.

"Okay, boys, so here's what I've got. I'm going to wait on the tox screen. It should be back in a few days. No blunt force trauma noted. Multiple stab wounds of different depths were counted for a grand total of forty-four, which leads me to believe this is a crime of passion. I was unable to ascertain what kind of knife was used as the weapon was never fully embedded into the victim. But I would guess, based on the width and diameter I could measure, possibly some sort of hunting knife. But, you're curious how I know the knife wasn't fully embedded?" Leavy looked at them with a smug smile. "Anyone care to take a guess?"

Manny and Deshawn looked at Dr. Leavy, then one another, then looked back at Dr. Leavy. Manny knew Allison well; she loved to explain things, almost "got off" on it.

"No takers?" Leavy waited, still smiling.

"Okay. My turn then. There were no hilt abrasions or bruising present. Therefore, I am unable to gauge the true length of the blade the assailant used. I can say the cause of death is exsanguination. The victim did have a horizontal throat slash, which due to the length, depth, and placement of the wound I can confidently say the vic got while on his back. Which came first, the throat or stabbing, I cannot confidently say. I will however offer this," Dr. Leavy paused to take a breath. "I strongly believe the assailant to be a woman."

Manny felt his mouth open slightly of its own accord. He closed it quickly.

*A woman? Very interesting.*

"Okay. Sure, it's very assumable, considering how we found him. Any other reason you believe that than the sexual inference based on the evidence we found at the scene?" Manny answered.

"I believe this because the depth of the stab wounds were not that great. Had it been a man I feel they would have been deeper; with more force comes more depth. I believe this is a woman of small stature. Petite." Dr. Leavy finished.

"Okay, thank you." Manny gave Dr. Leavy a grateful smile. "That helps a lot, Allison."

Dr. Leavy returned the gesture.

"No problem. I am always glad to help. You got lucky that I wasn't that swamped, and I was interested." Dr. Leavy smiled coyly at Manny. He tried to brush it off politely.

"Thanks Dr. Leavy." he returned to professional titles, hoping she would get the point. "So, I am assuming John Doe will return to the Decomp room for now at least for a few days until we are sure we either have a positive I.D. or we don't? Then you'll transfer him to the Froze Zone if we don't?" Manny asked.

Dr. Leavy frowned, but it didn't take her long to recover.

"Yeah, sure. I will buy you a little time." she winked.

Manny nodded. "Thanks."

"No problem, Manny. You know I am always here when you need me. And," she added as if to drive home her point. "I know you have my number." Dr. Leavy smiled once more at Manny, then turned her back to him.

"Alright, Sara, let's finish up here. I need some lunch."

Manny knew that was their invitation to leave. He turned to Deshawn and nodded towards the door.

"Okay D, let's roll"

"Nothing would give me more pleasure, buddy."

# CHAPTER FIVE

Alex sat, impatiently, at the kitchen table waiting for Manny to get home. It was ignorant of her, she knew, as there was never a specific time he could get home. Yet, she sat there at the table and waited. She was still upset, although her initial fury had subsided. She was a little irritated and maybe a bit resentful. Sighing, she laid her head upon her folded hands. Her coffee had grown cold some time ago and her stomach growled its own resentment at having not been fed all day, but she was in no mood for such mundane tasks at that moment.

Darkness blanketed the windows over an hour ago, leaving Alex in the tenebrous shadows of night, yet she made no move to brighten the kitchen. She continued her vigil at the table, mulling over how she would confront Manny when he returned home.

*Return home*, she thought. *How funny that sounds.*

Neither one of them had ever really spoken about it— it just kind of happened. After she asked him to stay with her, he had never returned back to his apartment. He still kept it. "In case." she whispered.

They never sat down to have any "official discussion" about anything. Everything that happened so far "just happened", and Alex was grateful for that. Talking about things was very difficult for her. It always was. She scoffed at the irony of it: a psychologist, someone who was paid to get people to talk about, and then listen to, their problems and give them advice, actually having difficulty discussing her own issues. Alex snorted out loud in the empty kitchen. The echo surprised her, and she jumped at the noise. Laughter burst from her lips when she realized how absurd she must seem. Just then, Manny walked in.

"Oh, well, what's so funny?" he asked, a half smile on his face, but confusion in his eyes.

Alex, embarrassed, swallowed her laugh as soon as she saw him.

"Nothing much, just some self-deprecating humor I guess." she answered, swiping at her tearing eyes. "You are home at O-dark-hundred."

Manny seemed to ignore the jab and took off his coat. He hung it on the coat rack near the door and removed his shoes, groaning slightly when he stood.

"Yeah, D and I wound up going down to the morgue to see the autopsy of the vic."

"You don't say!" Alex exclaimed.

*Hm, isn't that interesting, Leavy giving a private show,* Alex thought. A hot poker of jealousy stabbed at Alex's belly.

"And?" she prodded.

"You were right. Leavy concurs with you about the crime of passion. She counted forty-four stab wounds."

Alex sat for a moment, quiet.

"Is this coffee old and cold?" he asked.

Alex heard Manny from a distance, as if he were speaking

from behind a thick glass wall. Her mind was running on overdrive.

"Yup." she answered robotically.

Alex didn't seem to notice when Manny returned to the table and sat down to face her. She was deep in thought and for a moment she didn't see him. Then, as if being woken from a dream, she turned her gaze upon him.

"Listen…"

"Listen…"

They both spoke at the same time. They tried again, each speaking at the same time again.

"Go ahead." Manny, always the gentleman, invited.

"No, you go." Alex insisted, deferring to her usual "avoidance" of having to talk herself.

"Okay, if you insist." Manny sighed.

He smiled and managed a little chuckle. Alex would usually offer a giggle in return but tonight she only managed a half smile, out of courtesy. By the way he held his face, Alex could tell he understood he was in trouble.

"Okay, so, I have been doing a lot of thinking, and I was wrong." he blurted out.

*Wait, what? Did he say what I think he did?*

Alex studied him for a moment, but it was proving more difficult in the ever-darkening kitchen.

*I wish I had turned on at least one light.*

"Go on." she encouraged him— he also had a difficult time expressing his feelings.

"Okay, I was wrong to tell you what I felt you could and couldn't handle. You should be able to say what you can and can't handle. You know yourself better than anyone. I was only doing it to protect you. I love you, and I almost lost you once. I was only doing it out of fear of losing you again. I realize I cannot keep you in a bubble for the rest of your life. This is your work, OUR work, and I had no right to keep you from it. Especially when I need you. I need you with me. I have always needed you. I will always need you." Manny's voice trembled as he spoke.

Like an early morning mist dissipated when the sun radiated its heat upon it, the warmth in Alex's chest burned away whatever anger remained towards Manny. She knew he was trying to protect her but hearing the emotion in his voice made it real and tangible for her, not just an assumption. A tear slipped down her cheek and she shivered slightly. She reached up a hand and ran it against his rough stubble. He pushed his warm face into her soft palm, welcoming the contact. Alex's heart raced. She loved him deeply. He always thought of her first. How could she have been so angry with him? She was so selfish, so self-centered.

She moved closer to him until she could place her forehead gently against his. This close intimacy was something she had never had and couldn't imagine having with anyone else, ever. Manny's warm breath brushed against her skin, awakening something inside her. The desire to kiss him overwhelmed her. Before she lost her nerve, she gently placed her other hand on his other cheek and tilted his face to meet hers. Alex closed her eyes and took a deep breath.

Suddenly their lips were together, soft and connected, for the first time. A scary, yet exhilarating, feeling for Alex— like the time Abuela took her to the amusement park and they ventured onto the largest roller coaster there. Alex had been afraid of heights but Abuela told her that she must always try to face her fears. Alex remembered being at the very top of that roller coaster, right before it was about to descend— the fear and excitement that had coursed through her body—

then the flip of her belly as the roller coaster soared down its steep slope. That was the feeling she had now.

Manny's body stiffened at first in surprise, then it relaxed, and he was kissing her, gently. A small moan came from the back of his throat. Alex's entire body tingled excitedly. Manny moved closer and she felt a hand on the back of her head. Alex's heart began to race, and her breath caught in her throat. The hand grew strong, holding her tight. Panic rose like a tidal wave inside her.

*Oh my god, no,* she thought.

Fear gripped her from somewhere deep within. She pushed away from Manny's lips.

"No!" she screamed.

Alex broke free from the embrace and ran to her room.

Alex's lips were soft, and they tasted better than he had imagined they would. He wasn't expecting her to kiss him, but he certainly wasn't going to pull away. He moaned. He couldn't help himself. She felt amazing. Her hands were on his face, her lips were on his, and he had waited for what seemed an eternity for this moment.

Manny reached up and put his hand behind her head to steady her and hold her. He wanted to hold her and never let her go. His excitement was growing. His entire body quaked with it so much so that he missed the feel of Alex's body stiffening. He kissed her deeper, pulling her into him.

Suddenly Alex broke from his lips. She looked terrified.

"No" she screamed.

She looked at him as if she had never seen him before.

*What the...? Alex...*

Before he could say anything, Alex bolted for her room,
leaving him alone and confused.

*Oh, Alex, honey. Damn it, how could I have been so stupid!*
He walked slowly to her room. When he reached the door,
he knocked softly. Muffled cries found their way to his ears
from the other side of the door.

"Alex, honey."

No response, just quiet sobs.

He turned the doorknob. It wasn't locked. He walked in
slowly. Alex was sprawled out, face down on the bed, crying.
Manny's heart ached for her. He was angry at himself for
not going slower. She had finally made a move, and he had
botched it up.

*Damn it, Castillo,* he scolded himself.

"Alex, honey." he tried again.

"Oh, Manny." she cried, nearly imperceptible from the
pillow she had her face planted in.

"May I sit?" Manny asked.

Alex nodded; her face still buried in the pillow.

Manny sat next to her on the bed.

"May I touch you?" he asked.

Again, she nodded. Manny rubbed her back gently.

"You know as well as I do that you have PTSD and things are
going to trigger you. It is okay. We will work through this.
It's always much easier to be the doctor than the patient, isn't
it?" Manny asked calmly.

Alex lay still. The sobbing had stopped, for which Manny
was grateful. He knew what he had to say to her to make her
feel better, but how was he going to make himself feel better?
He felt horrible for triggering her like that. It was going to be
a long, tricky road to her recovery

Finally, after what seemed like hours, Alex rolled over to face him. Her eyes were red rimmed, and blood shot as if she had worn her contacts for too long. Manny gently brushed a piece of hair from her face.

"I'm sorry." she whispered.

"Don't you dare." he warned.

"But I am. I am sorry that I'm all messed up. I am a freaking psychologist for God's sake. I should be able to work this out and get myself up and running."

Alex went from sad to angry in seconds. Manny could see the fury flash across her eyes. Her cheeks flushed with more color than they already held. It reminded Manny of when he was a kid and his Abuelita used to pinch his cheeks every time she would see him and say" Mirate, Manuelito, volviendote tan gordito, mi querido." (Look at you, Manny, you're getting so chubby, my love). Manny had to refrain from smiling at the memory—Alex was pissed, and he was not about to feed her rage.

"It is going to take some time, honey. You have to give yourself a little time. You can't expect to snap back like a rubber band. You were put through the ringer. You know that and I know that. What would you say to a patient who had the same experience?"

Alex lay there contemplating what Manny said for a moment. She seemed somewhat satisfied with his reasoning for now because she didn't argue with him. She absentmindedly bit her lower lip, deep in thought. Manny loved when she did that, it was so sexy.

*Stop it,* he scolded himself. *That is what got you here in the first place.*

He took a deep breath and patted her gently on the leg.

"Yo tengo hambre chica— I'm starving." he announced.

"Hmm, actually now that you mention it, I am too. I didn't

eat today."
Manny frowned at her disapprovingly.
"I know, I know, but I was upset." she admitted.
"Okay, but still no reason to starve yourself." he reprimanded softly.
"Yeah, yeah, yeah." Alex waved a hand to shoo Manny off the bed so she could get up.
"Let's grab some Chinese." she smiled.
Alex pulled the sleeve of her sweatshirt down and swiped recklessly at her tear stained face. Manny smiled and shook his head at her.
*I love you woman. You have no idea.*
"What?" she asked quizzically.
"Hm?"
"Why are you staring at me like that?" she demanded.
Alex smiled and frowned at the same time. Manny knew that face. She was analyzing him. Honesty was always the best policy with Alex— she had a way of gazing right into your soul. "Like a beautiful bruja" his mother would have said.  Manny would have laughed and, respectfully, argued that Alex was not a witch, but rather, a woman with great intuition.
"I was thinking how beautiful you are, even when you cry." he murmured.
"Oh, brother." Alex scoffed. "I'll make you a deal." She offered.
"Depends what it is." He bartered. "Shoot."
"You don't say anymore corny stuff like that over dinner, and I will buy." Alex laughed.
Manny grinned.
"Hm, let me think about it." He rubbed at his thicker than most five o'clock shadow.

Alex slapped him playfully on the arm.
"Sounds yummy. Okay, you got yourself a deal, Aguilar."

# CHAPTER SIX

MANNY AND DESHAWN SAT AT THEIR DESKS playing
with their empty Sip N' Donuts wrappers and nearly empty
Styrofoam coffee cups. The Homicide Unit chattered with
the noise of phones, the click of keyboards and footsteps of
uniformed officers. A cacophony to any outsider's ears, but a
sweet symphony to veterans like Manny and Deshawn.
"Yo, I'm still hungry." Deshawn announced.
"Yeah, I knew two sandwiches weren't going to be enough for
you." Manny laughed, shaking his head.
Deshawn stood over six-foot-tall and weighed in at over two
hundred pounds but was far from overweight. His dense
sinewy muscle, from years of football and long, hard hours in
the gym, writhed under his dark, taut skin when he moved—
like tiny snakes trapped under saran wrap. He had declined
a pro football career to follow in his family's footsteps as an
officer of the law. His wife, Muriel, liked to joke about his
"feeding schedule". She insisted that it was not easy to keep
the man "maintained", calling it "quite the undertaking".
Manny remembered Muriel telling him one night over
dinner about their grocery store outings.

"Now I will tell you, sir, it sure is a sight to be seen. You should see us pushing two full shopping carts around, filt' — to the brim. Sometimes spillin' over." Muriel giggled, her Georgia accent even more endearing after a bottle of wine. "And the bill? Oh, my Lord, please do not get me started. Poor lil' Justice will have to get a job soon to pay for his own food so daddy can eat."

Manny smiled, remembering how they all laughed dubiously at Muriel's recount of the Freeman's weekly grocery outings.

"What is so funny?" Deshawn asked, smiling.

"Aw, nothing." Manny laughed.

"Uh huh."

"I was remembering the time Muriel was telling me about your grocery store visits." Manny chuckled.

"Ha!" Deshawn boomed.

The two laughed together for a few minutes before either was able to speak again.

"Well, I could seriously use another cup of Joe." Manny disputed.

"Yeah, me too. Another couple of sandwiches and another cup of coffee would set my belly just right." Deshawn sat back in his chair and patted his six pack. Amazingly it almost sounded empty to Manny's ears. Manny shook his head in disbelief.

"What did Muriel pack you for lunch?" Manny asked.

Like one of Pavlov's dogs, Manny's mouth began to water at the thought of Muriel's cooking.

"Mmm, I love that woman." Deshawn licked his lips. "She packed me half a smoked chicken, some corn on the cob, mashed potatoes and collard greens. I ate all the cornbread last night, so I didn't have any for today."

Deshawn shook his head sadly. Manny shook his head in

disbelief. Even after six years, Deshawn still astonished him at times. He had this way about him. Manny crumpled up his sandwich wrapper and threw it in the garbage pail that was regurgitating papers next to his desk, then regretted not throwing it at Deshawn instead.

"It would seem the cleaning fairy forgot to come by last night." he laughed.

Deshawn chuckled.

"Yup, they must have cut back on the janitorial budget again."

"Yeah, well, better their budget than ours." Manny snorted. There was a large stack of papers on Manny's desk, and they rustled when he shuffled through them. He picked one up and studied it before saying anything to Deshawn.

"It's been about forty hours since we found our vic and no I.D. yet. Leavy informed me she put a rush on the toxicology report so we should have that back shortly. If we don't get any leads soon, I'm thinking of heading back over to the Riverdale Inn and talking to the clerk again to see if I can jog anything else from his brain. I was hoping I could–"

"Excuse me." a timid female voice, raspy from crying by the sound of it, interrupted Manny mid-sentence.

"Yes?" Manny nodded.

A painfully thin brunette peered down at him with haunted eyes.

"Are you Detective Castillo?" she asked.

Her quiet voice was barely audible over the din of the hustle and bustle of the unit.

"Yes. Can I help you Miss…?" Manny encouraged softly, as he stood and reached out to take her hand.

"Mrs. Stanton." she informed him.

Her small, frail fingers were boney and cold in his large

hand.  Manny carefully closed his fingers over hers and shook
gingerly.

"Okay, Mrs. Stanton, how may we help you? Please." Manny
motioned to the chair that sat next to his desk for Mrs.
Stanton to sit.

Mrs. Stanton nearly fell into the chair, her meager frame
shaky. Her brittle brown hair was messy— a close resemblance
to a bird's nest of a bun sat atop her small head— and
threatened to unloose itself at any moment. Her puffy eyes
betrayed her lack of sleep and crying spells. Mrs. Stanton's
lower lip— chapped and red from repeated licking—
tremored. Manny found himself hoping he could help the
poor woman with whatever was ailing her.

"Hi, yes, I'm sorry to disturb you. I know, I mean, I'm sure
you are rather busy." She stumbled over her words, unsure of
herself.

"Go on, Mrs. Stanton, it's okay." Manny reassured her.

"Okay, well, you see, my husband Leo, Mr. Leo Stanton, he
hasn't come home." Mrs. Stanton choked out the last word
before she began to sob.

Manny snuck a peek at Deshawn, who was watching him.
Deshawn spied the box of Kleenex at the edge of his desk
and reached for a few tissues. He practically threw them
at Manny as if they were already contaminated with Mrs.
Stanton's snot. Manny raised an eyebrow at Deshawn before
he handed the snot cleaners politely to the distressed woman.

"Mrs. Stanton, can you tell us a little more information?"
Manny urged gently.

"Well," she sniffled, "he called me from work and told me
he and some of the guys were going to go over to The Lark,
you know the bar on Pleasant Street?" she looked at Manny
and Deshawn to make sure they were following her. They

both nodded in unison to show their engagement, so she continued.

"He said they were gonna go for a few drinks. They do that sometimes after work, ya know. Even on a weeknight. They don't always wait for Fridays, which I don't like, but Leo doesn't much care what I think anymore since…. Since…" Mrs. Stanton trailed off.

"Take your time, Mrs. Stanton." Manny urged.

"Gail." she insisted, "Please, call me Gail."

"Okay, Gail. Take your time."

"Thank you, Detective." Gail smiled at Manny and continued. "He, Leo, hasn't been into me, or our marriage since I lost the baby eight months ago."

Gail let out a deep breath and dropped her head. Manny sucked in the breath that Gail had let out and turned to Deshawn for help.

*Some information never gets any easier to hear*, Manny thought.

Deshawn shook his head back and forth, reflecting Manny's feelings.

"Gail, I'm very sorry for your loss." Deshawn spoke for the first time.

Gail seemed a bit startled by his voice. She had known Deshawn was there, but so far, he had just been a silent observer. It appeared from her reaction she may have wanted it to stay that way.

"I'm sorry, and you are?" she asked in a voice lined with distrust, all signs of timid, frail Gail gone momentarily.

"No, I'm the one who is sorry, Mrs. Stanton." Deshawn apologized. "I'm Detective Freeman. I should have introduced myself right away. I am Detective Castillo's partner. I am sorry if I startled you." Deshawn smiled warmly at Gail.

Gail studied Deshawn's face for a long while without returning his smile. Deshawn was undaunted. He waited patiently; his smile unwavering. An awkward silence held fast between the two for a moment longer, then Gail finally broke.

"Detective Freeman, nice to meet you. Yes, you startled me, but it is okay. I am easily startled these days it would seem." Gail managed a half smile for Deshawn.

"And thank you," she nodded at Deshawn and lowered her head slightly, "for your condolences."

"Of course." Deshawn urged softly.

"Gail, how long has Mr. Stanton been gone for?" Manny asked.

"Now? Near two days." she whimpered.

*That time frame matches the timing of our John Doe,* he thought.

"Gail, I'm sorry, but do you happen to have a picture of Mr. Stanton?" Manny asked.

"Yes, I brought our wedding photo." Gail handed a small wallet sized photo to Manny with a pale, shaky hand.

The photo was worn. The upper left corner dog eared from being repeatedly taken out and put back into the clear photo protector slot of a wallet. There was a slightly younger version of Gail in a plain white sundress standing next to a dark-haired man. The man, Leo, stood only a few inches taller than Gail and had an infectious smile. Manny studied the photo for a few minutes, but he knew the face the moment he held the photo.

"Mrs. Stanton, I'm afraid we have some bad news for you…" Manny began.

A banshee wail of grief and loss pierced the Homicide Unit,

freezing everyone in their tracks, as Gail Stanton collapsed on the floor.

# CHAPTER SEVEN

"I CAN'T BELIEVE SHE DIDN'T KNOW." Deshawn looked like someone just told him that Santa Clause wasn't real. "What's worse is that *he* didn't know." Manny said.

The purr of the Mustang's engine was the only sound between Manny and Deshawn when they were not conversing. Neither one had flipped on the radio when they got into the car. For Manny, at least, it hadn't seemed like a good time for music. He was happy to have the Mustang and not one of the unmarked sedans. The engine's vibration (only someone who has ever driven a V8 would understand) was especially soothing to Manny on days like these.

Manny restored the classic Mustang a few years ago and it was his "baby". His biggest pleasure was in knowing that he was able to find a rebuilt 289 HIPO engine and swap it for the old 289. The extra 46 HP had come in handy on more than one occasion and, even more importantly, made his metal steed unique. He made some smaller upgrades as well, including some unplanned repainting and recent repairs to the undercarriage a few months ago, from the damage it had sustained during the chase of Bobby Benson, Jr. at the old railroad container yard. Rocks and gravel had pummeled the car, although at the time Manny didn't care. The car could have exploded for all he cared, as long as he got to Alex in time. Now everyone and everything was safe, healed and repaired. He sighed. He wished it was the same for Mrs. Stanton.

After they told Gail about her husband, she had collapsed on the floor of the Homicide Unit and become unresponsive. They called 911 and rushed her to the E.R. Manny and Deshawn waited for the three hours it took for the doctors to evaluate Gail and for her to become stable enough for them to talk to her. Eventually, she agreed to see them for a few moments. She told them, when she felt strong enough, she would be by the morgue to see Leo to identify his body and claim him. She would have to wait for her mother to come into town as she needed the support. Gail then revealed to them that the doctors had drawn her blood and informed her that she was pregnant.

"Bittersweet, ain't it?" she had scoffed.

Manny thought of her pale face under the stark fluorescent hospital lights with the dark, sunken circles beneath her eyes. *Alex's eyes were like that not too long ago,* he thought. *Poor woman, what would she do now? Pregnant and widowed of a straying husband, all because he thought she couldn't bear his child.*

His stomach twisted in anger and disgust.

"You alright?" Deshawn asked.

"Yeah, I'm just thinking how ironic this whole situation is, ya know?"

"Yeah tell me 'bout it. Stupid dude goes out to get some cuz he can't stand being around his wife anymore thinking she can't have his babies. But hey, hey, hey now, guess what?

jokes on you, Leo." Deshawn voice was littered with fury.

"Yeah…" Manny sighed. "I tell you D, I'm getting tired, man."

"I know, Manny, I know." Deshawn sounded as weary as Manny felt.

They resumed their silence for the remainder of the trip to Deshawn's house, each of them deep in their own pool of thoughts. Manny pulled the Mustang up to the curb of Deshawn's house and put it in park. He dimmed the lights but left the engine idling.

"Wanna come in for supper?" Deshawn asked.

"No thanks, Alex will be waiting." Manny politely declined.

"Right."

"Tell Muriel and the kids I said hello."

"You got it. See you in the a.m. And, hopefully, not anytime sooner."

Deshawn gave Manny a quick fist bump and hopped out of the Mustang.

Manny watched as Deshawn strode up the walkway to his front door. Within seconds he disappeared into the house. Manny could imagine the kids yelping and climbing all over Deshawn as soon as he got into the front door. Muriel would be last, but not least, to reach him. Manny smiled.

*Family is so good,* he thought. *Maybe someday.*

He reached down and lit up the street with his headlights and pulled away.

# CHAPTER EIGHT

"DADDY, DADDY, DADDY!!!" little screams of joy echoed in the house as soon as Deshawn opened the front door.
*Ah, the very best part of my day,* he smiled.
"Yes! Bring it, you two little crazy babies!" Deshawn laughed. Two beautiful children, one girl and one boy, raced each other to greet him. Each one had on their respective pajamas and a giant grin.
Reagan, his two-year-old daughter, modeled her Cabbage Patch Kids nightgown, nearly tripping on it as she toddled over trying to keep up with her big brother, Justice. Her hair was only half completed with cornrows— the rest, tight curls of light brown— bounced zealously as she ran.
*Ha, she must not have let Muriel finish the rows,* Deshawn thought when he saw her.
Reagan was still getting used to having her hair pulled at. Cornrows took time and patience, neither of which his two-year-old had. Reagan would utter "ouchie" and try to get up from her seat each time Muriel would tug at her hair. Deshawn couldn't be around anymore for the process because he would laugh at first, but then he would swoop in and save

the princess, baby girl. Muriel was a saint in Deshawn's eyes for having the patience to even attempt to fix that little girl's hair. He had, at one-point, begged Muriel to take Reagan to the hair salon to have it braided, but Muriel was a stubborn woman once she had her mind set on something. Muriel had called Deshawn's sister, Ronnie, and had her come over multiple times to teach her how to braid Reagan's hair.

At four years old, Justice was much taller than other boys his age and his Transformer pajama pants were riding more like cartoon riddled Capris than pants. The arms on his pajama top were edging up close to his elbows. Deshawn watched as Justice yanked on them repeatedly with his long fingers to try and pull them down. Deshawn laughed at the dynamic duo with Muriel fast on their heels— hair flying out of braids that were made early that morning and untouched since.

"Yes, yes, Daddy is home isn't he!" Muriel exclaimed, an excited smile on her face.

Deshawn bent and grabbed a child in each arm sweeping them up easily into the air. They burst out in joyful giggles.

"Aww, D, be careful honey, please!" Muriel fussed.

"Again, Daddy!" Justice cried.

"Adin', Daddy, adin." mimicked Reagan.

"Uh, uh, you two need to go wash your hands for supper." Deshawn ordered softly putting them down.

"Aw, man." Justice whined.

"Aw, man." Reagan copied.

"Justice DeShawn. and Reagan Lee!" Muriel regarded them sternly.

Both children glimpsed up at their mother with big eyes.

"Do not make Mommy or Daddy ask you again, please. Now march." Muriel's voice dropped to a level the kids knew to mean business.

Muriel pointed a finger towards the bathroom and both children scurried obediently towards the bathroom to do as they were told. Muriel covered her mouth to stifle a giggle as she turned to face Deshawn. He covered his pursed lips with a long fingertip warning her to shush, but a smile broke through. He grabbed her and pulled her into him.

"Aw yes, a moment alone with Mommy." he whispered before kissing her deeply.

Muriel returned his kiss, passionate and strong. They stayed locked together for a moment, breathing heavy, wanting one another. Their foreheads pressed together as if sharing a telepathic thought. Giggles broke their love trance and they looked down to see their two children staring up at them giddily.

"Well, well now. Are your hands squeaky clean?" Deshawn asked them.

"Mhmmm." Justice nodded fervently.

"Mhmmm." Reagan nodded, nearly losing her balance. Deshawn stooped down and grabbed her, lifting her up and swinging her over to her highchair at the dinner table. This elicited a squeal of delight from the toddler's mouth.

"Come on y'all, let's eat." Muriel announced.

Deshawn belted Reagan into her chair and helped Justice into his booster seat. Reagan picked up her plastic spoon and banged it on her highchair table.

"Chow, chow, chow!" she chanted.

Deshawn raised a stern eyebrow at Reagan, failing to hide the laugh that snuck out of his mouth before he could stifle it. He (almost) regretted the day he had taught Reagan to do that little diddy. It had started out as a funny joke between Daddy and baby girl, but Mommy hadn't thought it was very funny when Miss Reagan started doing it at the dinner table.

What was worse, they couldn't get her to stop and Justice thought it was hysterical. Justice let out a gigantic belly laugh at his little sister's shenanigans. Every time he laughed, Reagan would jump with excitement and this would incite another round of chanting from the spirited toddler.

"Now, baby girl, you better quit that before your Momma gets back in here or your Daddy is gonna be in a whole lotta trouble." Deshawn warned.

He gently removed the plastic spoon from the chattering toddler's hand and finally sat with a "hmf" at the head of the table. Muriel hummed happily when she returned to finish dressing the table with the sides. Then as quickly as she entered, she exited again.

"Need any help, babe?" Deshawn called after her, suddenly feeling guilty for not offering before he sat down.

"Not one bit. You got the kids." Muriel smiled as she walked back in carrying the roast.

She blew a wisp of hair from her face and laid the pan, with the simmering meat in it, on the table. The room filled with the delicious aromas of pot roast, macaroni and cheese, green beans and homemade cornbread. Deshawn's stomach growled so loud everyone in the room could hear it. They all turned to stare at him.

"What?" he asked, pretending nothing happened.

Muriel roared with laughter. The kids jumped in their chairs, surprised at first, then joined in. Deshawn smiled. He basked in the beauty that was his family, each one of them, and memorized their faces in that very moment.

*It can't get any better than this,* he thought.

# CHAPTER NINE

THE PHONE ON MANNY'S DESK RANG for the fifteenth
time since his arrival to the office, which was, by his watch,
only thirty minutes ago.

*It's going to be one of those days.*

He sighed then reached begrudgingly for the handset. He
didn't bother to sit up all the way. He was comfortable in
his slightly slouched over position, his weary mind and tired
body both agreed.

"Castillo here."

"Detective Castillo, I have Frank Gianelli and Andrew
Pittman here for their interviews." Sergeant Cruz announced
dutifully over the phone.

Manny sat up in his chair at full attention, the hair on his
arms as straight as his back.

"Alright, have them escorted to Interview Room One and
Two. Offer them drinks and snacks. Thank you." Manny
hung up the phone.

"Here we go, Freeman."

"What's up, boss?" Deshawn swiveled around to face Manny.
The two uniformed officers Deshawn was gabbing with

chuckled as they walked away. Deshawn was always good for a funny story. He was somewhat of a celebrity in the precinct because of it. Manny would say to him, "yeah buddy, you're a real Stuart McLean." then laugh because Deshawn had no idea who Stuart McLean was. It also didn't hurt that Deshawn was easy on the eyes so there was never a shortage of female officers flocking around him. Yet, in all the time Manny had known him, Deshawn had never given any indicator that he was interested in any of them. He treated everyone equally. Manny knew Deshawn was as loyal a partner at home as he was to him, and that was one of the things that made him invaluable to Manny.

"Let's roll. We got the two guys downstairs waiting that were out with Stanton the other night. Each one is separated. One in Interview One and the other in Interview Two. We will go at it one at a time like we usually do. Press them if we have to." Manny discussed.

"Alrighty then." Deshawn smiled.

Manny chuckled. Deshawn loved interviewing perps and witnesses. Manny told Deshawn many times he should have been a lawyer— his interrogation skills were second to none. Manny wouldn't participate in an interview or interrogation with anyone other than Deshawn.

The two left the Homicide Unit and hit the stairs to descend the four flights to the main lobby. Sergeant Cruz pointed to Sergeant Baker who was waiting patiently for them.

"Good morning, Detectives." Sergeant Baker nodded.

"Morning, Baker." Manny and Deshawn greeted him in unison, both slightly out of breath.

"I have Gianelli in Room One and Pittman in Room Two." Baker reported.

"Alright, thanks." Manny nodded.

"Post outside, in case you're needed." Deshawn ordered.

"Roger that." Baker affirmed, handing Manny the keys to Interview Room One.

Manny jingled the keys around, searching for the one that had been etched with the number one. When he found it, he unlocked the door and entered the room with Deshawn behind him. The man at the table lifted his head to peer at them. His haggard eyes were laced with bright red blood vessels making it appear as if he had been on an all week bender with Jack Daniels and Captain Morgan. His black hair was greasy and disheveled. His clothes were wrinkled deep and far, as if he had slept in them for at least a few days. Manny could imagine that his breath was about as rank as the garbage can in the back of the bar that he was last seen at with his now deceased coworker.

"Mr. Gianelli?" Manny began.

"Yeah?" the man's voice cracked.

*Fear*, Manny thought.

"I am Detective Castillo. This is my partner, Detective Freeman. Do you know why you are here?"

"I uh, I am not so sure. No, I don't." Gianelli's voice was low with shaky uncertainty.

"You have no idea at all?" Deshawn prodded.

Manny held in his smile.

*And so, it begins.*

"Well, no." Gianelli tried again.

Manny figured he was most likely telling the truth since they hadn't released Mr. Stanton's name to the press yet, but he wasn't going to let Gianelli or Pittman in on any secrets. He needed to press them to make sure they didn't know anything.

"No? Hmmm." Manny challenged.

Manny sat down, facing Gianelli. Deshawn took his place, and stood behind Manny, his full six foot three inches a menacing presence for most. Gianelli's eyes grew wide for a moment, like a kid who had gotten caught with his hand in the cookie jar. He turned his eyes back to Manny and after a moment, seemed to lose his fear. Gianelli's wide eyes grew smaller as they closed into a squint.

"No, I don't." Gianelli's face flushed.

The tone of his voice morphed from guilty child to stubborn teenager.

"Well, what I will tell you is that we have your buddy Pittman next door. So now is your chance to come clean of anything before we go talk to him and get his side of the story." Deshawn goaded.

"And I can tell you we already have a lot of info on you and your partner," Manny stated "or else we wouldn't have you sitting here in front of us."

Manny could see the wheels spinning in Gianelli's head. Manny was half expecting smoke to pour out of his ears at any second. Gianelli tried again, once more halfheartedly.

"No, I… I don't have any idea."

Manny and Deshawn sat quiet. They used this a lot. Perps couldn't stand the silent treatment if they were weak. It broke them nearly all the time. Manny and Deshawn could do it for hours. Manny remembered how they had, in fact sat once, for five hours in silence waiting for their perp to break. They took turns coming and going, eating and drinking in front of him without giving him anything. It had worked, finally.

*It usually does if they're guilty,* Manny thought.

"I mean, I mean..." Gianelli began, stuttering. A magnificent sigh escaped his lips. "Fine! Okay… I do. I will tell you the truth." he sighed again, lowering his head and running his hands through his greasy hair.

*Ah, okay here we go. That was quick.* Manny thought.

"It's okay, Mr. Gianelli. We are here to listen." Deshawn coaxed.

Gianelli sighed again.

"Okay, okay," Gianelli whined. "Pittman told me it was cool. Like, he told me we could get away with it— that we wouldn't get caught."

Manny watched as a new flush of red moved from Gianelli's neck, up into his face and crawled into his hairline. From there, beads of sweat began to sprout and work their way back from where the flush of red had come.

"We get it, Mr. Gianelli. We have heard all kinds of things, we understand." Deshawn's voice oozed concern and non-judgement. Manny knew better.

"We were bored. You see? Like, our wives weren't… cutting it, ya know?"

Gianelli's querulous voice inflamed Manny's nerves, yet he nodded politely at Gianelli and waited. Gianelli was on a roll now, Manny didn't want to do anything to interrupt the flow. Manny knew he and Deshawn wouldn't have to do much now but sit back and listen. Gianelli was like a regretful sinner in the confessional on a Sunday morning, there to confess his sins and receive his penance.

"So, we bypassed the security firewalls on the computers. Pittman swore no one would find out because no one checks that kind of stuff at work. He said it would be less dangerous than opening it at home because then they could confiscate our home laptops and they would KNOW it was us. But, if we watched it at work no one would know it was us or be able to trace it back to us, because there were too many people who worked there. Like especially horny dudes. Ya know?"

Gianelli had diarrhea of the mouth now.

Manny sat, confused. He felt Deshawn's hand on his back, signaling his confusion as well. They had been doing this for too long to know that they couldn't quit the interrogation now though, because Gianelli was confessing to something, they just weren't sure of what yet. Manny needed to switch gears. He sat up in his chair and glared at Gianelli.

"We wanna know how much at this point." Manny played along.

"A lot." Gianelli confessed. He sighed again.

Manny could hear the remorse in his voice. Deshawn must have heard it too and stepped in to work his magic.

"How could you guys?" Deshawn was taking a chance, but he pushed.

"I know, man." Gianelli's voice cracked. "It was just so, I don't know. It was too tempting. It wasn't my idea. It was Pittman's. He was the one who picked the younger girls. I wanted to see the women. You know, actual women, like twenty-something year old women. But he, he is the one who decided on the younger ones. I didn't even know you could find little girls like that. I mean, he was searching for like thirteen and fourteen-year old girls. What kind of sick fuck does that? I was trying to spice up my life a little, you know?" Gianelli started to cry.

*Bingo! Child pornography.* Manny felt his stomach lurch. *They had no idea about Stanton. They thought they were here about downloading child pornography on their work computers illegally. Well, now they will be charged with something, just not murder.*

"Mr. Gianelli, I have to ask you a few more questions."

Manny mentioned.

"Okay." Gianelli sobbed.

"On the night you, Mr. Pittman and Mr. Stanton went to The Lark...." Manny began.

Gianelli looked up, his eyes glazed with tears and confusion, and sniffled. It took him a moment to focus on Manny. Confusion pushed the fear and embarrassment from his eyes.

"Mr. Gianelli, do you remember that night?" Manny nudged.

"Huh? Uh, yeah. It was Monday. We went out after work." Gianelli stuttered. "What about it?"

"Didn't anyone notice that Mr. Stanton didn't return to work after that night?" Deshawn asked.

Gianelli paused, considering the statement for a brief moment.

"Not really. Stanton does that sometimes. He'll go on a drinking bender on occasion and then call out for a few days. No one thinks anything of it. The boss doesn't care cuz he is one of our best salesmen when he's there. Like, I mean super good. Why?"

Concern began to deepen the lines that were already previously etched there from years of worry and anxiety. Silence followed.

"Why?" he asked again, more urgently.

Then, as if jerked awake from a nightmare and thrown into a pit of rattlesnakes, his face twisted with a sudden comprehension. Rabid fear replaced concern on his face.

"Wait!" Gianelli insisted. "Do you mean to tell me this isn't about kiddie porn?"

No one spoke. He was left to answer his own question through deduction.

"Fuck." Gianelli whispered.

"Mr. Gianelli, we called you down here to question you

regarding the night you were with Mr. Stanton. It was the last night he was seen alive." Manny interrogated.

Frank Gianelli's head snapped up so quickly Manny swore he should have heard it crack. The bright lights in the interview room created the perfect spotlight for Frank Gianelli's award winning performance of pure shock at Manny's news. Any color that remained in his face and neck drained away, replaced by a pallor matched only by the white of untainted, fresh fallen snow.

*If he is guilty of anything, he is a damn good actor,* Manny thought.

"H-h-hold up!" Gianelli stuttered. "You mean to tell me that Leo is dead? Leo. Leo Stanton." He emphasized Leo, then Stanton, as if they might have the wrong person.

"Yes, Mr. Gianelli. We are telling you that Mr. Leo Stanton is deceased, and it is believed that he was murdered. So, because you and Mr. Pittman were the last two people known to be with him when he was alive, you are now here with us." Manny said slowly, emphasizing each word so that Gianelli would understand.

Manny placed the manila folder on the table that he had been holding in his lap. He placed a long, manicured finger on it and tapped three times for emphasis.

"This, my friend, is a lot of information on Mr. Stanton and his murder." Manny said.

*Tap-tap-tap.*

Manny kept tapping the folder, *tap-tap-tap*, but did not open it. He stared at Gianelli. Deshawn shifted listlessly behind him, like a caged tiger waiting impatiently for its meal. Moisture formed at Gianelli's hairline again. He moved around in his chair like a little boy who had to use the potty but was afraid to tell his parents. His eyes darted from the folder, to Manny, to Deshawn, and back to the folder. Even with all of Gianelli's little idiosyncrasies, Manny didn't have a good feeling about this.

*This is not our unsub,* Manny thought. *This guy didn't kill Stanton. He's a mouse.*

"Man, I... I mean, Detective, sir. I don't know anything about that. Honestly. I am telling you the God's honest truth. Pittman and I met Leo down there at the Lark after work and Leo was already half in the bag. See, we stayed late after work to, well, you know what." Gianelli turned away, embarrassed, for a moment. "So, Leo, he left early actually. And the plan was to meet at The Lark. So, we did, and when we got there, Leo, as usual, was already two sheets to the wind. Dude had already had like eight beers. So, we stayed and watched the Pats play until almost the end of the fourth quarter, but they were sucking wind. Parcells has got some work to do. You know he replaced that chump MacPherson, right? Man, oh man." Gianelli shook his head.

"Please focus, Mr. Gianelli." Manny advised.

"Oh yeah, sorry. Anyways, so, Pittman's wife is super strict about him being home before the game is over or he catches hell. So, we told Leo it was time to go but he pitched a fit. Said he wasn't ready, and that Gail wasn't gonna give him any when he got home anyways so he was gonna stay there. We told him he should come with us so we could drive him. Told him he shouldn't be driving. He got pissed and told us to fuck off. Lately that's how a lot of our drinking nights end. It's nothing new." Gianelli glanced at Manny sland Deshawn searching for understanding.

"What happened next?" Deshawn asked, stone-faced.

The folder lay unopened. Gianelli shifted around, uneasy in his predicament.

*Tap-tap-tap.*

Gianelli eyed it anxiously.

"Pittman and I took off." Gianelli shrugged his shoulders. "When we left, Leo was still alive and breathing, if that's what you're inferring."

"Can anyone at the bar corroborate your story?" Deshawn asked.

Gianelli thought for a moment, then his eyes brightened. "Yeah, Cindy! That's the bartender. She knows us pretty well. She works there on Monday nights, when the games are on, and when we like to go in after work." Gianelli explained.

Deshawn jotted down the information on a small pad of paper then clicked his pen and put it away. Manny grabbed the manila folder and stood up.

"Can I go now?" Gianelli asked.

"I'm afraid not, Mr. Gianelli. We still need to speak with Mr. Pittman and make sure your stories jive. We will, of course, speak to some people at the bar. And then, there is this little matter of child pornography that you offered up to us. Thank you for that by the way. We will be in contact with the F.B.I. on that one. So, no, you will not be leaving anytime soon." Manny retorted.

Gianelli's mouth hung open. He sat, staring at Manny, the glaze of uncertainty returning to his face.

"Deshawn, could you do the honors?" Manny motioned to a small circular piece of metal that stuck up from the center of the interview table.

Gianelli's gaze followed Manny's pointing finger to the small metal loop that seemed to have been welded to the table. It was strange and archaic looking; quite a curious thing to have in the middle of a table. He watched as Deshawn pulled a pair of handcuffs from his back pocket and unlocked them.

Manny watched as realization spread across Gianelli's face. *The many masks of Gianelli,* Manny thought, stifling a laugh.
"Ah man, seriously?" he whined.
"Sorry, man. Precautionary. Regulation." Deshawn explained. "Please, give me your right arm."
Gianelli gave Deshawn his right arm. Deshawn clamped the handcuff on it and the other cuff to the metal loop on the table. Deshawn stuck his two fingers in between Gianelli's wrist and the handcuff to check the fit then, satisfied, let his arm fall gently to table.
"How long do I have to stay in this room?" Gianelli moaned, as Manny and Deshawn were exiting.
"As long as it takes." Manny answered, then he locked the door behind them.

# CHAPTER TEN



"WELL, PITTMAN IS GIVING THE SAME STORY from The Lark." Deshawn muttered.

Manny peeked up from his paperwork to see Deshawn walking towards him, a frown on his face.

"Okay, so the stories match up." Manny shook his head. "That's okay, I guess."

"I called and spoke to Cindy, the bartender. She gave me a quickie statement over the phone. Says she will come down to the station and give a sworn statement later today to Sergeant Baker. But, according to her, Pittman and Gianelli left shortly before the game was over, but Stanton stayed. Cindy says she remembers seeing Stanton sitting at the end of the bar at some point during the night with a woman with long black hair. But then he was gone, and that is all she can remember." Deshawn plopped down in his chair with an exasperated "humph".

Manny sighed and shuffled his papers again. The photos of Stanton's body were strewn like paint samples from Home Depot on his desk; a tie dye menagerie of different shades of crusted red and brown strewn across a pale canvas of white corpse.

"So, she never served her a drink? Did she get a look at her face?" Manny asked.

"No, she never served her one iota of a thing. There were no other bartenders that night either. It's apparently pretty slow on Monday nights, even during football season. And of course, she never saw her face. Come on man, that would have been too easy." Deshawn smiled.

Manny gave Deshawn a halfcocked smile.

"Well, we kinda figured he was with a woman at the hotel, didn't we? Okay, we have a woman with long dark hair. Great. We can at least rule out the blondes and reds." Manny chortled.

Deshawn snorted.

"Oh good, I can take Muriel off the list."

"Well, that's good, cuz I was beginning to worry a little." Manny jibed.

"Yeah, me too. She's been going out a lot lately. Leaving them darn kids to fend for themselves. That's why Reagan's hair's been lookin'a holy mess. Ha!" Deshawn laughed.

"I'm going to tell her you said that, D." Manny warned.

"You serious man? You trying to throw me to the lions?" Deshawn's eyes widened.

*Worse*, Manny thought, *the lioness.*

"Hmm, "Manny feigned consideration. "I will think about it. Maybe you will have to bribe me with a couple of those famous pulled pork sandwiches of hers." Manny raised his eyebrows at Deshawn.

"Okay, okay. Deal." Deshawn laughed.

"Sorry to interrupt Detective Castillo," Sergeant Baker cleared his throat as he approached.

He stood next to Manny's desk waiting for Manny to reply.

"Go ahead, Baker." Manny allowed.

"I thought you'd like to know that an Agent Willis is here with a few other Feds to take Gianelli and Pittman into custody. They are downstairs waiting for you and Detective Freeman." Baker shifted on his feet.

"Alrighty then. Thanks." Manny acknowledged Baker without taking his eyes away from the photos of Stanton. Manny turned to Deshawn.

"Okay hermano, you ready to go release those punks to the Feds?"

"I was born ready, my man." Deshawn smiled.

# CHAPTER ELEVEN

MANNY PULLED THE MUSTANG INTO THE DRIVEWAY
and turned the keys in the ignition until the rumble of the
engine ceased. He dampened the headlights and sat back in
the bucket seat for a moment with his eyes closed. The day
had seemed like it would never end. His entire body ached,
and his mind wouldn't stop racing. It was as if his brain's fast
forward button was stuck and there was no way to unstick it.
He wished like hell he could find the remote control.
The last few days had been a whirlwind of craziness, a roller
coaster of ups and downs. They found out the identity of
their John Doe, but the news that came with finding out
who he was had been painful to hear. Manny knew that
for himself, it would take a long time to work through that
particular part of the case. Children having to grow up
without fathers was a particularly difficult pill for Manny to
swallow. They had also unknowingly caught two men illegally
downloading child pornography by bringing them in for
questioning for something completely different, thanks to the
blabbermouth Gianelli.
*More innocent kids! What the fuck?* Manny felt sick at the

thought.

Manny's own father had spent Manny's entire childhood, and most of his adult life, behind bars at the State Penitentiary in maximum security for committing a triple homicide during an attempted bank robbery. Manny was only four years old at the time. His father had died of colon cancer eight years ago while still in prison. Ramón Castillo was on his second of three consecutive life sentences without the possibility of parole. Manny never went to see his father during his incarceration. He never even went to his father's burial. Manny's mother had, on a few occasions, tried to get Manny to reconcile with Ramón, but Manny had nothing to reconcile. His mother had done a perfectly good job raising him, other than his poor attendance at church as he grew older. Manny smiled at the thought, then he opened the car door and ungracefully hefted himself out.

The porch light was on, and as he neared the house, the floodlight hit him in the face making him feel like he was Tom Jones in the spotlight on a Vegas stage. He instinctively raised a hand to shadow his eyes from the floodlight's intense glare.

*Damn, I always forget how well that thing works,* he laughed to himself.

He was glad that he had it installed, even though he wondered if the bright ball he saw when he closed his eyes would go away soon. He found his house key and went to put it in the keyhole when the door swung open.

"Wow, are you okay?" Alex asked breathlessly, her face riddled with anxiety.

"Yes, I'm fine." Manny smiled a tired greeting at her.

He could see the concern on her face.

*She's been worrying. I should have called her earlier,* he thought.

The deep lines that pinched Alex's brows together softened, and Manny noticed her shoulders drop as the tension left her body. He put a gentle hand on her arm to let her know he was there and felt her tremble slightly from his touch.
"Sorry, I was worried." she admitted.
"Don't be sorry, Alex. I understand, believe me, I do."
"Oh jeez!" she exclaimed. "How insensitive of me, Manny. I'm so sorry. ¿Estás cansado? You must be so tired."
Alex rolled her eyes in exasperation at her lack of consideration and grabbed Manny's keys, briefcase and windbreaker. Manny watched her for a moment as she moved about, putting his things away, before he turned to shut and lock the door.
*Even when she is upset at herself, she is gorgeous*, he smiled. Manny turned back, still smiling, and walked into the kitchen where Alex had situated herself at the stove. The smell that wafted over to his nostrils from the pot that was boiling on the stove top was exquisite. He knew the smell well, and it never failed to evoke growls of hunger from his belly and memories of his childhood from his mind.
"Ah, habichuelas, I mean frijoles!" Manny pulled out a kitchen chair and plopped down with a tired thud.
"Sí, Manuelito, con arroz, with rice." Alex answered from the stove, her back to him.
Manny loved it when Alex spoke Spanish with him. They had both grown up in Spanish speaking homes. Her family was of Mexican descent and his was of Puerto Rican descent, so their Spanish was at times slightly different but enough the same that they could communicate with one another fluently. He thought back to the time Alex learned how to cook rice and beans from Manny's mother, "Puerto Rican style", as Alex liked to call it. It was after they had become good

friends so that she could "cook him some of his favorite meals".

*That act alone would have been enough to make me fall in love with her. It was a bonus that she is also beautiful, intelligent, funny and amazing,* he thought. He smiled.

"What are you thinking?" Alex asked him, pulling him from his thoughts.

"Oh, I'm remembering the first time you made rice with my mom." Manny started laughing.

"What about it?" Alex dared him; her voice lined with playful intimidation.

"Oh, you don't remember?"

"Oh, I remember. Go on…" Alex prodded, daring Manny once again to say something.

"Do you remember that the rice was so jacked up that if you threw it on the wall part of it would have made a hole in the wall and the other part would have stuck to the wall?"

Manny burst out laughing.

"Hey!" Alex blurted out.

Alex jumped into Manny's lap and started tickling him.

"Take it back! Take it back!" she insisted, laughing.

"Nope!"

"Take it back!"

"No way!" Manny laughed.

He wrapped his arms around Alex so she wouldn't slip off his lap.

"Manny, take it back or I'm gonna… I'm gonna…"

"Or you're gonna what?" Manny dared her.

They both laughed harder.

Then Manny was the one tickling Alex. Her laughter was full and happy. Manny felt his body tingle with warmth.

*Dios mío, I love this woman so much,* he thought as he stared at her face, laughing.

Alex noticed Manny staring at her and stopped laughing, but the smile remained. Her eyes fixed on his and they sat, face to face, quiet and staring. Manny felt the familiar tingle, the familiar tug of desire he always felt around Alex. It had been there since the first day he laid eyes on her. It only grew stronger with each passing memory they made together. He vowed a long time ago to be patient, and at that moment more than ever, it was the hardest but most important vow he had ever made.

"Manny?" Alex breathed.

"Yes, Alex."

"Would you mind if we tried kissing again?"

Manny sucked in a breath.

"Of course not." he blew the breath out.

Alex also breathed out.

Her hand found his face and then the back of his neck. Then her other hand found the back of his neck and she was close, so close.

*God, her touch feels so amazing, so good.* Manny waited. *Be patient.*

Alex's lips touched his, and he closed his eyes. Her lips were soft and tasted of Sangria and Adobo seasoning. Manny kept his arms and hands where they were. He wasn't about to make the same mistake as last time. He was going to let Alex drive this time.

Alex kissed him again, this time with a little more pressure. Her lips parted and Manny felt her tongue slip into his mouth.

*Oh God. Patience. Stay in control.* Manny returned her kiss, carefully, gently.

Alex's fingers curled into Manny's hair, and he could feel her pull herself closer to him. Her breathing quickened, as did his.

*God, she feels so good. Tastes so good. Stay in control.*

Manny reminded himself that he could not slip up. Yet, he could feel himself growing excited. Alex moaned as if to test him even further. How was he going to control himself? Alex's breath came quicker than before and Manny was having a hard time trying to keep his hands still.  Alex moved even closer, as close as she possibly could. There was no longer any space between them.

"Alex." Manny whispered between kisses.

"Hmmm." she moaned.

She kissed him harder, her tongue moving deeper into his mouth this time. Manny felt like he was going to explode. This was torture for him. Manny hadn't been with a woman in a long time. Finally, the woman he had been waiting for was there, kissing him, wanting him, and he had to be careful not to ruin it. Alex pulled back and started to unbutton Manny's shirt, startling him. He tried to peek at her face, but she was still kissing him on his neck, his cheeks, his lips.

"Alex, honey."

"Mhmmm" she murmured.

"Wait." he whispered.

"It's okay." she whispered back.

"Alex!"

"It's okay!" she insisted aloud, this time.

"No, Alex!" Manny demanded her attention.

Alex stopped and glared at him, shocked and confused.

"Manny, I…"

"Alex, no honey, the beans…!" Manny exclaimed pointing, as the hissing from the overflowing beans on the stove finally caught Alex's attention.

"Oh crap!" Alex exclaimed.
"Holy frijoles!" Manny yelped, laughing.

# CHAPTER TWELVE

MANNY SAT AT HIS DESK SMILING, remembering the events of last night with Alex, even though the takeout Chinese food was still causing a strong desire for a shot of Pepto Bismol. The beans had charred to the bottom of the pan— thick like black tar— by the time they tried to save them. The once glorious smell replaced by something scorched and biting— caustic to the nostrils. They had laughed until their sides ached. Of course, the damn beans ruined whatever might have transpired with Alex, but he was content with the way things were.

The phone rang, jarring him out of the cloud of last night's memory.

"Detective Castillo.", Manny barked.

"Hey, it's me." Alex announced.

He could hear her smile through the phone.

"Good morning, beautiful." Manny smiled back.

"Good morning, yourself." she giggled.

"What are you up to?" he asked.

"Well, I was going to head in and discuss the Slasher case with you." she solicitated.

Manny opened his mouth to tell her "no way" then he

paused for a moment, remembering what he had promised her.

"Okay, see you soon." he gripped the arm of his chair tight to stop himself from telling her no.

Manny heard Alex sigh lightly. He felt a pang of guilt. He knew at that moment she thought there was a chance that he was going to tell her no. And, for a moment, he almost had. Manny wrote a mental note to make it a priority to stop trying to shelter Alex. He hung the headset on its cradle and stared at the phone for a very long moment.  It was good that Alex was coming in because he never had the chance to mention Mrs. Stanton last night. Not that he was very enthused about revisiting the events of Mrs. Stanton. The vivacious mood Manny had five minutes ago was suddenly replaced by sullen dread. He readied himself to discuss Mrs. Stanton with Alex and to invite Alex back into the dangerous world of the Homicide Unit. Manny found himself wondering every day if it was his fault that Alex had been targeted by Bobby Benson, Jr. He considered the idea that if he had never asked Alex six years ago for her opinion on that first murder case, and she hadn't gotten "hooked" as she liked to call it, if she would have stayed safe. Manny shook his head back and forth a few times to clear his mind, as if shaking his head to and fro would somehow cause the bad thoughts to fall from his ears. He could hear his mom's voice in his head "Manuelito, déjalo, mijo leave it alone, my son."

"Sí, mamá." he whispered to the air.

"Yo, 'morning gorgeous." Deshawn bellowed.

"Yeah, yeah." Manny grumbled.

"Oh man, what's got your panties in a bunch?" Deshawn asked.

"Alex is coming."

"What's wrong with that?" Deshawn asked cluelessly. Manny shook his head back and forth slowly. He wondered how one person could be so attuned to him at times, and other times have absolutely no idea what he was talking about. Deshawn stared at him, waiting for him to answer his question, still unsure as to what Manny was referring to. Manny gave it a few more seconds to see if Deshawn could figure it out. When he still had a blank look on his face after an entire minute had passed, Manny answered.

"I still don't want her in the action, D." Manny frowned like a petulant schoolboy.

"Dude, you can't hog all the action for yourself." Deshawn jibed.

"D, you know that's not what I meant." Manny barked.

"Okay, okay. But seriously. You cannot keep doing this. We already talked about this. You have to let it go, Man. I mean, honestly. It is getting ridiculous now. You are going to seriously piss her off. She is adamant about jumping back in. Do you blame her? You and I do it for a living. You've heard her say it a million times. I know I have. She is "hooked". If she isn't giving it up after what happened to her, she isn't going to. So, you are going to have to, somehow, figure out a way to accept that." Deshawn was playing Devil's advocate and Manny wanted to hug him and smack him for it. Instead, Manny sat back in his chair and listened to his friend's words of advice.

*He is right. There isn't much I can do and pushing back is only going to drive a wedge between us*, he thought.

Manny leaned back in his chair balancing on the two back legs, an old habit from his childhood that would often land him in trouble. He could hear his mother saying…,

"Cuidado, be careful." Alex's voice floated to him from behind.

The chair came slamming down on the floor, and Manny felt his butt bounce on the seat. Deshawn let out a howl of laughter loud enough to be heard within a four-mile radius. Alex giggled. Manny glanced at them both, surprised at first, then chuckled at his own expense.

*Yes, mamá, all those years and I still haven't learned.*

"Hey." he smiled sheepishly.

"Hey, yourself." she smiled, the giggle still caught on her lips. "I know, I know."

She glanced at him, a mischievous twinkle in her eye.

*I could stare at you all day,* he thought as he watched her. Alex must have felt the heat from his gaze. She held it for a moment, then bit her lower lip and turned away toward Deshawn. Manny felt his stomach flutter.

"So, D, how is the family?" Alex asked.

"Great, thanks for asking, Dr. Aguilar." Deshawn answered.

"Okay, D, I have to say it." Alex's voice took on a different tone.

*Uh oh,* Manny thought, *she has her stubborn voice on. He is in for something.*

Deshawn must have heard something in Alex's voice as well. He gazed up at her from his chair like a child who was about to be scolded for writing on the walls with his crayon. He sat, quietly waiting for his punishment. Manny smiled at the picture before him. It was comical to see Deshawn, a six foot plus a few inches, former linebacker, brick house of muscle cowering to a hundred- and twenty-pound beauty. Manny knew exactly how he felt.

"Listen, I do not want you to call me Dr. Aguilar anymore. That is enough. I am Alex from now on. We've talked about this before. I am serious this time, okay? Got it?" Alex demanded sweetly.

Manny did all he could to stifle the laughter that was building up inside of him. He would catch hell if he let it out. From both of them. He sat silently watching the situation unfold before him. He found himself pushing himself back on his chair's two hind legs again, this time more out of anxious energy.

Deshawn gave Alex a crooked smile.

"Yes, ma'am." he grinned.

"Uh oh, oh no." Alex protested. "None of that either. JUST ALEX!" Alex insisted.

"Okay, Alex."

Deshawn's tone was filled with the aroma of discomfort. Deshawn was brought up in a very strict home where title meant everything, and respect meant more. Everyone that earned it had worked hard to get it and to not give it was the ultimate sin. Manny had the pleasure of hearing many stories about Deshawn's family history, going as far back as the 1800's when his family took on the surname Freeman once they literally became "free from slavery". Deshawn hailed from a long line of service men, and he did everything he could to make them proud. Manny smiled at Deshawn. *If only half the men in this country were half the man he is,* Manny thought.

Alex seemed satisfied.

"Please, tell Muriel I send my best." Alex smiled.

"Will do." Deshawn returned Alex's smile.

*Ah, good, everything is copacetic,* Manny nodded.

"Now that all the pleasantries are done with..." Manny mused. "Let's get down to business, shall we?"

Deshawn and Alex turned to Manny, both appeared

interested and agitated at the same time.

*Oh, now we are getting back to normal,* Manny grinned.

"What?" they chimed simultaneously.

"Oh nothing." Manny chortled.

Before either one of them could interrogate Manny any further, the phone on his desk blared, interrupting their conversation.

"Detective Castillo."

"Hello, Manny." Dr. Leavy's voice came through the line, static breaking here and there.

"Hello, Dr. Leavy, how are you?" Manny asked.

"Great, great." she answered, even though to Manny she sounded winded.

"What's up?" Manny asked.

"I got the tox screen back and thought you might be interested in hearing it rather than waiting on the official." Leavy breathed.

"Oh yeah, definitely. Thanks." Manny said.

He glanced over to see Alex and Deshawn staring at him intently. He held a finger up at them, signaling for them to wait, that the phone call was important. Deshawn nodded. Alex watched him with a blank expression on her face. Manny wondered for a brief moment if she was okay but remembered Dr. Leavy had possible substantial information for him and returned to the phone.

"Go ahead." Manny urged.

"Okay, so the hematology report was insignificant. CBC was normal. Toxicology however came back with elevated levels of alcohol and get this..." Leavy paused. Manny didn't know if she was searching for information or doing it for dramatic effect, but he waited.

"...3,4MethelenedioxyMethamphetamine." she finished.

"Molly?" Manny asked.

"Yes, that's one of the street names for it. The other is Ecstasy. It depends on the form in which it is in." Dr. Leavy added.

"Yes. I am familiar with it." Manny indicated. "What is interesting is that our vic doesn't quite fit the profile for a Molly banger does he?" Manny spoke, more to himself than to Leavy. "Okay, anything else, Dr. Leavy?" Manny asked.

"Nope. That's it. That's all she wrote." Dr. Leavy snorted. Manny didn't laugh.

"Okay, well thanks for letting me know as soon as you knew. I appreciate the early heads up, Allison. Have a good night." Manny hung up the phone without waiting for Dr. Leavy to say goodbye.

"Well, I'm sure you figured out that was Dr. Leavy. She was calling with the tox screen results on Mr. Stanton. Seems like he had some Molly in his system." Manny divulged the information to Deshawn and Alex.

Alex spoke first after a few moments of silence.

"Well, it makes sense that the unsub would use something like Molly to drug Mr. Stanton. It alters mood and perception. It gives a sense of pleasure, emotional warmth, and can distort sensory and time perception. All those things would help someone smaller than the vic, if they are trying to harm him, to be able to control him or the situation better. Right?" Alex offered.

"Makes sense." Deshawn agreed.

Manny nodded.

"Okay," Manny began. "So, we have a female unsub, long black hair, between the ages of twenty-two to late thirties. She was last seen at The Lark with our vic. The bartender, Cindy, doesn't remember seeing her face or serving her a drink. There were no fingerprints lifted from the hotel or from the body. No blood or body fluids found at the scene or on Mr. Stanton, other than his own, to help identify our unsub. So basically, what I'm saying is that we haven't got shit to go on." he sighed.

"Welp, it wouldn't be the first time. So, let's do what we do best." Deshawn chimed in with his usual upbeat, positive self.

Manny smiled.

*Leave it to D to put a positive spin on things.*

"Has Muriel been teaching you some cheer leading meditation at home?" Manny teased.

"She's been teaching me something!" Deshawn snorted.

Manny and Deshawn laughed, sharing their "man jokes", forgetting for a moment that Alex was there. She cleared her throat, glaring at them from the corner of her eyes. Her left eyebrow raised, in a feigned disapproving scowl.

Manny and Deshawn quickly choked back their laughter and cleared their own throats. Manny stood up straight, smoothing his shirt. Deshawn shuffled his feet around like an uncomfortable schoolboy who was being reprimanded by his schoolteacher for leaving a whoopee cushion on her seat. He couldn't quite wipe the grin off his face completely, it hung there still, half exposed, so he hid his face instead.

"You boys done playing?" Alex inquired sternly.

"Yes ma'am." They answered in unison.

"Alright then, let's find us a slasher."

# LITTLE
# BLACKBIRD

# CHAPTER ONE

THE NIGHTS WERE GROWING WARMER. The moon sat high against the onyx backdrop of night, casting a glow along the sidewalk. It lit her way like a shimmering gold runway laid out for her, and only her. The sky was clear making the stars seem like untarnished diamonds floating in black water. Raven Rivers walked at a leisurely pace, the heavy bag with all its contents felt like nothing against her. She loved to walk at this hour— the witching hour. The streets were almost always quiet between two and three a.m.  The only sounds were the buzzing of the electricity from the streetlights and power lines. An occasional random car might pass, but it was rare. She was exhilarated, filled with a newfound energy that paralleled the humming of the current in the power lines. The initial fear and nervous energy from the hotel room long since dissipated.

*It had been easy. Almost too easy,* she thought.

That scared her a little, but she had her reasons and they were much too important to let a little fear get in the way.

Raven turned the corner and approached her neighborhood. The streets were lined with older homes. Most were Colonials and split-level homes, all well maintained and owned for generations.  Her family had also owned their home for generations, and her uncle and mother inherited the old Victorian with its dark windows and shadowy corners when her grandparents passed.  Her mother, however, forfeited any rights to her inheritance when she was sixteen and ran away to New Orleans.

The old Victorian stood stoic, positioned further back away from the street. The driveway was a long and narrow path, riddled with potholes, for the grand entrance to a dilapidated garage that had gone unused for many years. The house was unkempt, it's multicolored facade like layers of old makeup peeling from years of neglect and weather damage. At night, the shadow cast by the Victorian was monumental. Raven imagined in the Victorian's prime— with her massive turrets, elaborate shingled shapes, and steep gabled roofs— the painted lady was once quite beautiful. Now, her age and years of solitude showed, even through her mask of darkness. Her uncle would be sleeping at this hour, allowing Raven a question-free entrance, for which she was grateful.  She climbed the cracked and splintering wood stairs and entered the house. The grandfather clock chimed four a.m. announcing her arrival as she closed the front door, causing her heart to skip a beat.

*Shit!*

No matter what, the damn clock still scared her every time it chimed. She had been living here with her uncle for years now and she still wasn't used to the clock. She caught her breath and waited until her heart slowed before she climbed the stairs to her room.  She purposely skipped the fourth step on the way up knowing it would creak loudly. At the top of the stairs she waited, listening for a moment.  After a few seconds, she heard the comforting sound of her uncle's deep snores coming from the first bedroom on the right and knew she was safe to continue on to her room at the end of the hall.  The carpeted hall floor beneath her protected her the rest of the way.

Raven entered her room and smiled. The room decor was still that more to the likings of a thirteen-year-old girl. She hadn't changed it much from the original way her uncle had decorated it for her when she came to stay with him when she was almost fourteen. Now at the age of twenty-two she added a few touches of her own here and there but left most of the things the way that he fixed it for her so that he wouldn't feel bad.  She appreciated him letting her stay with him. She didn't have anywhere else to go. Her uncle was her only living family. She loved him dearly. He was good to her like no other man had been.

Raven laid the bag down on a chair by her desk and sat down on her bed. A single tear slipped down her cheek. She let it fall, barely noticing it.

*Oh momma, I'm sorry,* she thought.

Sadness enveloped her suddenly, replacing the fevered excitement that warmed her only moments ago.

The loss of her mother was unexpected and hurt as much at that moment as the day it happened nine years ago. Raven fell over on to her bed and cried, heavy weeping cries.

*Oh momma, I'm so, so sorry.*

Raven cried until there were no more tears left to cry. Her eyes ran dry and her body grew limp from being wracked with sobs.

After a few moments she reached up and rubbed her face absentmindedly. Raven thought about the hotel again. She didn't know what happened to her, really. It wasn't supposed to go that way. That wasn't how she planned it. The plan was to tie him up, draw his blood, and slice his throat.

*Yes, slice his throat humanely, right? That was the plan.*

But something went wrong. Something in her head just snapped.

*Yeah, something went terribly wrong,* she thought.

She frowned. She didn't mean it.

"I didn't mean it, Momma." she whispered. "It wasn't supposed to happen like that, I promise."

After a moment in silence, Raven stood up and went over to the bag.  She picked it up and set it on the bed, opening it to peer inside. Still frowning slightly, she began to remove its contents, laying them on the bed to take inventory. A few butterfly needles, a wad of vinyl gloves, fifteen filled vacuum tubes of blood and twelve empty ones, a small hunting knife, a few plastic adapters, three half burned black candles, a book of matches, some condoms, a few capsules of Molly, and her Gris Gris bag.  She had two Gris Gris bags, both made by "Aunt Lalla"— one given to her when she was five and the other when she turned thirteen. This was the latter of the two. It contained stones, crystals and herbs with a tiny scroll that held a miniature script on its face. Raven rubbed it out of habit like she had many times before, comforted by the soft leather pouch beneath her fingertips.

Raven remembered the tubes of blood and returned to the bed, gathering them up gently to place them in the mini fridge she purchased for her room.  She checked to make sure the temperature gauge read thirty-nine degrees Fahrenheit, that was the temperature needed for the blood to stay good for seven days. She only needed it to stay good for that long. She smiled. That's all the time she needed to find a new donor.

# CHAPTER TWO

THE SOUND OF THE ALARM jarred Raven from sleep. She rolled over and slapped at the blaring plastic box until her hand accidentally found the off button. She rolled over again, groaning as she went. The pounding in her head matched the rhythm of the deceased alarm clock *beep-beep-beep-thud-thud-thud.* She could hear the pulse throbbing in her temples.

*Thud-thud-thud.*

Raven reached up and rubbed her forehead— her cold fingers gave only minor, temporary relief to the pain.

"Ugh!" she exclaimed to the empty room.

Silence answered her complaint.

She kept her jade green eyes shut, willing them to remain closed. She was afraid the light that filled her room might singe her eyeballs from their sockets if she dared open her lids and expose them. She wished momentarily for the weekend again, despising the mundane schedule of weekdays and work. *It has to be done, lazy child.* Raven heard her Momma's voice echoing from far away, chastising her for her insouciance towards work. Raven's momma had always been a hard worker and taught Raven that you had to work for what you had.

"It's the only way to get what you need and what you want in life, little blackbird" was what momma would say.

"Well, Momma, you were right. One does need to work for the things they need and the things they want." Raven whispered to the empty air.

She sighed and let out a groan, once more complaining of the task at hand. When she realized no one was coming to her rescue, she shoved the blankets from her warm body and forced one eye open, awaiting its obliteration. When her eyeball didn't evaporate, she knew it was safe to open the other eye. Other than a little stinging that bright light brings to the eyes that have only seen darkness for so long, no harm had besieged them as she had feared. She smiled. Her mother had always told her she had a flare for the dramatics. "Quite the imagination" momma had called it. Raven always chalked it up to the fact that she had been an only child to a single mother, so she had been forced to be her own playmate.

*When you're your own playmate, you become quite cunning in the imagination department,* she thought.

A screeching came from the plastic alarm clock again causing Raven to nearly fall off the side of the bed.

"Shit!" she yelled.

She stood and made sure to really hit the off button this time instead of the snooze.

*Man, I truly despise that thing. One day I am going to throw it out the window.*

Raven smiled at the picture forming in her mind of herself taking an elevator in the tallest building in Boston to the top floor, walking out on the rooftop where the cold winter air would blast her in the face, and flinging the stupid alarm clock into the traffic below where it would meet its demise.

After a moment of dreamy satisfaction, she grabbed her towel and walked towards the bathroom in fluffy socked feet.
The house was quiet, as she knew it would be. Her Uncle Jack would still be sleeping. (Well, passed out was more like it.) He was a night owl, like Raven was. As was her mother. *When she was alive*, Raven thought, sadly.
Her mother and uncle had been alike in just about every way. They were fraternal twins. Raven's momma told her that being fraternal twins wasn't a guarantee of being exactly alike, but somehow her momma and Uncle Jack had forged a deep connection from within the womb.
Raven smiled, thinking of the pictures she grew up looking at, of her mother and uncle, and listening to the stories of the mischief they had caused. Raven remembered thinking how funny it was that her mother and uncle were twins but didn't resemble one another. They were both beautiful children, neither one lacking in the looks department. Uncle Jack with his stick straight hair, black as ink and emerald green eyes. Then there was Momma with her blonde curls and blue eyes. One would think they belonged to different fathers. When Raven brought it up to her mother, a curious look would come across her mother's face. Her mother would suddenly clam up for the remainder of the day.  Raven's mother had been good at avoiding many conversations about "family". Raven grew up knowing very little other than the thin exterior of her family's history— a fragile Faberge eggshell broken sometime before Raven was born— glued back together with only the pieces Raven's mother chose to share with her when Raven asked.
The nozzle on the shower wall creaked its grievance at being called upon, but put forth a spurt of water, nonetheless.
The old pipes knocked their usual sequence of bangs they

occasionally issued as the water traversed through them. They didn't always do it, but when they did it was loud and somewhat unnerving. Raven remembered being scared as a child when she first came, her imagination running wild with ideas of what might be lurking below, knocking on those pipes.

She waited until the water was hot enough to nearly scald her skin and stepped gingerly into the porcelain tub, careful not to slip. The water burned her almost painfully, but that was how she wanted it. It was a cathartic cleansing of sorts for her. She would scour her skin until it was bright red and let the hot water pelt her until she felt as if every sin had been washed away.

"Every sin, momma." She told the air.

When she was fully bathed, Raven turned the water off and stepped out of the shower, splitting the steam that filled the small bathroom with her petite body. The exhaust fan still needed to be replaced. Her uncle Jack was supposed to do that a month ago.

*I will have to remind him again,* she thought, as she did every day when faced with the mist. *It's okay, Uncle Jack,* Raven thought.

She thought of him sitting in his chair by the unlit fireplace, his thin hand wrapped protectively around the nearly empty bottle of bourbon. She always knew to find him there, or in his room. He never ventured out anymore unless it was to go to the liquor store. Raven did the grocery shopping now and any other shopping or errands they needed done. At the young age of thirty-eight, Uncle Jack seemed more like he was in his early sixties. Years of heavy drinking and drug use had taken its toll on his body and mind. He had gotten clean of the drugs but still used alcohol as a means of escape. He would have it for breakfast, lunch and dinner. But to her, he was still the only man she loved and trusted.

When Raven had first come to live with him, her uncle had been the picture of health. Young, vibrant, handsome. Now, he was a mere exoskeleton of the man he used to be. She was sure it had everything to do with her mother's death. It had killed something not only inside of Raven but inside Uncle Jack as well, she was sure of it. They had each other at least. *If we didn't have each other to turn to, we would have both surely died.*

Raven sighed, wrapped herself in her towel and tiptoed with wet feet back to her room to get dressed for the day.

# CHAPTER THREE

Newbury hospital was bustling with the usual conglomeration of scrubs, white coats and civilians; some doctors, some patients, some workers. Raven walked through the revolving door, making sure not to get too close to it or else it would stop.

*Anyone with no patience would have a serious issue with this thing,* she smiled impishly.

She considered messing with it for a moment. There was an elderly man behind her.

*That would be too easy,* she thought.

She giggled mischievously and instead made a smooth exit out of the moving door, past the welcome desk in the main lobby, and headed down the hall. The two elderly women that manned the welcome desk waved and murmured their "good mornings" to her.

"Good morning, Gloria. Good morning, Vera." she waved and smiled as she passed.

Raven took a right at the end of the hall and walked briskly to the elevator. She pushed the "up" button with her elbow to avoid touching it with her hand and waited for the familiar "ding" that would signal its arrival. A gaggle of nursing students chattering nervously exited the silver reflecting doors when they opened, nearly barreling Raven over. Raven expertly maneuvered around them and swiftly entered the elevator as the doors were beginning to shut.

*Phew*, she blew out a breath from the corner of her mouth. After pushing another button with her elbow, this one for floor four, she turned to watch the people in the atrium move about below as she ascended in her glass encased mobile box. When her ride came to an end, as it always did, she exited the doors and headed to Suite 488.

The reception area was empty for now.

*It won't be like this for long,* Raven thought to herself.

The front desk was enclosed with a sliding glass partition that had a typed paper sign taped to it. It read "Please sign in and be seated. Thank you". Raven opened the door that separated the reception area and led into a hallway. They all called the door the "gateway". To the right was an area where the patients would check out without anyone in the reception area hearing them. Then there was the hallway, which contained a door marked "bathroom", a door marked "staff only", and one marked "Lab".

Raven entered the "staff only" room. It was tight and cluttered with a small card table and folding chairs where the staff could eat meals if they chose to. A set of six lockers stood against the wall like rusty, metal sentries keeping watch. Beside the lockers sat a water cooler and a small college dorm sized refrigerator almost identical to the one in Raven's bedroom. On the front of the mini fridge was a sign stating that it was for "FOOD USE ONLY. Do not place Laboratory Reagents or supplies in this unit". She put her sweater in locker number five along with her bag and padlocked it for the day. She turned and headed out the door down the hall to the lab.

Raven scanned her keycard and waited for the light to turn green, then pushed on the door. It opened for her, exposing her to a cold rush of air and bright fluorescent lights. The television was already on broadcasting Channel Four CBS news.

*Charlie*, she thought.

"Good morning." a voice sang.

*Speaking of the devil,* Raven smiled.

"Morning, Charlie." Raven grumbled.

"Aw, my dear Raven, when will you learn to love the mornings?" Charlie smiled cheerily at Raven as he rounded the corner, his rotund belly leading the way, followed by the rest of him.

"When the mornings learn to love me." she replied.

"Well, well." Charlie chuckled.

Charlie resembled Santa Clause very much. He was round, his cheeks were ruddy, and his laugh was boisterous and contagious. His entire body would shake when he laughed. Charlie's white beard, however, was kept short and neat according to hospital regulations. But from all the movies, pictures and descriptions Raven had ever seen and heard, Charlie was as close to the real Santa Claus as Raven had ever gotten. Unfortunately, Raven had found out very early on there was no such thing as Santa Claus. Christmas was never a great time in her home when she was younger, even though Momma had tried her best to make it good.

Raven's smile faded and her eyes glazed over.

"Hey little lady, you okay?" Charlie asked, playfully adding a drawl to his voice.

Raven didn't hear him. She stood, staring off into a memory

only she could see.

"Raven." he tried again, a little louder.

"Huh?" Raven peered at him through foggy eyes.

"Honey, you okay?" Charlie asked, concerned.

"Yeah, sure. I'm good Chucky, honestly. I'm sorry, I didn't sleep great last night. I'm tired." Raven managed a smile. Charlie peered at Raven for a moment longer, his kind eyes trying to discern whether or not she was telling him the truth. After a moment, he seemed satisfied and his smile returned. Raven felt relieved. She was not up for questioning today. She was feeling weak again.

*Today is the last day,* she thought. *I have to go out tonight. I need a new donor.*

"You ready to start the day, lil' lady?"

Charlie tried out his best New Orleans accent on Raven. She smiled. He always had a way to get her to smile.

"You betchya!" Raven responded, willing herself to get through the day.

*Get through today, you can go out tonight and find a donor,* she encouraged herself.

"Alright," Charlie recited as he held the clipboard. "It looks like Mrs. Murray is here for her monthly INR draw."

"No problem. I will grab and draw today. You can check in and out if you want." Raven cajoled.

"You sure?" Charlie said. "You said you were tired. I don't mind doing it."

"I am sure, Chucky. If I sit up there, I will fall asleep. You know that. I have to keep moving or I will go crazy. Come on now, trust me, you'll be doing me a favor." Raven coerced Charlie further.

"Oh, alright then." Charlie conceded.

Raven went to the reception area and found Mrs. Murray,

petite eighty-four-year-old, Mrs. Murray, sitting patiently waiting to be called. Mrs. Murray's cane lay next to her on the chair, the end jutting out like a metal tongue waiting to strike the next person that dared try to sit next to the old woman.

"Mrs. Murray? Hi, Mrs. Murray." Raven called.

Mrs. Murray didn't move.

"Mrs. Murray." Raven called louder.

Mrs. Murray didn't budge.

"Sorry, Raven. I forgot to tell you she's hard of hearing." Charlie poked his head through the glass at the front desk.

Raven glared at Charlie for a minute.

"You sure it isn't my accent?" she smiled, thickening her New Orleans drawl.

Charlie chuckled, closing the sliding glass so that Mrs. Murray wouldn't hear him.

"MRS. MURRAY!" Raven raised her voice.

Mrs. Murray jumped in her chair. Raven and Charlie glanced at one another, barely able to contain their exposure.

"Yes." her feeble voice answered.

"Mrs. Murray, please come with me." Raven motioned Mrs. Murray towards her, kindly.

Raven felt a twinge of guilt for startling the old woman. *She must have dozed off,* Raven considered. *I shouldn't have almost laughed,* she chastised herself.

Raven waited patiently as the elderly woman slowly gathered her things and met her at the "gateway".

"Please follow me." Raven smiled warmly.

"Oh, you're a pretty little thing." Mrs. Murray smiled.

"Thank you. I'm Raven."

"Hmmm, yes, like the bird. Interesting." the old woman mused.

Raven watched Mrs. Murray curiously. She thought if she gave the old woman a minute maybe Mrs. Murray might offer a follow up to her open-ended comment, but she uttered nothing further. Mrs. Murray stood patiently, considering Raven.

"Well, okay then." Raven sighed. "Follow me."

The two walked silently down the hall to the door marked "Lab", Raven leading the way and Mrs. Murray shuffling behind with her awkward three-legged dance; *two-step-knock, two-step-knock, two-step-knock.* Raven again used her keycard to gain entry, as she would multiple times throughout the day for the rest of the day.

*Beep-beep goes the key card, beep-beep goes the card,* she thought as they entered the lab together.

"Okay Mrs. Murray, I'm sure you know the routine. Pick a chair, any chair. Pick an arm, any arm." Raven giggled inside her head at her wittiness.

Mrs. Murray did not laugh.

*Okay, I am 0 for 1 so far,* Raven thought.

Mrs. Murray shuffled over to the first chair (*two-step-knock, two-step-knock)* and sat with a decisive "humph"— cradling her purse, overcoat, and cane all on her lap like a newborn baby. Raven had to stifle a laugh at the sight of Mrs. Murray, so small, nearly swallowed by the overly large lab chair made that way a few years ago to compensate for an overgrowing population of a literally overgrowing population. She blew out an exasperated breath as she situated herself and her things in the gigantic chair. After taking a few breaths and steadying herself, Mrs. Murray rolled up the sleeve of her pink blouse, exposing a thin, pale arm of sagging, crepe-like skin. Raven cringed inside.

*Oh boy, this should be a fun challenge.*

"Okay, Mrs. Murray. You ready?" she smiled.

"About as ready as I will ever be, I suppose." Mrs. Murray did not smile.

"Any allergies?"

"You have my information. I am assuming you should know that, but no. I do not have any." Mrs. Murray answered.

*Shit, what a feisty old woman. Wonder what crawled up her ass today,* Raven brooded.

"Okay, well. I like to make sure. I use nitrile anyways, but I always ask. Thank you. I also have to check your date of birth." Raven sighed, waiting for another smart remark from the old crank.

"September third, 1909." Mrs. Murray answered.

"Thank you."

Raven pulled on her nitrile gloves and put out a vacuum tube for the blood draw.

"I'm going to feel right here in the crook of your arm for your vein and then I will place the tourniquet." Raven explained.

"Just get it over with. I do this every month. I am very familiar with it, so you don't have to walk me through it, dear little bird." Mrs. Murray replied.

Raven swallowed. She was usually very good at reading people, but she could not read Mrs. Murray. She was unable to tell if Mrs. Murray was being kind or condescending. Raven decided it didn't matter. She was there to do her job and she tried to treat everyone the same, no matter what. Raven palpated Mrs. Murray's skin on the inside of her elbow. Her veins were visible there; thick green lines of lumpy, venous roads, mapped out against a vast faded land of thin skin. But feeling them and sticking them without them rolling on her was another thing.

Raven tied the tourniquet and wiped the area with an alcohol gauze pad.

"Please pump your hand three times in a fist opening and closing it, then hold it in a closed fist to the best of your ability until I ask you to release it." Raven tried to muster some form of sweetness in her voice.

Mrs. Murray complied, silently.

Raven could see the green vein road plump up slightly. She found her small butterfly needle and waited for another second then plunged it into the vein.

*First try, baby.* Raven celebrated silently.

Raven opened up the line to the butterfly needle tubing and attached the glass vacuum tube. She watched, mesmerized, as the blood spurted into it.

*Amazing.*

As monotonous as the other parts of her job were, this part of her job never got boring.

Raven placed the tube to the side, attached another tube to draw one more sample, then as gently as possible she removed the needle. She replaced it with a two by two pad of gauze and asked Mrs. Murray to hold pressure for a moment. Raven placed a white label on the tubes of blood that contained Mrs. Murray's name, date of birth, and medical record number; then put them in a holder labeled "transport" where they would be taken down to the actual laboratory, placed in a centrifuge, then analyzed.

Raven removed the two by two pad of gauze and replaced it with a new one. She put a small piece of medical tape over it to hold it in place.

"Mrs. Murray, please leave the gauze until the bleeding has stopped completely. Can you please confirm your name and date of birth for me once more?" Raven asked, awaiting a snarky comment. To her surprise, nothing came.

"That was the easiest blood draw I have ever had. Painless." Mrs. Murray smiled sweetly. "Ellen Murray, September third, 1909, beautiful little blackbird." Mrs. Murray grabbed Raven's hand with her small, thin one— its withering skin shifty but soft under Raven's fingers. Mrs. Murray put her other small, bony hand on top of Raven's and patted it gently. "Good girl, Little Blackbird."

Raven smiled.

*My momma used to call me little blackbird...*

# CHAPTER FOUR

Raven sat in the only single seat available in the train car she was in. Each car had the same seating plan made up of mostly double or quadruple seats. There were two singles on each car and Raven always tried to grab one if she could so that no one could sit near her. The seats were hard and made of plastic, definitely not made for comfort, but for cheap durability. Although they were uncomfortable, she was grateful for the single seats. She wasn't much of a conversationalist on the ride to and from work. That was her time for reflection. Besides, the train smelled like piss and body odor, and there always seemed to be some kind of perv trying to talk to her. She hated the train, but it was necessary for now.

"No, fuck you!" someone snarled.

Raven saw what she assumed was a young couple, arguing. They were both thin with dirty, ripped clothing. When the man grinned, Raven could see he was missing one of his front teeth and his skin was pockmarked, scarred from years of untreated acne. The woman had long, straggly hair that was tangled and matted, like it hadn't been washed in several weeks. Her face was peppered with cystic acne that appeared painful, red and swollen. Raven could briefly see the distinguishing features of track marks on the woman's thin inner elbow before the man grabbed at it, obscuring her view. The man was trying to hold the woman, but it appeared she didn't want to be touched. The woman ripped her arm from his grasp. Raven's body stiffened.

"I said no, Junior. Why don't you fucking listen for a change?" the woman hissed.

It was obvious she was trying to keep her voice down, but it was getting harder and harder for her as her anger with her partner increased. "Junior" was either very hard of hearing or was stupid because the more "angry lady" hissed, the more he put his paws all over her.

"Junior!" (much louder)

Heads began to turn in their direction.

"Keep your fucking hands to yourself. You're drunk and you stink! Don't touch me! You wanna fuck that bitch and then fuck me like it ain't nuthin'. Well, I ain't nuthin'. I'm somethin'. I ain't gonna go for that shit! And don't tell me you fucked her for that hit of crack cuz that's some bullshit and you know it!" Angry lady growled.

*Aw, there it is.*

"Baby, baby, you know I wasn't gonna hit it all myself. I was gettin' it for US!" Junior whined.

Junior went to try again, but the train lurched to a stop, throwing him off balance. Junior fell, not so gracefully, to the floor. Angry lady and many others burst into laughter, and some people clapped. Junior laid there for a moment making out with the floor of the train instead of what was now, most likely, his ex-girlfriend. The doors to the train opened and angry lady stood up on slightly wobbly legs and exited the train. Others did as well, many stepping around, and over, Junior to do so. Junior rolled slightly to his left to examine his surroundings, then with surprising swiftness for his supposed state, hopped to his feet and stumbled after his hissy-faced lover.

Raven sighed.

*There's never a shortage of entertainment on the train.*

She rode peacefully to the Newbury depot and got off. The air outside was warm and fresh, unlike the stale train air. Raven took a deep breath in and gazed up. The sky held beautiful pale pinks and purples shed in the war between night and day as they fought for space and time on its heavenly land. But soon, the black of night would come and swallow up the remains on the field of battle leaving nothing but darkness.

*Darkness always wins,* Raven thought.

# CHAPTER FIVE

THE BAR WAS DARK. A few people were scattered here
and there. She sat in the corner far from the chatter of the
patrons, the televisions, the bartender. She always started
out there, in that very spot. It was a good spot to watch
from. To wait. She wasn't sure that anyone could, or would,
even see her there in that corner. There was no table there.
There was no light. She had snuck in quietly, her Red Sox
cap concealing her face. It was never difficult to be stealthy
in a bar of self-centered, halfcocked people. It was easy to
camouflage yourself. She had been perfecting the art of
invisibility since she was a child.

Cindy, the bartender, was doing her usual "single lady"
routine. Raven had become quite accustomed to it. After
dinner time the bar would thin out a bit, leaving Cindy with
a manageable number of customers, most of which were
men. Raven imagined Cindy made quite a chunk of money
on nights like these. Cindy was, in her prime, a good-looking
woman. From a distance, she seemed like she could be
someone's trophy wife. Tall and thin, but round in all the
right places, and a pair of legs that kept on going. No need

for heels on that one. Yet, up close, anyone could easily see Cindy had lived a hard life in the fast lane. As much as she tried to cover the deep wrinkles with caked-on foundation, makeup couldn't hide the damage from years of sniffing white lines of the powdery kind in dirty bathrooms and back seats, or from pounding your bar's supposed "spill tab" all day. That was why Raven wasn't too worried about Cindy seeing her. Cindy's brain cells had been cooked a long time ago, like an egg on the asphalt of the Vegas strip on a 105° day.

Raven would wait and watch. She was very patient. Cindy would start to chat up a man or two, or three or five, at the bar. Her usual routine was to buy them a shot and after a few of those, for every shot Cindy bought them, she would bang back two of her own. Once Raven was sure Cindy was nice and oiled up, Raven would advance on her chosen donor. Until then, she would wait. Wait and watch. As she waited, Raven thought about her momma.

Her beautiful momma in the kitchen at the stove. She was boiling up a chicken head and chicken feet with Mr. Mackey's hair in it. Mrs. Mackey had given it to momma because "Mr. Mackey was keeping company with the neighbor lady" momma revealed to her. Beside the stove was a small doll Momma had sewn of Mr. Mackey, another piece of his hair glued on the head of the doll. Momma had told Raven she couldn't play with the Mr. Mackey doll. It had "done some bad things and didn't deserve to have any more fun.".

"Cheating is a horrible sin, little blackbird. You hear me?"

"Yes, momma."

"Raven, baby, all men desire is sex and money. They are Satan's creatures, born from the fires of lust and greed.

You'll be able to use that to your advantage someday, little blackbird. When you are older, I will teach you how."
Momma kissed her head then.

Momma stirred the hoodoo soup on the stove while she sang "Blackbird" by the Beatles. It was her favorite song. Raven smiled when momma sang that song. The sun shone through the kitchen window, casting a halo around momma's blonde curls.

*Oh momma, I love you so much*, Raven thought.

"Ha! Damn it!" someone yelled, ripping Raven from her memories.

"Man, that sucks!" another man yelled.

"Come on ref! What the fuck game were you watching?" Raven despised Monday night football, but it was the best night to find a donor. More drunk, stupid men hanging around the bar to choose from. Cindy's laugh, hoarse from years of smoking, floated over to Raven. Just by its reckless volume, Raven could tell Cindy was well on her way to shitfaced.

*Soon*, she thought. *A few more "one for you and two for me" rounds and she won't remember a thing from tonight*, Raven grinned.

"Touchdown!" a drunken patron yelled.

"Fuck, yes!" another yelled.

"Wahoo!" another followed suit.

*Perfect.*

"Touchdown round on me." the fat man called out, eliciting a whooping loud applause.

Cindy poured and passed the drinks. Raven watched and waited. Cindy poured herself two shots and missed her mouth on the second one.

*Okay, here we go.*

Raven stood and walked slowly over to the end of the bar, where a man had been sitting alone for the evening. She sat next to him without a word. She wasn't worried about Cindy. Cindy was drunk and had a reputation for "ignoring women". Raven waited for a moment, then purposely brushed her arm up against the man's elbow.

"Oh, excuse me. I'm terribly sorry." Raven's husky New Orleans drawl fell like a slow country song from her crimson lips.

The man looked at her and she locked eyes with him trying to gauge his interest. His face flushed and he turned away, a shy smirk on his mouth.

"Don't worry 'bout it, Sweetheart." he slurred, still avoiding her shyly.

*Perfect*, Raven thought. *Already halfway there.*

The drunken man mulled something over in his head. Raven could see him struggling with it, the conflict. When he seemed to come up with a decision, with that decision came a little nerve. He turned to steal a glance at her.

"How are you doing tonight, lovely lady?" he asked, the smell of whiskey and cigars drifting to her on his heavy breath with each word he spoke.

"Better now." she half lied.

The thought of having to press her lips against his made her stomach twist with disgust, but she knew it had to be done. Once it was over, she would have what she needed, and all would be right again.

"Well, is that so?" he slurred.

"Jameson?" Raven asked, pointing at the man's glass.

"Absolutely." he nodded, teetering slightly, then catching himself before completely tumbling to one side.

"Well, looks like you're in need of another." Raven smiled

with crimson colored lips.

"Oh no, no. Thank you, but a woman doesn't buy a man a drink where I come from. The man buys the woman a drink. He..." The man stopped mid-sentence to bark a painful sounding hiccup from somewhere deep within his bowels. Surprised, he cleared his throat and continued. "Pardon me. As I was saying, he should buy the woman a drink."

Raven watched the pitiful man trying hard to impress her in his wrinkled clothes and messy hair. She could see his brain working hard to find its way through the drunken haze in order to form intelligible conversation. Raven had enough experience to recognize that the Jameson was winning the battle. The man's brow creased. Raven waited patiently, expecting nothing clever to follow. She wasn't disappointed.

"So," He drew out the word as if he were trying to think of something else to say.

*Intriguing.*

"So." Raven parroted.

"Another Jameson, Billy?" Cindy's voice sounded as garbled as Billy's thought must have been.

Cindy focused right on Billy, completely ignoring Raven. Nonetheless, Raven turned her head away from Cindy and pretended to watch one of the televisions mounted behind her so that Cindy could not see her face.

*The rumors are true,* Raven thought. *That's all well and good for me and my situation. I don't want her remembering one little thing about me.*

"One more, Cin." Billy answered.

"For you, friend?" Cindy asked.

*Don't turn around,* Raven thought.

Billy turned to Raven.

"Would you like one?" he asked.

Raven thought of politely declining, then reconsidered. *You're going to have to kiss him and he is going to taste like it. You're gonna need it to get through tonight.*
Raven nodded without turning around.
"Yeah." Billy barked at Cindy.
Cindy walked away to get two glasses of Jameson.
"Thank you, Billy." Raven cooed. "Sorry, didn't mean to seem rude, I wanted to catch that." She turned around to face him and pointed at the television.
"Ah, yes," (slur)" You're welcome, Miss?" Billy looked at her, eyebrows raised, a question on his face.
"Oh yes," Raven extended a hand to him. "Aeval." she smiled warmly.
Raven had taken on the alias Aeval Eiram. Marie Catherine Laveau, the voodoo queen herself, was Raven's inspiration. Raven used Marie's first and last name and turned it into a palindrome, (dropping the U at the end), and she became Aeval Eiram. She had come to enjoy becoming this other persona, this dangerous, wild woman free of inhibitions and fear.
Billy squinted at Raven as if he couldn't see her. Raven wondered if him seeing her had anything to do with the fact that he couldn't pronounce her name. She resisted the urge to roll her eyes and moved in a little closer making sure he could see her lips. Like a Bingo caller, she repeated herself, loudly and precisely.
"It is pronounced A-vel," Raven moved her lips for him slowly.
Recognition replaced the confusion.
"Nice to meet you, Aeval." Billy shook Raven's hand.
His hand was thickly padded with doughy skin, clammy from sitting in the warm bar and nervous energy. It

was that time of year when the weather was stifling but establishments, especially lower level ones like The Lark, were too cheap to put on their air conditioning units. The sweat beads that clung to his forehead glistened intermittently from the flashes of light off the televisions surrounding them. Raven struggled to stay seated next to him, her repulsion growing for him.

*It's gotta be done.*

Cindy dropped the drinks in front of Billy and walked away. Raven watched her throw back two shots of her own, then put the lid back on the Jameson bottle, sealing the revered amber liquid until called upon again. Raven despised what liquor could do to some people. She had seen it in action many times, and it was a slow working poison for most. Tonight, however, she was grateful for its help.

Billy handed Raven her drink then took his own, swirling the liquid around a few times before sipping it. He nudged Raven gently with a nod. She picked up her glass, mimicking Billy and sipped at her own golden liquid. It burned every inch of her throat and esophagus as it made its way down, but she forced herself to make no visible signs of distaste. He smiled at her approvingly. She returned the smile, then cocked the tumbler back and threw the remaining liquid down her throat, swallowing hard.

"Thirsty, pretty lady?" Billy asked her with mixed surprise and admiration.

"No. Bored." Raven answered sarcastically, but only enough to tease.

"Ah, I see. Well, I don't blame you. It is quite a boring football game, and there aren't any good-looking fellas here, I suppose." Billy hinted.

*Brother! Captain Obvious,* she thought.

"Well now, I can think of one," Raven drew out the last word and thickened her voice.

She knew her New Orleans accent was still audible in certain words, but when she wanted to, she could pour it on thick. She had been told on many occasions that it was "sexy", so she utilized it to her advantage. She watched Billy closely. She could see new sweat beads forming on his forehead. He could not hold her gaze. He viewed the patrons around the bar and shifted around on his bar stool.

*I make him nervous. Good.*

Billy shifted his attention to the television.

"Which one is that?" he probed.

"Well, you, silly man." Raven giggled.

Billy snorted— a piggish sound. He shifted in his chair again. A moment passed, then he turned to face Raven, his cheeks colored red as if Cindy had applied rouge on them. His brown eyes were wide with surprise.

"Oh yeah?" he asked, truly shocked it seemed.

*Poor man,* she thought, but only for a moment.

"Sure." Raven smiled sweetly.

"W-wow." he stammered.

Raven got closer to Billy. He started and backed up slightly. Raven put her hand gently on his arm to steady him and moved in closer. Billy stopped his retreat. It was as if her touch paralyzed him. Her hand was on his arm and her thumb was touching the skin on the underside of his wrist. She could feel his radial pulse, pounding through the skin. She knew if she counted the beats, they would read in the low hundreds. The heat radiating from his skin could have melted the ice in his glass had Cindy not been lazy and actually put some in it.

"What do you say we get out of here?" Raven coaxed.

Billy's breath shuddered.

"I, I, um, okay." he stumbled.

Billy scavenged through his pockets for a couple of singles and threw them, mostly crumpled, upon the sticky bar top. He turned, timidly, toward Raven.

"Okay, now what?" he asked, like a new employee waiting for instructions.

"Alright, let's go." Raven announced and hopped down from her stool. "No need to say goodbye. Let's not disturb anyone." Raven whispered in Billy's ear seductively. She didn't want to draw any attention towards them.

Billy's body shuddered.

"I, I, okay." he stumbled, again.

Raven had to stifle a laugh.

*Could I have chosen a bigger idiot? He is perfect.*

"Okay, Billy. Follow me."

# CHAPTER SIX

"Go in and get a room for yourself and once you have the key and room number, I will join you." Raven sat in the passenger seat of Billy's car and tuned her head away from him so she could roll her eyes.

"Okay, but how will you know what room?" Billy asked her timidly.

*Oh boy this one is not a bright one, but I guess that is good for me. Positive thoughts, Raven, positive thoughts.*

Raven blew an exasperated breath from her mouth. The air coming from the vents in Billy's car smelled stale, and it made her feel nauseous and agitated. She tried desperately to keep her cool. She couldn't show any contempt toward this dull man or she may ruin her chances.

*Take a deep breath of the nasty air and try.*

She did just that. She breathed in through her nostrils and slowly spoke as she exhaled, trying not to sound condescending.

"I will be hanging back behind the magazine rack over there and that fake plant. The clerk won't see me, but I will still be able to hear everything." Raven ordered.

"I don't see what you are talking about." Billy squinted his eyes and tried to peer through the car window into the entrance of the hotel's check in desk. "How do you know..." he began.

"I came here last month on business." Raven cut him off, growing more impatient by the second.

*This fucking air is stifling.*

"And why are we doing this again?"

*Jesus, we are never going to get this done and over with,* Raven thought, aggravation brewing inside her like a pot of water reaching its boiling point. If Billy wasn't careful she was going to blow her top.

"Well, Billy, do I have to explain that to you?" Raven forced a girlish giggle and ran a finger up his inner thigh.

Billy jumped in surprise and snorted.

"No, no..." He stuttered. "I know why we are here."

Billy blushed, his skin flushing so red it was visible in the minimal light that peeked through the windshield.

"I meant, why do I have to check in by myself while you hide?"

His face was twisted with confusion.

*It won't be the only time tonight that I see his face like that,* Raven thought with pleasure.

"Because, silly, I don't want you to have to pay for two people. Only one. Now get going before I lose interest." Raven turned her face from him and frowned.

Her last words set a fire under Billy's rear.

"Okay, I'm ready. Are you?" he asked.

"Billy boy, I have been ready." Raven answered, trying to sound enthused but failing. Billy seemed to have missed it. He opened the door to his car and a warm breeze hit Raven in the face. A scintilla of humidity lingered in the air; the perfect concoction of summer weather. Raven loved warm nights; they reminded her of New Orleans. She missed the late nights in July, thick with humidity and sparsely clad bodies roaming the French Quarter—echoes of laughter and Creole reflecting off the faint breeze, along with the smell of booze, tobacco smoke, seafood, and vomit.

Raven opened her door and followed Billy after he was safely inside, and she could see him at the clerk's desk. She posted herself behind the magazine rack and decorative plant like she told him she would. She stood quietly and listened.

"Yes, one. For one night."

"Okay sir. Check out is at eleven a.m. There is no smoking in the room. There is a mini fridge and a small microwave. We will hold an incidentals charge on your credit card for..."

"I'm paying cash." Billy interrupted the clerk.

"Oh, okay, well then I will ask you for an extra deposit of thirty dollars which you will get back once you check out and there are no extra charges we have incurred on your behalf." the clerk recited his lines.

"Okay." Billy rummaged through his wallet.

He handed the clerk a small stack of bills. The clerk took it and counted it.

"Great, thanks. Here is your room key. You are in room thirteen. It's outside to the left about six doors down." the clerk handed Billy the keys, then as an afterthought added, without looking up, "Call if you need anything."

"Thanks." Billy raised a grateful hand as he headed out the door.

Billy turned to leave. He glanced at Raven on the way out. *Idiot*, she thought. *Thank God that damn kid isn't paying attention to anything but whatever he's got going on in his lap.* Raven waited a few minutes watching the clerk. Fortunately, he stood and went into the back office giving Raven a moment to escape out the front door. She walked down to join Bumbling Billy in room thirteen.

She knocked quietly on the door. It took a moment for him to answer.

"H-hi"

"Hey." Raven pushed past Bumbling Billy to get into the hotel room.

He didn't seem to mind.

"This is nice, right?" he gawked at her, following her back into the room like a duckling following its mommy.

"Yeah, sure. Nice." Raven laid her bag of tricks on a chair next to the table and surveyed the room, ignoring Billy.

"What is nice is all the hot things I'm going to do to you, Billy." Raven plastered a playful smile on her lips and turned to face Billy at last.

For the second time that evening, she saw him shudder.

"I, um…"

"It's okay, sweetie. You don't even have to talk. In fact, I prefer it that way."

Billy mouth gaped.

"I have a little something for you. It's to take the edge off. You know, make you feel good. Less… nervous."

"I-I, what is it?"

"It's a little something that will make you feel extra good before I make you feel even better." Raven smiled.

Raven pulled out the baggie with the Molly in it.

Billy's eyes opened wide.

"I don't do drugs." Billy exclaimed.

"Oh honey, don't be such a nerd. It's not anything that can hurt you. I have done it a ton of times. I will do it with you." Raven persuaded.

Billy eyed Raven closely, then eyed the bag. Raven could see him swaying slightly on the bow of his invisible ship as it tossed in the rough seas of crapulence.

*I can't believe I let him drive me here,* she thought. *He's shitfaced.*

It was a good thing The Lark was only a few blocks away. Bumbling Billy slowly returned his gaze back to Raven. She could tell he was indecisive about the Molly. Thankfully she had mastered the art of the pill under the tongue.

"Listen, I will take mine first if it makes you feel safer. Then I'm going to take my bag and hit the little girl's room to freshen up." Raven flashed a beautiful smile Billy's way.

"Trust me you're gonna feel so damn good after you take this. And by the way, the orgasm on this is amazing."

Raven went to the sink in the bathroom and filled two plastic cups with water. She returned to Billy and handed him one. She opened the baggie and handed Billy a pill and grabbed herself one. Raven placed hers on her tongue and closed her mouth. She skillfully maneuvered the pill so that it sat below her tongue, then she sipped some water and pretended to swallow it.

"Okay sexy, you're turn." she coaxed.

Billy fidgeted nervously.

"It's okay. I wouldn't do anything to hurt you." Raven lied. She moved in closely and planted a lingering kiss on his trembling lips. Then, backed up and stared at him expectantly. His eyes were closed, and he stood, wavering like a sparse tree in a heavy wind. But now, she believed it had more to do with his intoxication with her than the alcohol.

"Billy Boy." she prodded.

"Okay." Billy murmured as he opened his eyes, woken from his dream.

Billy regarded the pill in his hand. Raven gently pushed Billy's hand towards his mouth. He glimpsed at her once more for reassurance. Raven smiled brilliantly at him. Billy smiled back then threw the pill down his throat and chased it with the water from his plastic cup.

Raven grinned happily.

"Great job, Billy. Now we are going to have some fun. I am going to freshen up." Raven turned and headed to the bathroom.

Raven switched on the light in the bathroom and listened to the familiar buzz of the fluorescence as the electricity surged into it, bringing it to life. It crackled a few times leaving Raven to wonder when the electricity had last been upgraded, or better yet, even checked. She leaned over the toilet and spit her Molly capsule into the bowl. She peered at herself in the mirror. A large crack ran diagonally from the lower left corner up to the top right corner of the glass, distorting her image.

*A split face,* she thought, *a two-faced monster. How fitting.* She ran water into her cupped hand and sucked it up into her mouth, swishing the cold liquid around in her mouth. Raven puffed out her cheeks from side to side with the water, admiring her chipmunk-like appearance, then spit the water into the sink. One of her teeth screamed at her from the cold, but she ignored it for the moment, as the urgency to urinate took over. She squatted over the toilet seat to pee and watched with amusement as the little pill was pushed around from the pressure of her urine hitting the water. It reminded her of the time she chased an ant around with a stick— how it scuttled away every time she got near it, running back and forth until she finally just squished it with the bottom of her sneaker.

*Run little pill, run.* Raven giggled to herself.

When she was finished, she sat on the edge of the tub and put her chin in her cupped hands. She wasn't ready to go back out to Bumbling Billy quite yet. He disgusted her. She could feel the cold of the porcelain tub seeping through the thin material of her skirt into the back of her thighs. It felt good, calming. She looked down to the left of her at the lip of the tub and considered what she saw there. A small, black spot with an irregular border of chipped porcelain that exposed dark cast iron beneath it stared at her. A black eye—all seeing, all knowing. It held her there, for how long she did not know, but she finally broke free from its hypnotic spell and shook her head. She stood and returned to the beautiful, two-faced monster in the mirror and spoke silently to her.

*You have hidden long enough. For fuck's sake, it's going to take a while for the Molly to hit Bumbling Billy. You are going to have to keep him entertained.*

The thought of doing anything sexual with Billy made Raven want to wretch up the Jameson she had floating in her belly. Her mouth filled with saliva in preparation for vomiting. She took a few deep breaths and swallowed hard.

*You can do this.*

Raven splashed some cold water from the faucet on her face and wiped her fingerprints off the handles. She took a deep breath and checked herself out in the mirror one last time. Raven smiled deviously and opened the bathroom door.

"Well there you are. I thought you fell in."

Billy was sitting on the edge of the bed waiting for her, a mousy smile on his face.

*My, haven't you grown some balls.* Raven gritted her teeth together. *Bumbling Billy is now Ballsy Billy, I see.*

"Yeah, well, a girl needs to freshen up, doesn't she?" Raven answered, trying to hold in her annoyance.

"I don't mind." Billy answered, the smirk still on his face. Raven couldn't wait for the Molly to kick in. She didn't want to have to even kiss him again. His face was pale and fat, his brow slick with nervous sweat. Raven felt a surge of saliva fill her mouth again.

*Oh God, please, don't let me vomit. I have to get through this. Come on, think,* she urged herself.

Ballsy Billy shifted on the bed; his flat brown eyes shifted nervously. Raven knew she had to do something soon, or Ballsy Billy was going to be Bye Bye Billy.

"Do you like music, Billy?" Raven asked, thickening her New Orleans drawl again.

Billy's pale complexion disappeared, replaced with the pink hue of nervous excitement. Raven imagined his skin tingled with electricity as much as hers crawled with disgust. Raven turned her attention to the small radio alarm clock that sat on the side table next to the bed. The digital numbers read eleven twenty p.m. She walked over to the plastic timepiece and examined the buttons. After a moment she found the AM/FM button and pushed it. The black plastic box came alive with screaming static.

"Shit!" Billy exclaimed.

Raven started laughing.

"Sorry. Hold on."

Raven searched for the volume control and when she found it, turned it until the static was no longer at an ear-piercing level. She checked on Billy, who instinctively put his hands over his ears, to make sure he had survived the audio attack. He sat, watching her, hands held a few inches from his ears, as if another static ear perforating assault was imminent. Raven found the radio dial and searched for a station. She stumbled through two talk radio stations and a station with a commercial for Howard Stern's talk show. Raven was beginning to wonder if she would ever find music when the dial found it, the last station, playing rock.

*Okay, this may work,* she thought.

The black box pulsed a rhythmic beat through the cheap speaker slits. Raven loved rock and this was a new kind of rock that was becoming popular. The song playing was from a new, upcoming grunge band from Seattle. She knew they were going to make it big.

*Perfect, this is exactly what I need. This will help me get in the mood.*

She turned to face Billy. He had since laid his hands in his lap. His eyes were wide and curious. Raven moved to the sound, shifting her hips back and forth and moving her feet. To anyone watching, she would have appeared like a well-practiced belly dancer— hips undulating perfectly to the rhythm of the music, sexual and seductive. Raven closed her eyes and listened to the melody, allowing it to take her somewhere other than here with pudgy, pale Ballsy Billy. With her eyes still closed, she spoke to him.

"Do you like what you see?" she murmured.

"Y-yes." he stuttered.

"Do you *want* what you see?"

An audible, trembling sigh.

"Y-yes. I do."

"Do you know what I want" Raven asked in her most enticing voice.

"No." Billy answered, breathless.

"I want to play a game." Raven's face flushed with excitement.

She opened her eyes to see Billy's reaction. He was staring

at her with tangible desire. Raven continued to sway to the music. She rocked back and forth, tugging slowly on her blouse, exposing her bare shoulders, arms, and belly. Her black, laced bra sat snug against her breasts, cradling them as she danced. She could see Billy suck in a breath at the sight of her. Raven took her hands and ran them up the sides of her head, knocking off her hat and pulling her long, black hair up and away from her face – exposing her long, elegant neck. She dropped her hair and it fell wildly around her face. Her own hands were all over her body, touching, caressing. She rolled her head back and forth to the beat of the music, letting herself get lost in the tribal beats of the drums. She knew he wanted her. She could *feel* him wanting her. That's how all men were. Her momma had taught her that. Her body was a tool she could use to get what she wanted or needed. Raven had honed her skills for getting what she wanted.

"What, um, what kind of game?" Billy stammered.

"It's kind of a kinky game, Billy. I am not sure you can handle it." Raven's voice was thick with seduction.

Billy moved around on the bed awkwardly, as if he didn't quite know whether he was supposed to stand or stay seated. Raven thought his eyes appeared glossier than before.

*I hope that means the Molly is kicking in.*

A goofy smile moved Billy's lips, baring his teeth. He laughed suddenly, as large and goofy as his smile was. Billy seemed surprised at himself. He clapped his hand over his mouth as if to catch the laugh and jam it back into his lips.

"I can play that kind of game." Billy's voice quivered.

His lips were twisting, working hard. Raven couldn't understand at first what was wrong with them, then she realized he was trying not to laugh. She struggled for a moment to calm herself. She couldn't ruin his mood by yelling at him.

*It's the Molly making him giddy. Go with it.*

"Are you sure?" she dared.

Billy's face lost its foolish expression. His glazed eyes fixed upon her.

"Yes, I am very sure." Billy said with indisputable assuredness.

"Okay. But you'll have to trust me."

"Okay."

Raven walked over to her bag. She reached in and removed a pair of long, plastic zip ties and laid them on the table. Billy watched her intently. She knew she had to give him a little more to entice him. Raven turned her back to him and slowly unzipped her skirt, letting it fall to the floor. She turned to face Billy, standing in front of him with only her black, laced bra, black stockings held in place with garter belts, and black lace panties. Billy's mouth fell open again.

*And that folks, is the ticket,* Raven thought.

"Billy, I am going to tie you up." Raven purred.

"You, huh? What?" Billy asked, bewilderment spreading across his face.

"I am going to take these plastic zip ties and tie you to the bedpost. Gently, of course." Raven giggled.

"Oh, um, okay. I have never done that before." Billy said nervously.

"Oh Billy, silly Billy Boy. You are going to enjoy yourself, Billy Boy." Raven moved her body, twisting it enticingly. "I promise."

"Okay, what do you want me to do? Like, what should I do?" Billy resembled a teenage boy on his first date. His flustered state may have been endearing had Raven been attracted to him, but he was exhausting. Raven was actually going to enjoy slicing this one's throat.

"Get naked, Billy Boy." Raven demanded.

Billy scrambled like a firefighter called to a four-alarm fire. Raven thought for a moment he might rip his clothes as he pulled them off of his body. She found herself wondering when the last time poor Billy had gotten laid was. He seemed starved for affection. Within a minute Billy had stripped himself bare. His pasty skin reminded Raven of the bread dough her Momma used to make lumpy and blanched. Billy awaited further instruction.

"Lay on the bed, Billy Boy."

Billy did as he was told.

Raven went to him with the zip ties.

"Please place your arms above your head, Bad Billy Boy." she growled.

She could see Billy's excitement growing rather quickly. It still amazed her that a few words, spoken a certain way could make a man become fully erect within seconds. Women did have magic powers like momma promised. Raven tried hard not to see Billy's pitched manhood. She only had to make him believe she wanted him for a few more minutes, when in reality the thought of even being this close to him and his erection had her stomach bile fighting its way up into her throat.

Raven swallowed.

Billy swallowed.

Billy was frightened; the fear was evident in his eyes.

Raven took the first zip tie and fastened it with Billy's wrist inside, to the bedpost, until the skin hung over it slightly.

"Ouch." Billy complained.

"Sorry, sweetie. Didn't mean to make it that tight." Raven lied sweetly.

Raven fixed the next one the same exact way.
"OUCH, Aeval!! Be careful! You said you would be gentle!" Billy yelped.
"Oh Billy Boy, honey. I know I did. I know I did."
Billy whimpered in surprise and discomfort.
"Billy Boy, pain can mean pleasure. Pain can actually make pleasure so much better. It intensifies the orgasm."
Raven smiled as she grabbed a candle and the book of matches from her bag. Billy watched like a young child in the doctor's office about to get a shot, wide eyed and scared, yet unsure of the situation that was unfolding. Raven sauntered over to Billy and lit the candle. The wick sizzled to life, spitting a few sparks off, making Billy jump. Raven giggled.
"Aeval, what are you doing?" Billy asked, fear coating his voice.
"I'm having a little fun, Boring Billy." Raven groaned. "Billy, are you boring? If you're boring, I am not going to wanna play with you anymore."
Billy shifted uncomfortably on the bed. His eyes moved from the candle to Raven, then back to the candle.
"No, I-I am not boring," he replied.
Raven stood next to the bed and held the candle over Billy's chest. Billy's eyes widened as if someone had pinched him. His mouth opened, but nothing came out. Raven tilted the candle allowing a small stream of hot wax to fall against Billy's sallow skin.
"Arrrgh!" Billy cried out.
Raven smiled. She blew on Billy's chest. Billy's body stiffened, everywhere, including his small endowment that had started to go limp with apprehension.
"See? Feels good, doesn't it?"
"Mhm." Billy moaned.

*Ah, finally, the Molly is hitting him. Thank God.*
Raven dropped another stream of candle wax on Billy's chest eliciting another cry. She blew on his chest again, giving rise to more moaning from Billy. Billy's eyes were closed. Raven did this until she had made her three completed marks, then she blew out the candle.
*It's time.*
She walked to her bag and retrieved her gloves, pulling them on tightly.
"Aeval, what are you doing?"
Raven peeked at him to see his eyes still closed.
"Getting ready to finish our game, Billy Boy."
Raven removed the hunting knife from the bag. The light glinted off the blade. Billy opened his eyes and looked at Raven. A rush of satisfaction flooded her when she saw Billy realize what was about to happen. Raven smiled at him sweetly as she moved toward the bed.
"A-A-Aeval" he stammered.
"Billy Boy. Shhh." Raven put a gloved finger to her lips.
"Please." he whispered.
"Shh." Raven whispered to him.
Billy's stomach rose and fell quickly. Raven imagined it wouldn't take much for him to start hyperventilating.
*Fear.*
"This is just a game, right Aeval?" Billy whimpered.
"Yes, Billy Boy, just a game." Raven repeated.
"Please don't hurt me. I have money. I can give you money." Billy bartered.
"Billy Boy, I don't want your money, honey."
"I can get you anything you want, Aeval. I will get you whatever you want but please don't hurt me. I have a wife and kids. What do you want?" Billy begged.

"Oh, Billy Boy, that's so ugly. You just made this so much easier for me. Why would you wanna go and do a naughty, nasty thing like that?" Raven hissed.

Billy's face was wet with tears and drool seeped out of the corner of his gaping mouth. Snot bubbles expanded and contracted with each labored breath he drew. Raven laughed at the sight of him.

*Serves him right.*

"What? What did I do?"

"Billy Boy, why would you wanna be unfaithful to your wifey? That's just bad form, Billy Boy." Raven taunted through teeth gritted.

"Please, just tell me what you want?" Billy cried.

"I want your blood." Raven laughed as she sliced Billy Boy's throat.

# CHAPTER SEVEN

RAVEN RUSHED TO HER BAG to grab the needle and glass vacuum tubes inside. She didn't have much time. She only had a few minutes before Billy's heart would stop pumping. Billy's blood spurted from his throat with each beat of his heart and he garbled inaudible words as he began to choke on his own blood.

"Stop it!" she hissed. "Stop talking! I can't stand it!"

Raven cut Billy's left arm free of the zip tie and tied the rubber tourniquet around it tightly. She quickly found his vein and plunged the butterfly needle into it. Red blood flowed quickly into the plastic tubing. Raven removed the clamp and attached the glass vacuum tube to the connector and watched as the tube filled with warm crimson liquid. *Liquid life,* she mused.

She removed the tube once it was filled and replaced it with another empty one and watched as it filled with Billy Boy's life force.

Billy was still trying to talk, but his attempts were becoming more futile with each passing second.

*Only a few more tubes.*

Raven hurried as fast as she could. She grabbed the last tube and pulled it off of the needle.

*That makes twelve.*

Raven gathered the tubes gently and placed them in the box they came in, then back into her bag. She walked over to Billy to remove the needle and tourniquet. Billy was gurgling. "Glub-Glub-Glub."

The sound reverberated in Raven's head. It reminded her of something torturous, like nails on a chalkboard, grating in her ears.

*Stop it.*

"Glub-Glub-Glub."

"Stop it."

His eyes were bulging— the whites of his eyes were enormous ping pong balls ready to pop from their sockets.

"Shut up!" Raven warned him.

He didn't stop. The gurgling continued. It echoed in Raven's skull, ricocheting off the thin bones like a bullet off of bullet proof glass. Raven grabbed at the sides of her head and pulled at her hair. She squeezed her eyes shut, trying to push out the sound from her mind. It didn't work.

"SHUT THE FUCK UP!" she screamed.

*Make him stop, Raven. Make him stop.* That was all she could hear in her head…. *Make him stop, Raven, please make him stop….*

Raven opened her eyes.

There, on the bed, the shiny metal caught her eye. Raven grasped the cold hilt of the hunting knife. Something took over her. She was no longer in control. It was as if she were floating above her own body watching as she slashed with the hunting knife at Billy's body too many times to count. Violent. Stabbing. Anything to make him stop. She had to

make him stop.
*Make him stop, Raven baby. Make him stop!*

*The kitchen was bright, full of sun, warmth and love. Momma was at the sink singing Blackbird. Raven listened intently while she colored on the floor. She could hear the cardinals outside, singing their background music for Momma's song, while they nibbled from the bird feeder. The day was already growing thick with humidity, and Raven found herself having to wipe her forehead of the perspiration that continued to appear there. Momma didn't believe in air conditioners, nor could she afford one. She made just enough money making her hoodoo potions and giving treats to her "gentlemen callers", whatever that meant. Raven had asked her on more than one occasion to explain what "treats" were, but momma explained she would understand when she was older. Although, at nearly thirteen years of age and between the dirty boys and the gossip girls at school, Raven had already pretty much figured it out.*

*Today was a day when momma was going to have a gentleman caller. Raven would have to swing outside or walk down to the French Quarter and buy a beignet. Momma would give her some money for one. It was Raven's special prize for being a good girl while Momma worked. Raven loved the warm, doughy texture and the sweet powdered sugar on top. It melted in her mouth when she held it in there for a while, savoring it, like butter melts on a warm piece of toast.*

*"You goin' to go get yourself somethin' yummy for your tummy?" Momma asked her from the sink.*

*Momma turned to look at Raven, her piercing blue eyes gazing down on her, one blackened by a recent gentleman caller.*

*Momma tried to tell Raven a story of how she fell down the cement steps in the back that led to the "yard" of dirt and patches of brown grass. Mr. Jackson, the elderly next-door neighbor, had been nice enough to hang an old tire swing for Raven a few years ago in the makeshift "backyard" to make it more appealing and "user friendly" for a child. Raven went out there to the tire swing often, mostly when Momma had her "business" to do. There was something in the solace of swaying back and forth on that tire swing with her face against the rubber and the smell of it in her nostrils. It kept her from acting on the anger she felt towards the men that came in and out of her home. Raven was no longer ignorant to the stories her Momma gave to her regarding her occasional bruised skin from rough encounters with her "business partners".*

*"Not today, Momma. I'm goin' to hang around the yard."*
*Raven was waiting for a dispute, but Momma glanced at her with quiet acceptance. Raven smiled. Momma smiled back. Raven gathered her things from the floor and stood. She was almost as tall as Momma now, and she stood next to her with her colored pencils grasped in her hand. Momma smelled like Confederate Jasmine and wine. Her black tourmaline crystal hung around her neck, sitting in the nape, glinting beams of sunlight when she moved just right. Raven had the same crystal around her own neck but cut smaller and shaped slightly different. Momma explained that it was a powerful stone for protection against negative energy. Raven often found herself wondering if that were true, why hadn't it kept the bruises off of Momma's body.*

*There was the signature knock on the door. Raven jumped.*
*Rap-rap-pause. Rap-rap. Pause. Rap. Stop.*
*It was the "code".*
*Raven rolled her eyes.*

"Oh, little Blackbird, you know Momma needs to work. How else can we survive?" Momma kissed Raven's forehead.

Raven grabbed an apple out of the bowl on the kitchen counter, wiped it on her t-shirt and smiled at her mother.

"Okay, Momma."

Raven opened the back door that led from the kitchen to the yard of crusted dirt and humidity. The neighborhood's mascot was standing a few feet from the tire swing staring at Raven. The stray mutt was excruciatingly thin, each rib visible through his taut skin. His fur was matted and tangled in places, missing completely in others. Raven imagined he was probably a beautiful golden yellow hue at one time, but the elements had been unkind to him, dusting him a dirty coyote brown.  His tail wagged slightly at the sight of her. The pair often kept each other company on hot summer afternoons. Raven walked over to the ragged pup and spoke to him softly.

"Hey there, Poopsie. How is your day?"

Poopsie swung his tail full force at the sound of her voice. He opened his mouth into a panting grin, welcoming her to the tire swing. Raven tucked her apple into her bra and held the rope while she got her feet into the tire, one at a time. She scooted her body into the tire until her thighs were planted on it securely and she could plop her butt into the hole. Once she was in safely, she was able to let go of the rope and grab the apple. The tire swung lazily to and fro from being jostled about. Poopsie came closer, used to the routine, knowing what was coming next. Raven smiled at the expectant mutt.

"I see you, Poopsie. I know what you are waiting for."

Raven opened her mouth wide and took a big chunk out of the apple, but instead of chewing and swallowing it, she pulled it out of her mouth. The dog sat down, his tail flicking back and forth, kicking up dust behind him.

*"Good boy." Raven giggled then threw the chunk of apple into the air above the dog's head.*

*The mutt jumped slightly and caught the piece of apple in his mouth. He chomped on it twice and swallowed. Then sat down next to the tire swing again with an impatient whine. He whined again and licked his chops twice when Raven didn't move quickly enough.*

*"Hold your horses, man." Raven chided.*

*Poopsie stared at her with wide, brown eyes, panting with excitement.*

*Raven again took a large bite of the apple and removed it from her mouth without having any. She swallowed the sweet and sour juice mixed with saliva that filled her mouth, then threw the piece to the dog, who wolfed it down within a matter of seconds.*

*"Aw, who is a hungry..."*

*Something crashed in the house, cutting Raven off mid-sentence. Poopsie jumped. He gawked towards the house then at Raven, his tail between his legs. Raven sat, frozen. Then another crash and a scream came.*

Momma.

*That was momma's scream. Raven's heart jumped into her throat. She nearly fell out of the tire swing trying to get out of it. Poopsie ran away with the commotion, leaving a trail of dust behind him. Raven barely noticed. As she got near the back steps she slid on the dirt and gravel. She tripped and slammed her head on the concrete step. A lightning bolt of pain shot through her skull, crippling her and showering a grand finale of fireworks before her eyes. Searing heat traveled up and down her face. She reached for her scalp, cradling it as the blood poured out of the one-inch gash the concrete had opened up in her skin. Something else crashed in the kitchen this time. It was enough to forget the pain.*

*Raven stood on shaky legs and opened the back door to the kitchen. Everything was painted red as the blood dripped into Raven's eyes. He was above Momma, a hulking body of a man, wailing on her. His fists connected over and over. A sick, thudding sound followed each blow. Broken dishes lay strewn around on the cheap linoleum floor. A small kitchen knife lay a few feet from Momma, the tip painted red. The man was gurgling.*

*"Please, make… Him… Stop!" Momma begged between each hit.*

*Something snapped inside of Raven. Something crazed and feral arose from the darkest depths of fear inside of her. Raven's eyes searched for what she already knew she needed.*

Ah, yes, there it is.

*The metal glinted in the sunlight as if calling to her. She ran to the counter and grabbed the butcher knife out of the dish strainer. The man still had his back to her, oblivious to her presence.*

*Raven ran at him and plunged the knife into his back as hard as she could. The man screamed in surprise and pain. His back arched and his arms flailed around trying to reach behind himself and remove the knife from his back. He turned and faced Raven. The red monster that was beating Momma to death.*

*"Gurgle-Gurgg!" he exclaimed.*

*Raven swiped at her eyes, trying to clear some of the blood. Now she could see why the man was making that awful sound. Momma must have gotten a stab into his neck before he started breaking her bones. The red monster was moving towards her, still trying to remove the blade from his back and garbling nonsense from his monster mouth.*

*Raven ran back to the counter and grabbed another knife. She turned to attack the red monster again when she heard him cry out and fall to the ground like a tumbled oak tree. He grabbed at his ankles and screamed like a child. Raven glanced and saw Momma on her belly holding the knife, her face nearly unrecognizable. The red monster turned on Momma.*

*"Bithhh! I KILL OUU!" he managed to spit.*

*Raven remembered the many times Momma had shown her how to slice an animal's throat. A chicken, a turkey, a goat.*

*"You make sure you grab right here, and you hold that head tight. Then you make a clean, but deep, slice, little Blackbird. You hear me baby girl? Deep. Make sure it's deep."*

*Raven charged at the monster that sat before her Momma. She got behind him and gripped her fingers into his mess of sweaty hair so tightly that she ripped some out. Before he knew what was happening, Raven took the cold blade of the carving knife she grabbed and did as she had many times before, as Momma had taught her. She sliced the red monster's throat wide open. More gurgling ensued.*

That sound. Oh my God.

*Raven couldn't take it. It was like glass shards in her ears. He had to stop soon, he had to. The red monster grabbed at his throat, then fell to the floor, face down. Raven stood above him, watching, waiting. His body twitched. Raven stiffened. Then, nothing. The red monster was still.*

*A soft moan came from Momma.*

*"Momma!"*

*Raven ran around the lump on the floor to reach her mother. She knelt down to pick her up.*

*"No!" Momma screamed.*

*"Oh Momma, I'm so sorry."*

*"No, baby. No, no." Momma whispered.*

*Raven's body shook all over. Her face was wet with tears and caked with blood. She felt like a hero and a helpless nothing all at once. Momma was so broken. All of her, every bit. Her blue eyes weren't blue anymore, they were bloody red. Her left arm bone was sticking out of her pale skin; the tendons, fat and muscle exposed. Raven thought it resembled a chicken drumstick after a bite had been taken out of it, when you can see all the way down to the bone. She shuddered again.*

*"Momma, what should I do?" Raven whimpered.*

*"Stay here with me, little Blackbird." Momma whispered. Momma's skin was quickly losing its color. Her blood was pooling beneath her head, painting a crimson halo around Momma's beautiful crown. Her eyes were nearly swollen shut, fat with dark purple bruises. Raven didn't know what to do. She wanted to scream, to cry, to run, to stay.*

*"Momma, please. Let me go get Mr. Jackson. He can get us help." Raven pleaded.*

*"No, little Blackbird. Please, stay. Rest. Let's rest together. It has been such a long road. Such a long journey. Let Momma rest a bit. Let me close my eyes and rest, Raven, my beautiful little Blackbird. Momma loves you."*

*Raven did as Momma asked. She sat with her and rested. She sat next to Momma and waited. She watched and listened as Momma took her last breath.*

Raven sat with her back up against the bed breathing heavily through the burn in her chest from the anxiety and exertion. Her nostrils teemed with the smell of blood, urine and feces; a combination that only comes with a fresh corpse. Yet, it was still not enough to move her from where she sat. Her mind raced as fast as her heart, a new thought replacing the old with each fresh heartbeat in her chest. The alarm clock radio was jamming out a new song but Raven only heard it in muted tones. It was as if she were under the ocean, the waves crashing above her where all the noises around her were warped by the surrounding water. She stared straight ahead of her with open eyes but saw nothing in front of her. All she saw were flashing movie scenes of the last few hours in the hotel room, and they were on repeat in her mind. If she were actually seeing, she would be disappointed by the peeling wallpaper and the decaying drywall it denuded beneath.

A loud noise came from the wall jerking Raven from the scene that replayed in her mind where she was slicing Billy's throat. The air conditioner jumped and hummed to life as the heat index rose outside. Raven grew nervous.

*It must be later than I thought.*

She searched for the alarm clock's digital numbers and found them, red and glaring at her angrily.

*Four forty-two a.m.,* she thought. *Not much time left.*

It was enough to get her moving. Raven stood with a groan and began to methodically retrace her steps. She donned a fresh pair of gloves and moved inch by inch about the hotel room, wiping down anything that might have her fingerprints on it. She cleaned the alarm clock and shut the music off, allowing the air conditioner to provide the solo background music for her clean up routine.

After some time, the air conditioning unit bumped twice, then shut off, leaving behind a deafening silence. The hair on Raven's arm stood on end. She knew that was a spirit telling her she needed to get a move on and get out of there. The air in the room was ice cold even though it should have become stagnant and humid when the air conditioner stopped. She stole a glance at Billy. His fleshy carcass lay rigid, staring at her as stupidly as when he was alive.

"Don't look at me." she hissed at him quietly.

Raven turned her back to him and gathered her things.

She needed to make her escape under the guise of darkness before the dawn broke and threatened to expose her face.

She grabbed a swath of toilet paper and wrapped her hand around the hotel room door, opening it to the wide expanse of predawn. Raven peeked her face out carefully and scanned the parking lot for on-lookers.

*No one. Thank Goodness.*

Raven strode quickly out of the parking lot and towards the main road.

She smiled triumphantly.

*Soon I will have enough life force to try the spell.*

# CHAPTER EIGHT

RAVEN PUT ALL BUT ONE OF THE TUBES OF BLOOD into
the mini fridge and sat on the bed. She was exhausted. The
heaviness of her body gave her the feeling that she had liquid
cement coursing through her veins. She pulled the rubber
cap off of the glass vacuum tube of blood and drank it down.
The lukewarm liquid was viscous and tasted metallic in
her mouth, as if she were sucking on a copper penny. She
still hadn't gotten used to the flavor of it, but it was more
palatable than when she first started drinking it. She had
originally started with chicken and pig blood but didn't
think the animals' life forces were strong enough. She needed
human life essence. Black magic was tricky. She was a novice
at best, but she had to do whatever she could to make this
work.

"I'm doing my best, Momma." she whispered.

Her body throbbed. Even her skin ached to be touched.
Raven tossed the tube into her trash can and laid back on
the bed. She stared up at the ceiling with tired eyes. She was
glad she hadn't turned on the ceiling light, just the side table
lamp. It cast a soft, buttery glow upon her things; enough

light to throw shadows on her walls. She thought she may
have caught a small shadow crawling up the wall out of the
corner of her eye. She ignored it. Momma always told her
not to talk to *them*. If you did you would invite them in.
"Best to just ignore them, baby." Momma would say.
Raven always listened to whatever Momma taught her.
Momma was her everything.

The water stain on the ceiling shifted slightly under Raven's
squinted eyes. She could expand and shrink it with her eyes.
If she stared at it long enough, she could sometimes see
Momma's face there, staring down at her. She knew Momma
was there with her, all around her, protecting her. Raven
touched her tourmaline crystal absentmindedly and took a
deep breath in.

"I'm gonna see you soon, Momma." she whispered to the
ceiling.

A soft knock made Raven jump.

"Yes?"

"Raven?" a muffled voice came from the other side of the
door.

"Come in, Uncle Jack."

The door opened slowly. Uncle Jack stood in the doorway
hidden partially by the shadows of the hall and the half open
door. He smiled at her from the shadows. She knew if she
got up close, he would smell of bourbon and cigarettes. She
loved his smell. She smiled back at him.

"So, you want to come in?" Raven asked, patting the bed
beside her.

"I, um, I was going to let you know that I fixed the exhaust
fan in the bathroom today. I'm tired, honey. Not tonight."
Raven considered Uncle Jack for a moment. He was wire
thin. His pale skin was almost sickly. He was not the Uncle

Jack she knew, not even the Uncle Jack of even six months ago. A pang of sadness hit her. She knew he was drinking himself to death. She tried talking to him about it many times, but he shooed her away gently. She smiled at him lovingly.

"Thank you. That was very kind of you."

He smiled at her shyly.

"Well, sorry it took so long."

"It's okay. Better late than never."

"I was going to make some coffee. Would you like some?" he asked.

"Yes, please. This is going to be a very long day at work." Raven sighed.

"Well, if you didn't stay out all night galivanting around town, ya know, it would be a lot easier."

Her uncle chuckled and headed down the hall. Raven stared at the empty doorway.

*He's the only one I have left.*

She wanted to grab him and glue him to his lazy boy chair by the fireplace and never let him leave again. Losing your loved ones was the most painful thing one could ever experience, and Raven didn't know if she could do it again. She sighed.

*Time to get up and face the real world again.*

"Ugh, I don't wanna!" she groused to the ceiling.

She was wishing that she had asked one of the other girls from work to take her shift today. She felt like she had been in an eight-round fight with a heavyweight boxer and that she had not come out the victor. Every inch of her body was gripped with aches and pains. It always happened to her after she had a surge of adrenaline course through her body.

*Well, it was worth it. Now, get your ass up and move, girl. Lazy do nothings don't become "somethings".*

Raven stood and readied herself for a new day.

# BIRD TRAP

# CHAPTER ONE

Manny lay watching Alex sleep. Her face was that of the most beautiful creature he had ever seen. He never imagined he could love something or someone so much as he did her. He gazed upon her, committing to memory every inch of her, as he had many times before. The rise and fall of her body under the blankets was barely noticeable, but it was comforting, nonetheless. The blush of dawn was just bright enough to light her features — her high cheekbones, her slightly arched eyebrows, her smooth chestnut skin, the two small scars from the gravel at the railyard that had embedded so deeply into her skin. It had taken weeks to work itself out. He was glad she was finally sleeping. Only an hour ago he woke to her screaming. She suffered night terrors often. Not as many as she did right after she had been kidnapped and repeatedly raped but still, even a single night terror was one too many. He wished so badly he could take away her pain and trauma. It tore at his heart to see her in any anguish. Alex's nose started to twitch like a bunny sniffing the air. *Adorable.*

Manny smiled, trying hard not to laugh out loud. He wanted

to grab her and plant kisses all over her face. Manny started to laugh but held it in the best he could. The bed shook with his laughter. He tried to stop, but he couldn't.

Alex stirred.

*Uh oh.*

"What are you doing?" she asked, sleepily, with her eyes still closed.

"Nothing." he giggled his words.

"Mentiroso… Liar, you are up to something." she accused, lovingly.

Manny released a booming laugh.

Alex's eyes opened.

"What?" she exclaimed.

"I'm sorry. I can't help it. You're so damn cute. You were scrunching your nose up like a bunny rabbit." Manny giggled between words.

Alex stared at him perplexed and with feigned anger.

"I am *trying to sleep here!*" she scolded him.

Manny stuck his lower lip out like a dejected child. He knew this would elicit a smile from her. He waited patiently for the spell of the Sandman to lift from her beautiful face. A small grin curled the corners of Alex's lips.

*Yes! Paydirt.*

"Good morning, gorgeous." he smiled at her.

"Good morning." she whispered.

Alex yawned, stretching slowly and lazily, resembling her little feline counterpart that Manny could hear purring loudly under the covers. Manny took his index finger and lightly traced the inside of Alex's arm that she held, outstretched, towards the sky. Alex shivered with his touch.

"Are you cold?" he asked.

"No." she whispered.

Alex's blue green eyes were locked on Manny's face. He could feel the warmth of her stare on his skin. His body responded immediately. Goosebumps covered his flesh, raising the hair on his arms. An electrical current of desire ran through him, reverberating through his body like the musical notes in the pipes of an organ at church during procession. He traced the outline of her face with his finger gently, sending more electrical shocks through his body and leaving a residual throbbing. Alex closed her eyes when Manny touched her face allowing him to caress her. Her breath came out slow but unsteady.

Manny moved in closer, his body touching hers. He expected Alex to become rigid, but she didn't. He breathed out relief. With cautious care, Manny gazed upon her face. Alex opened her eyes and they were full of desire and fear.

"Alex…" Manny whispered.

Alex placed her hand gently on Manny's cheek and rubbed his lower lip with her thumb. It felt like silk. A surge of heat coursed through his body. Alex pulled Manny's face to hers until their lips were nearly touching.

"It's okay, Manny. I want to." she whispered.

Manny wasn't sure he heard her correctly. He didn't move. He stared at her. She must have felt his hesitation because she wrapped her hands around the back of his neck and pulled his lips in to meet hers. Before he knew what was happening, she was kissing him.

*She is kissing me.*

His lips were on fire.

His body was on fire.

*Oh my God. She is kissing me.*

Manny kissed Alex back. His heart pounded in his chest. His body throbbed. He could feel the heat between them,

the skin that was exposed and touching felt as if it would
sear each other if it made contact for too long. He could feel
Alex's breath getting heavier and shorter. Her hands were
moving along his back, rubbing and grabbing. Their tongues
were touching, teasing, getting tangled up in a passionate
dance of yearning. Manny pulled back from Alex to check in
with her. She was surprised, confused and a little frustrated.
"What's the matter?" she asked, breathless.
"Are you okay?" he asked, concerned.
"Yes, baby. I am fine." she smiled.
Her smile was beautiful. He believed her this time. Her eyes
were solid, locked on his, no aversion.
"I am sure." she said with conviction. "I want this. I have
always wanted this. But now I know I am ready for this. For
you, for us. I am ready, Manny."
Alex leaned forward slightly and grabbed at the hem of
her t-shirt. Before Manny knew what was happening, Alex
pulled it up and over her head and tossed it on her chair.
Manny sucked a breath in. Alex lay next to him, her bare
chest and arms lit perfectly by the now morning light that
broke through the bedroom window. She was completely
naked except for a small pair of panties. She was like a
golden goddess to Manny. His already throbbing body grew
painfully so. He needed her so badly. Alex held her hands out
to him, beckoning him to her. Manny sighed and nearly fell
on top of her to get to her.
Alex moaned as Manny kissed her, deep and hard this
time. He could feel Alex's heart pounding in her chest as
thunderous as his. They kissed each other like two lovers,
separated for months, reunited. Each moment that passed
their breathing grew faster and heavier, their need stronger
and less controllable. Manny knew that Alex could feel him

between her thighs now. There was no getting past that. She didn't seem uncomfortable. She hadn't moved away from him or turned her back to him.

*Stop analyzing things. Go with it. She will stop if she gets uncomfortable.*

He knew she would. They had talked a few weeks ago and decided they would let things "happen". But Manny had also insisted on Alex having a "safe word" in case she ever felt unsafe or out of control. She thought it was silly at first. She insisted she could never feel unsafe with him. But Manny knew the weight of PTSD and what it did to people. He knew that even with someone's most sacred lovers, people could still have flashbacks or blackouts and not even know, causing them to say or do things irrational things.

"Manny, please." Alex whispered.

"What baby?"

"I want you." Alex murmured in Manny's ear.

"Huh?" Manny asked. He wasn't sure he heard her, or had he made it up in his mind?

"I... want ...you…" Alex's eyes were on his, clear as glass.

*She is sure*, he thought, more for his own sake than for hers, reassuring himself.

Alex touched Manny's chest, placing her hand near his heart. Manny closed his eyes. She moved her hand up along the nape of his neck, placed it behind his head and gently pulled him to her. Manny felt Alex's lips on his, making him burn with hunger for more. Alex's tongue slipped into his mouth and searched for his, until they met once again to resume their tango.

Manny felt Alex's hands on him. He gently placed his hand at the small of her back, pulling her into him. Alex moaned. He knew she could feel him, hard against her body.

*Oh my god, I'm going to explode.*
Manny moaned. He kissed Alex's neck, then planted gentle kisses along her jawline and chin. He ran his tongue lightly from the nape of her neck up to the tip of her chin and to her lips. Alex's body shook, and she pulled at his hair when their lips met again.

Manny moved against Alex, rubbing his body against her. She moaned again. He could feel the heat coming off her. It matched the warmth coming off of him. He couldn't take it anymore. He reached down and gently tugged at Alex's panties, then paused to see if he met any resistance. Instead, Alex raised her hips off the bed, allowing him to pull her panties completely down. A deep groan escaped Manny's lips. The tension he felt inside his groin was so immense he wasn't sure how much longer he could hold on. Alex pulled at Manny's waistband on his sweatpants, trying to push them down. They were both breathing hard and wanting each other so badly they were near desperation to have one another.

"Oh God, Alex." Manny moaned.

He kissed her all over. He reached down and cupped her breast in his hand, sucking her nipple into his mouth gently. Alex gasped in surprise and pleasure. She ran her fingers through his hair while he licked each of her nipples playfully. Alex giggled. Manny was mesmerized by her beautiful face, her beautiful, naked body. Love and desire pulsed through his veins.

"I want you so badly. I love you so much." he whispered.

"I love you, Manny. You have me, mi amor." Alex whispered.

Manny leaned in to kiss her. Alex opened herself to him, and Manny entered her slowly, gently. She was warm and wet. He wasn't sure how long he would last. His entire body tingled with excitement and he felt lightheaded with elation. They both moaned together as they moved slowly, as one. Manny locked eyes with Alex, and she did not turn away. She held his gaze. He moved inside her, loving her, every bit of her. Alex laid her head back and closed her eyes. Her body shivered.

Manny could feel Alex's body tightening up. He needed to see if she was nervous. Her eyes were closed, and her head was turned slightly, her lower lip caught on the edge of her upper front teeth. Alex sucked in a breath and let it out in a moan. Manny could feel what was about to happen. It excited him beyond anything he had ever felt before. He didn't think he could get any harder, but he did. He moved inside her, faster, but still as gently as possible. Alex moaned louder and wrapped her arms and legs around him.

"Oh God, Manny, yes." she cried.

It was enough to bring Manny to the brink. He could feel the surge, the rush of pleasure, explode from him into Alex. His body tensed, on the verge of convulsing, then went weak. He fell, half on, half off of Alex.

They lay, entwined and breathless, for what seemed like hours. Neither one spoke or moved. Gradually, their breathing and heart rates slowed. Manny was able to move after a few minutes of post orgasmic paralysis. He traced Alex's hip with his finger as he mentally replayed the events of only moments ago. She smiled at him.

"Are you okay?" he asked.

"Yes." She smiled.

"God you are so beautiful." Manny touched her face.

Alex grabbed his hand and held it to her cheek.

"Thank you, Manny."

"For what?" Manny asked, surprised.

"For being so patient. For being so loving. For being… for being you." Alex explained.

A small tear fell from the corner of her eye and slipped down her cheek. Manny kissed it, tasting the saltiness of it. He kissed her forehead and her other cheek. Then, he gently kissed her lips and looked at her.

"Alex, you are worth every bit of time that I have waited. Every day, every hour, every second. I would do it all again." Alex stared at him. He could feel her searching for deceit, for something to mistrust. Her eyes bore through him. He could feel it. He understood. She had so much pain all throughout her life; losing her parents at a young age in a tragic car accident, Abuela's death, her own recent experience of trauma. Manny had been the only constant in her life for over twelve years now. Alex softened. Her cheeks were wet with more tears. Manny wiped them gently.

"No more crying, my love." he whispered. "There is nothing to cry for any longer."

Alex looked up at him with something Manny had not seen in her eyes in a long time.

Hope.

# CHAPTER TWO

THERE WAS NO TREPIDATION. No hesitation. All she could feel was love and desire. His lips were on her, and she welcomed them. Alex wasn't expecting this to happen, but it was, and she didn't balk. There was no anxiety as there had been in the past. Just desire and passion.

*It feels so good.*

She never knew it could feel this way, never even imagined. All she knew of it before was pain. Of course, she had read of pleasure in books. Silly romance novels depicting two lovers embraced in the throes of love making, bringing one another to the brink of explosive gratification. Then riding off into the sunset on their horse or ship, or whatever means of transportation they had for whatever period of time it was she was reading. Then there were her patients who talked about love so deep and severe it was debilitating, but she had only known that kind of love for her parents and Abuela. This, this was different. Now the only fear was of losing it. Manny smelled so good. His skin radiated devotion. How was it possible that it warmed her to her core, yet she shivered? Alex breathed him in deeply, wanting to remember

what he smelled like. His lips were on her face, her neck.
*Oh God, Manny, don't stop.*
She closed her eyes for fear that if she opened them, she
would awaken, and this would have all been a dream. Why
had she waited so long? Why had she pushed him away?
She was tingling between her thighs. Alex could feel Manny
stiffen against her, his excitement growing with each passing
moment. She moaned in consonance. Manny's hands were
on her. Gentle and loving. He was kissing her all over, his
tongue licking her neck in little circles, tickling her skin.
Then his fingers pulled gently at her panties. He paused,
waiting for her permission. Alex couldn't speak, her emotions
were running wild inside her head and her body, so she raised
her hips towards him. He removed her panties and cast them
to the floor. Without thinking, Alex found herself pulling
at Manny's sweatpants, trying to push them down. A small,
throaty groan came from Manny's lips. It excited her.
"Oh God, Alex." Manny groaned.
Manny traced the line of Alex's neck with his fingers until
he reached her breast, then gently grasped it in his hand. He
bent and took her nipple into his mouth, teasing it with his
tongue. Alex gasped with pleasure and surprise.
*Oh my God, it feels so good.*
Alex grabbed at Manny's head and ran her fingers through
his hair. He had his tongue all over her breasts. It tickled her
and made her tingle, eliciting a throbbing from her down
below that she had never felt before. She giggled.
Manny gazed at her with eyes that could have seared her soul.
"I want you so badly. I love you so much." he whispered,
breathlessly.
Alex felt her heart jump into her throat. Her body tingled
everywhere.

"I love you, Manny. You have me, mi amor." Alex murmured. Manny kissed her deeply and it was more than she could take. She wanted him. No, that wasn't it. She *needed* him. She opened her legs to him, inviting him into her. Manny entered her gently.

*He feels so good.*

He moved inside of her slowly, gently. Alex felt no pain, only love and ecstasy. She laid her head back on the pillow and closed her eyes, biting her lower lip. She could feel something building up inside of her. She didn't know what it was, but it was an amazing feeling. Alex opened her eyes and saw him looking at her, his gaze steadfast upon her.

*I am so in love with you.*

She moaned and wrapped her arms and legs around him, pulling him into her. The feeling, it was intensifying. It made her body stiffen and shiver all at once. Manny must have felt it because it excited him, and he moved faster inside of her.

*Oh, that feels so good.*

Alex's breath quickened, the feeling inside her grew so much so that she felt as if her entire body might combust.

"Oh God, Manny."

Alex heard Manny groan loudly and he moved even faster than before. She thought the feeling couldn't get any more intense than it was, but it did.

*This is crazy,* she thought.

Suddenly, a flood of physical and emotional feelings burst from her all at once. Alex's body shuddered. At the same time, Manny uttered something inaudible and his body trembled then stiffened. Alex felt him move inside her a few more times, then Manny fell half on, half off of her, exhausted. Alex couldn't help the smile that moved her lips. They lay together, bodies tangled up and breathless. Neither one could speak or move, nor did they need to. It was a comfortable silence. After a while, Manny traced Alex's hip with his finger, sending more shivers along her spine. The smiled remained.

"Are you okay?"

"Yes." she whispered.

Alex smiled. He was so caring, always thinking of her, never himself.

"God, you are so beautiful." Manny gently touched her face. Alex grabbed his hand and held it to her cheek. She loved his touch, his closeness.

"Thank you, Manny." she whispered.

"For what?"

"For being so patient. For being so loving. For being… for being you."

She felt a tear slip down her cheek. She didn't mean to cry, but the emotion of making love, feeling love, needing and wanting love, had all gotten to her. Manny kissed away her tear. He kissed her forehead. He kissed her other cheek. Then, her lips. His brow wrinkled with concern; his eyes filled with love.

"Alex, you are worth every bit of time that I have waited. Every day, every hour, every second. I would do it all again." Alex stared at him. She searched for any sign of untruth. A pair of unwavering hazel eyes stared back at her, not a hint of deceit to be found. She needed him to be real. She needed him to be here and to stay. She couldn't take losing him. She had lost too many people that she loved in her life. Her parents, Abuela. This love she had allowed herself to feel, if she lost it, could kill her. Alex could feel more tears falling down her cheeks. Manny wiped them gently.

"No more crying, my love." he whispered. "There is nothing

to cry for any longer."

She gazed up at him. He was right. She had to stop living in fear. It was no way of living, with one foot in the grave. She needed to try and let things go, to live each day. Live in the moment.

*I died for God's sake,* she thought, with conviction. *It's time to start living each day like it's my last. No more fear of the future. No more fear of what I cannot control.*

Alex glanced at Manny, a sparkle in her eyes and warmth in her soul. At that moment, she gave him her heart.

# CHAPTER THREE

"GOOD MORNING, PRINCESS." Manny grinned contagiously as Deshawn shuffled into the Unit.

"And a good morning to you, Sunshine." Deshawn greeted him brightly.

Deshawn stopped and stared at Manny. He raised an eyebrow appraising Manny like an art lover in a gallery trying to decipher an abstract piece on display. He studied Manny's face for a long moment. Manny stared back wondering what Deshawn was peeping at.

*Do I have a moco hanging out of my nose?*

If he had a booger hanging out of his nose, why was Deshawn staring at it? Manny reached up and swiped at his nose to make sure, pulling in a precautionary sniff through his nose.

*Nope, nothing.*

Finally, Manny couldn't stand it anymore.

"What?" he barked.

"I can see it." Deshawn smirked,

"See what?" Manny protested.

"The afterglow." Deshawn grinned from ear to ear.

*What the hell is he talking about? Afterglow?*
Then, as the clouds in Manny's brain parted, exposing a bright, shiny light bulb, his eyes opened wide and he began to realize what Deshawn meant. He didn't know whether to laugh or punch him in the arm.

"D, what the hell?" he snarled.

Deshawn giggled like a hyena.

"Sorry, buddy, did I hit a sensitive nerve?" he laughed, but lightly this time. His tone was apologetic, hidden in the guise of jest.

After a moment, a half smile lifted the right corner of his lip. Manny felt a rush excitement fill him as the memories of the previous night flashed in his mind like Polaroid photos being passed in front of his eyes. He turned away, slightly embarrassed.

"Aw, man, I know you so well. That's all. We have been partners for so long, how could I not know? I think it's awesome. It's about time, that's for sure." Deshawn chuckled. "It would be a bad thing if I didn't know you that well, don't ya think?" he added as an afterthought.

"Yeah, actually, I guess you're right." Manny agreed.

The phone on Manny's desk wailed. Manny grabbed at it and smiled, grateful for the distraction.

"Yup, saved by the bell." Deshawn laughed.

Manny nodded, grinning, as he answered his phone.

"Detective Castillo."

"Castillo. Dickerson here." Dickerson's voice, official and curt, came over the line.

"Hey, Dickerson. How's it hanging?" Manny jibed.

"I got another one for you, all processed and ready to go. We are back here at the Riverdale Inn. Looks like the same M.O. as the last one." Dickerson said, not skipping a beat.

Manny paused. His mood shifted instantly to all business. *Another body? Same M.O.?*

He held the phone to his ear and listened while Dickerson gave him the rundown of what they found. It matched the Stanton murder almost precisely. Manny glanced up to see Deshawn watching him intently. He took his finger and made a horizontal swiping motion at his own throat as if he were slashing himself, then pointed at the phone. Deshawn's eyes widened and he nodded. In another minute Manny told Dickerson thanks and hung up the phone.

"Let's roll." Manny told Deshawn.

"The Slasher?" Deshawn asked.

"It's gotta be." Manny answered. "Riverdale Inn. Same M.O." Manny and Deshawn looked at the stairs, then the elevator, then back at the stairs. They grinned at one another at the same time. Deshawn was usually the instigator of the schoolboy antics, but Manny always fall prey, no matter how serious their current situation. Deshawn darted for the stairs with Manny on his heels. They raced down the steps, slowing only slightly to maneuver past the few uniformed officers who were trying to make their way up the stairs, mumbling their obligatory apologies. Then speeding back up again until they reached three stairs before the bottom, at which point they stopped, straightened themselves, caught their breath and proceeded professionally, minus their boyish smirks. They competed for the lead towards the main front hall, Deshawn slightly in the lead, Manny following close behind. A few officers moved out of their way like an obedient herd parting for its master. The precinct had started to come to life with the hustle and bustle of early morning traffic and they manipulated their way through sporadic bunches of uniforms, plain clothes officers, hookers and junkies being brought in for booking, and the random law abiding citizen there to make a complaint or file a missing person's report.

"Hey, watch it asshole!" a high-pitched screech came from their left.

Manny and Deshawn spied a thin, dark haired woman being detained by an officer. Her breasts, the only large thing on her, were bulging out of her "one size too small" bra, threatening to burst from their restraints. Her tube top was stretched so tight the neon pink paled to a pastel and her faux leather skirt was torn and dirty. It shifted up her stick legs as she twisted around. She was not cooperating by the looks of it, and the male officer that held her cuffs appeared frustrated and uncomfortable. Manny glanced at Deshawn, who shrugged and rolled his eyes at him for the second time that day.

"Carla." Deshawn smirked.

Carla was a regular face at the precinct, picked up often for prostitution.

"I was NOT whoring around, man. I was walking to the library." she yelled at the officer.

Deshawn rolled his eyes again and scoffed.

"Yup, and my name ain't Deshawn Freeman." he snorted.

It was Manny's turn to snort.

"You keep rolling your eyes like that they're gonna get stuck in the back of your head, D." he said, then laughed.

They both burst out in laughter so loud that the uniforms at the front desk turned around to see what all the commotion was about. Once they settled down, they stopped at the front desk where the administrative officers stood post. A young blonde officer, short and stocky, had his back to Manny. He was chatting the ear off of another officer who was typing furiously on their keyboard.

"Hey, Davis, can I have the keys to one of the sedans?" Manny asked.

Officer Davis turned from his conversation with the other uniformed officer to acknowledge Manny. His face was that of a teenager, hairless and acne free, with a strong jawline. His green eyes were pale but clear, and Manny imagined he didn't have any trouble in the dating department. Davis beamed a perfect chiclet white toothed grin Manny's way. "Oh hey, Detective Castillo. Sure, you can take car four." he obliged.

Officer Davis walked over to a gray box that hung on the wall and opened it, revealing a collection of keys for every squad car and unmarked car in the precinct. Each set hung kissing its twin set on a hook marked with a number above it, its matching number engraved on each key. Officer Davis removed one of the two sets of keys from hook number four and brought it over to Manny. Davis pulled out a notebook, thumbed quickly through its weathered pages until he found what he was looking for, and grabbed the ballpoint pen out of his breast pocket. Officer Davis, in small, neat penmanship, wrote down Manny's name and badge number, the date and time, and turned the notebook to face Manny. "Please sign her out, Detective." Officer Davis requested. Manny took the pen from Davis' hand and scribbled his signature on the dotted line. Officer Davis retrieved his pen from Manny's hand and closed the logbook. He handed Manny the keys to car number four with another cheerful smile.

"It's been a pleasure, boys." he joked.

"All ours." Deshawn chimed in.

Manny chuckled and turned to head towards the elevator, waving his hand that held the keys in the air, signaling his thanks to Davis as he walked away. When they reached the elevators, Deshawn punched the button and they waited for the number above the doors to light up. The doors opened after a moment and a few suits shuffled out murmuring their hellos and good mornings. Manny and Deshawn returned their greetings and stepped in once the square moving death trap was clear of bodies. Manny was not a fan of elevators, but they served a purpose, so he used them, even though he'd rather not. Claustrophobia was a real, and at times, very disabling fear.

The elevator doors opened up to the parking garage and the smell of rubber and exhaust hit their faces. Manny never understood why they would build an underground parking garage without any air circulation, but the precinct had been built over fifty years ago and only a few updates had been done since. He was sure they hadn't thought much about it back then, and now with budget cuts, their lungs weren't going to see any reprieve.

"You gonna call Alex and let her know?" Deshawn asked.

"No, not yet. She is at the office today seeing patients." Manny answered.

He knew she would be upset that he waited to let her know, but he didn't want to distract her from her day. She had recently started seeing clients again and he wanted her to concentrate on her practice, not on helping profile for his cases. He knew she loved it, but she also loved working with her patients, and that had somehow become dampened for her when she was thrown into the depths of the Homicide Unit's murder cases. He hoped by spending time at the office, her passion for helping her clients would be rekindled.

"Alright, your call, but we know how that's going to go." Deshawn warned.

"Yeah, yeah." Manny mumbled.

Manny and Deshawn opened the doors to the unmarked sedan and hopped in, swallowed up by the smell of old coffee and stale cigarette smoke. Manny started the car and pulled out of the parking space, squealing the tires slightly as he went.

"Damn surveillance teams. I hate when they smoke in here." Manny growled.

"Hell, do I know it." Deshawn agreed.

Manny pushed the automatic window button and breathed in deeply through his nostrils as a fresh breeze found its way into the car. The late morning air was quickly growing thick with humidity, and the smell of rain replaced the acrid smells that had assaulted Manny's nose only moments ago. He welcomed the sultry atmosphere.

Manny weaved through the city traffic while Deshawn reviewed the Stanton file from a little over a week ago. Manny wanted them both to be fresh on the details of the body presentation so that they could compare once they reached the Riverdale Inn. If Dickerson claimed it was the same M.O., Manny wanted to make sure he was right. A car honked as Manny swerved to his right to avoid a jaywalker.

"Damn it, people!" Manny cursed.

Deshawn didn't flinch or even pause, he kept reading through the file. Deshawn read a few more lines before closing the folder and laying it on his lap. Manny watched the cars ahead of him and the cars passing him in the oncoming traffic. He watched as people drove their cars, going about their lives. It was just another normal day for them, not one of them knowing another murder had taken place in their city.

"See these people, D? Unsuspecting. Fearless. Going about their business. No clue that we're headed to another crime scene. Not just us either, but that there are multiple crime scenes being worked in the state of Massachusetts. One of these people could very well be our unsub. Who knows?" Manny rattled on.

Deshawn sat quietly listening. Manny appreciated when Deshawn let him ramble. Sometimes he had to vent, and Deshawn was the only one who truly understood how he felt. He couldn't talk to Alex about it because she would worry about him. Manny was also a lot more cynical about mankind than Alex. She always searched for the good in people. Manny searched for people's ulterior motives. He wondered sometimes if that made him a negative person. He didn't think so. He thought it was more logical, more realistic, than anything. He was pragmatic, that was all. Alex was more of an idealist, yet he loved her for her ability to still have faith in humanity.

Manny turned into the entrance of the Riverdale Inn. The familiar assemblage of vehicles and personnel was present, clustered in the parking lot like a group of teenage girls gossiping quietly about the table next to them in the lunchroom. Manny pulled the car up next to the C.S.I. van and turned the engine off. He and Deshawn got out and scanned the area.

"Over here." Deshawn motioned towards a small bundle of bodies hovered around an open hotel room door.

Manny followed.

As they approached, Manny recognized the back of Mike Dickerson's balding head, its patchwork of age spots unmistakable. Fragile Irish skin and years of sun damage had created an interesting pattern of multicolored freckles and sunspots on Dickerson's near hairless noggin.

*I hope he sees a dermatologist for that,* Manny thought as they approached the men.

"Hey, fellas." Manny joined in.

The huddled group turned to greet Manny and Deshawn. Dickerson stuck his hand out and Manny took it, returning the strong gripped hello.

"Mike." Manny nodded.

"Manny." Mike Dickerson nodded; his voice raspy with exhaustion.

"How's it going?" Manny asked.

"Same ol' same ol', ya know?" Dickerson shrugged.

"How's it going in there?" Deshawn asked.

"Well, like I told Manny, it presents near identical to the Stanton case. White male, naked, bound. His throat slashed. Multiple, I mean multiple, stab wounds. No I.D. found. Only his clothing." Dickerson reported.

"Wow! That's great." Manny smiled facetiously.

"Yeah, so we will head back and run the fingerprints. Should have something back in about forty-five minutes or so, depending on how busy the Staties are. Hopefully. That, of course as you know, is assuming he is in AFIS. If not, we have ourselves another John Doe." Dickerson put his hands in his pockets, looking less than satisfied.

"Alright, well let's hope he did something wrong in his life." Manny tittered trying to sound optimistic.

Manny observed the movement of bodies. Most were Dickerson's C.S.I. team returning their equipment to the van and truck. A few others were uniformed officers tasked to secure the area and keep watch for any suspicious people in the area that may be the unsub. In some cases, killers liked to return to the crime scene and watch as things unfolded, especially as the media showed up. He couldn't see anyone he didn't recognize.

"You guys all done here?" Manny asked, peering back at Dickerson.

"Yeah, sure, just wrapping up. You two can head in and take a peak if you want before the M.E.'s transport takes the body." Dickerson allowed.

"Ready, D?" Manny turned to Deshawn expectantly.

"I am always ready, Castillo."

"Okay, then let's go see us a dead body."

# CHAPTER FOUR

ALEX SAT, LISTENING TO MR. JOHNSON TALK about his overbearing mother, but she found herself peeping at the clock more than usual.

*Stop that,* she reprimanded herself. *Pay attention. This poor man needs your full consideration.*

Alex cleared her throat and refocused her eyes on Mr. Johnson. He must have felt the weight of her stare, because he shifted in the chair slightly. He rubbed his hands together as if trying to warm them then methodically wiped them on his thighs, hip to knee, four times. When he was done, Mr. Johnson pushed his glasses up on the bridge of his nose and counted to six. Mr. Johnson's OCD was becoming better controlled, but it revealed itself more readily during times of anxiety. Alex made a quick note in his chart before she spoke. "Go on, Ted." she encouraged.

"I, uh, I was saying that she doesn't make me feel like I do anything right. I feel like nothing is good enough for her. I feel like I could win the Nobel Prize and she would tell me that I could have done better, like 'win two of them, Teddy' she would say." Mr. Johnson whined.

Mr. Johnson's voice grated on Alex's spinal cord. She cringed inside. She felt a twinge of guilt and hoped neither showed through her skin. She couldn't understand why she was feeling this way lately, but in the last few weeks as she had been starting to see patients again, she found herself becoming almost irritated with having to sit and listen to them snivel about their "issues". Alex knew that to her patients they were major problems. But after what she had endured, and what the victims of the serial killers she had been helping Manny and Deshawn find had suffered, these minuscule complaints were taxing to her devotion.

Alex took a deep breath in and let it out slowly, trying to make it so that Mr. Johnson wouldn't hear her. She concentrated on releasing her breath in the littlest amount possible without feeling the tingle of lightheadedness. She could hear Mr. Johnson speaking, but could not make out his exact words. He sounded as if he was speaking from inside a glass bowl and Alex was on the outside, looking in. Alex allowed her mind to drift back to last night with Manny, and a tingle instantly awoke between her thighs. Surprised, she squeezed her legs together, hoping Mr. Johnson didn't notice. She checked in on him and was relieved to find him still mumbling along about his mother and her incessant griping. Alex touched her lips lightly as the memory of the weight of Manny's lips on hers flooded her head. Mr. Johnson's face blurred, obscured by flashbacks of Manny caressing her, kissing her, inside of her. Alex instinctually squeezed her legs together again, trying to stop the pulsing between her thighs. She had never felt like this before. Thoughts and memories had never provoked such physical feelings from her. It was confusing and exhilarating all at once.

"Dr. Aguilar? Dr.?"

Alex could hear Mr. Johnson from somewhere far away, calling to her.

*Hmmm? What? Stop trying to interrupt,* she thought.

"Dr. Aguilar, are you okay?" Mr. Johnson asked again.

He began counting. Alex pulled herself from the cloud of last night's memories and focused on Mr. Johnson. He stopped counting and started rubbing his hands together as if to warm them.

*Next will come the hands on the thighs,* Alex thought.

Then, as if his hands heard her, Mr. Johnson's palms moved from the top of his legs to top of his knees, rubbing in a specific motion, four times, as before. Then, he counted again.

"I'm fine, Ted, thank you. Sorry, I was daydreaming a bit. I apologize. I'm a bit tired. Do you mind if we end the session a few minutes early today?" Alex asked sweetly.

Mr. Johnson seemed uneasy for a moment, unsure how to answer, so he pinched his forearm four times and took a deep breath. Alex could see him counting in his head because his lips were moving ever so slightly. She waited patiently for him to finish his rituals. It was best not to rush him or interrupt. Once he worked his way though he was usually very amicable. After a moment longer, Mr. Johnson smiled a thin smile and agreed that it would be best for both of them if they ended a little early.

"I should head home and feed the cats before Ma gets up and moves around." he stated. (Mrs. Johnson was an extreme hoarder and was known for having, at last count, nine cats.) Mr. Johnson rose from his seat, and Alex stood with him. He thanked her for the session and made sure he had another booked for two weeks from this visit. Alex assured him that he indeed had a standing appointment for two weeks from today. Not to worry. But that was like telling the sun not to rise. It was going to happen no matter what. It was inevitable. Mr. Johnson had OCD, Obsessive Compulsive Disorder, and GAD, General Anxiety Disorder; worrying went along with his other symptoms. Constant reassurance and schedules were very important for him.

Alex shut the door behind Mr. Johnson and exhaled as if she were blowing out one hundred trick candles on a birthday cake.

*What a relief to be done with that,* she thought guiltily. She leaned against the office door and laid her head back, feeling the cold of the frosted glass against her skull. It soothed the aching in her head slightly. Alex closed her eyes and inhaled, willing the stress of the day to leave her body with her next exhale. She let it out slowly. Steadily. Purposefully. She could feel her body starting to relax, the tension it held, letting go.

The phone on her desk beeped twice signaling an incoming call from Lola Martinez, the brightly dressed, slightly plump, fifty something, transplant from Puerto Rico, secretary whom Alex adored. Alex started at the sound. She walked briskly over to her desk and grabbed the handset before it could beep again.

"Yes, Lola." Alex breathed into the phone.

Alex cringed. She knew she sounded agitated and regretted it instantly.

Lola was sensitive, and she would feel Alex's frustration over the line and most likely take it personally. Alex didn't know what was wrong. She had such an amazing night with Manny last night. There was absolutely no reason she should be feeling stressed at all. If anything, she should feel elated, untouchable. She was confused as to why her mind was all over the place. She felt trapped in her head like a pinball in a pinball machine, her emotions bouncing back and forth— pinging from joy to frustration to excitement to perturbation.

"Sorry, Miss Alex, but Mr. Manny is on the phone." Lola apologized.

Alex closed her eyes and rubbed the brow above her left eyelid.

*I'm sorry, Lola, I'm such a jerk. ¡Qué idiota!*

Alex used her middle finger to rub with moderate pressure under her left eye as if removing makeup, then blinked a few times to clear her vision.

"Okay, Lola, thank you."

"Okay, Miss Alex, he is on line two."

"Lola?" Alex stalled.

"¿Sí?"

"I'm sorry." Alex repented.

"No hay problema, Miss Alex."

Alex could hear Lola's smile through the phone.

*Sweet Lola.*

The "line 2" button was flashing on the phone face. Alex pushed the button next to the flashing light and waited for the familiar clicking sound.

"Hello, Manny."

"Hello, bella." He sang into the phone.

*He sounds so happy.*

Alex felt a series of flips in her belly...the kind you feel when the roller coaster has reached the tippity top as it is about to roll over the crest and begin its descent from its highest point. She sucked in a breath hoping it would ease her stomach back to its anatomical home, instead of sitting in her throat, like it was at that moment. She swallowed, trying to push it down. It didn't work. The minnows in her belly swam around again tickling her and making her queasy at the same time.

*¿Oh, Dios mío, qué es esto? My Lord, what is this?* she thought.

"Hey, you there?" Manny asked.

"Yes, yes sorry. I was, my throat is dry." Alex cleared her throat and managed a small laugh.

"Okay. I thought you hung up on me for a second. Ha!" Manny's laugh was like an old song through the phone, recalling memories and flashbacks in her mind.

Alex's knees felt weak and her skin tingled

*I wonder if he feels even half of what I am feeling.*

"No, silly." she laughed, grateful they were on the phone. She knew if they were face to face, he would see her cheeks flush with embarrassment and exhilaration. Funny how two feelings could coexist.

"Good, por qué si estás triste, I would be sad, mamacita." Alex smiled again.

*I am smiling uncontrollably when ten minutes ago you couldn't rip a smile out of me.*

She was feeling like a schoolgirl with her first crush. Her knees felt weak again. Without checking, Alex reached back for the familiar feel of the soft leather of her Captain's Chair that sat stoically behind the massive cherry wood desk the interior designer insisted she needed. She played the "trust" game with her chair hoping it would catch her as she fell into it. She allowed her body to fold into it safely.

*What is this man doing to me?*

"As would I." she responded.

"I would hope so, mi amor."

There was a moment of silence, but it was not

uncomfortable, it was the opposite.

"So, last night…" Manny began.

Alex's face grew hot. The tingling she had felt earlier between her thighs returned, tenfold. Her stomach flipped past her throat. It may have disappeared at that point for all she knew or even cared. She was hanging on his last words with the edge of her fingertips, white knuckles bared.

"Yes?"

Alex suddenly felt a little short of breath.

"It was… amazing!" Manny sounded as out of breath as she felt.

Alex melted the rest of the way into her Captain's Chair. Her body felt like a rubber band that had been stretched millions of times to its capacity then left to lay, all elasticity gone.  She almost dropped the phone. It took all her energy to catch it from falling to the floor.

"Alex, you okay?"

She heard him from far away.

She knew he heard her drop him.

*Ugh, idiota.*

Despite it all, she giggled. She brought the phone back to her ear, still giggling.

"Sorry, I dropped you."

"I heard. Silly girl. You okay?" he chuckled.

"I'm great now."

She didn't want to ruin the moment by going into detail about how only a bit ago she was feeling tired and unable to focus on her client. How sitting with him sland having to listen to him lament about, what Alex now felt were, insignificant problems was torturous. She felt a rush of guilt again for even thinking what she was, but something had changed in her. Something she could not undo. Some paradigm shift had occurred in her thought process and she could not grasp what was lost.

"Hey, so I called to let you know that D and I just got back to the precinct from another crime scene matching the one from almost two weeks ago." Manny paused, waiting for her to reply.

Alex sat up in her chair. Apparently, she hadn't lost all her elasticity. Any cloud of thought or emotion she was feeling was pushed instantly away. Her brain focused on what Manny said. She repeated it in her head again to make sure she heard and understood him.

"The same modus operandi?"

"To a tee."

Alex wrapped the phone cord around her index finger a few times and then let it unwind itself. She did this once more as she pondered what Manny told her.

*The implications.*

"Well… you know what that means."

"Yes." Manny replied.

"We have ourselves another serial killer." Alex declared, just as she wrapped the cord around her finger again, one too many times, cutting off the circulation.

"It would appear we do." Manny agreed.

"Manny?"

"¿Sí, mi amor?"

"Why didn't you come get me before you went to the crime scene?"

# CHAPTER FIVE



MANNY PAUSED; CHOKING ON HIS VOICE, the lump of it lodged in his throat.

*Damn it. I should have known this would happen. D called it.* He scratched his head then ran his fingers through his hair a few times, more a soothing mechanism for himself than anything. He took a deep breath in and readied himself for an argument.

"I knew you had patients today and I didn't want to interrupt you, Alex. I know it has been hard on your practice for the last five months, what with Abuela and then…" he paused not wanting to even say the words.

There was a corporeal silence that followed so thick he could feel its tentacles reaching into his eardrum through the phone line. Manny clenched his teeth together and waited. There was no point in trying to dance around the subject. One of the things he found so attractive about Alex was also one of the things that could make her difficult. She was a very strong, independent woman who could be as stubborn as a mule.

*A beautiful mule.*

Manny pulled his lips into his mouth between his teeth and brought his teeth together against his lips with enough pressure to elicit a little pain to keep from laughing at the image that had popped up in his mind. He could hear his mother's voice in his head.

*Manuelito, this is no laughing matter. Basta! Stop it! Sé serio— be serious. She is going to cut off your huevos.*

Manny bit down hard on his lips. If he didn't, he was going to lose it and burst out laughing. He was already in enough trouble. The pain arrested his laugh. He tasted the slight tinge of blood. A minor price to pay compared to what Alex would do to him if he laughed at that moment. He could hear her sigh over the phone after what seemed like a never-ending silence.

"Okay, so I am assuming Leavy has the body now?"

*She sounds less angry, but angry, nonetheless.*

"Yes. D and I are going to go over the reports and photos from the scene. Would you like to join us when you are finished with your patients for the day?"

Manny's face wrinkled in a small wince. He was waiting for a barrage of accusations and angry questions for his actions, but nothing followed except a calm response.

"I will be there, yes."

Manny wasn't sure what was happening, but this was not his Alex. Any other time he would do something that she felt was overbearing or overprotective, he would hear about it multiple times on many levels. This new silence and calm demeanor were eerie; it was not like her at all. He waited a few more seconds before he spoke, almost wishing for her to bite his head off. Nothing. No Venus Flytrap. No snapping dragon.

"Okay, so we will see you soon then. Te quiero, I love you."

"Okay, me too." Alex said, then the line went dead.
*Okay, there it is. The smoking gun.*
"You're in big trouble, aren't you?" Deshawn remarked from behind Manny.

Manny didn't turn to answer him. He put his hands up near his head as if he were surrendering and slowly raised the middle fingers of each one, successfully flipping Deshawn a bilateral bird.

"Hahaha!" Deshawn burst out laughing.

Manny joined him.

After a few moments the chuckles died down and the air morphed from playful to serious. Deshawn sat in the chair at his desk facing Manny and rested his chin on his fists, his eyes fixed on Manny. Manny shook his head.

"Nope. We aren't talking about it. Any of it. I don't want to." Manny said sternly and stared down at his desk for the file on "John Doe Two".

"How did she take it though? That's all I wanna know." Deshawn probed.

"How do you think?" Manny barked.

He peered up at Deshawn with wary eyes. They had been partners for over six years, friends for almost the entirety. They knew each other so well that neither one needed to speak if they didn't want to. They knew one another's' facial expressions, body language and intricacies. They could get angry with one another, but they generally let it blow over quickly. Most of the time though, thankfully, they didn't let it get that far. They generally knew when to stop pushing each other's buttons. Deshawn nodded.

Manny grabbed the file for "John Doe Two" and opened it up. He grabbed the 5x7's and handed them to Deshawn. Deshawn picked them up and spread them out on his desk, creating a photo collage of the crime scene. Manny pulled out the preliminary CSI report that was given to him a few minutes prior to him calling Alex. He knew what it would say. He and Deshawn had already seen "John Doe Two" at the Riverdale Inn. But it was necessary to review the report once, twice as many times as needed to lock in the information and possibly see something that might have been missed or overlooked.

"So, we officially have a serial killer." Manny sighed.

"Yeah, we do, don't we! Question is, what do we do about it? She isn't leaving us much to go on. No DNA, no fingerprints. She is like a ghost." Deshawn stared down at the glossy photos in front of him.

Deshawn was right. This unsub was difficult to profile. She was deliberate and systematic in everything she did it seemed, except for the stabbing frenzy that had now occurred twice. The first could have been chalked up to a crime of passion, but two? It seemed much less likely at that point.

From where Manny sat, the sheen on the photos obscured the image of "John Doe Two". It made him seem like every other murder victim in every other photo Deshawn had placed on his desk over the years, like a makeshift game of murder memory, for their viewing pleasure. Manny squinted his eyes to see if it made a difference, but it only added a tent of black spider leg eyelashes to his vision.

"Hey." A familiar voice called from behind him.

Manny jumped.

Deshawn's head popped up and he smiled.

Alex came around the side of Manny and walked over to Deshawn's desk, peering at the photos as she went. She reached out a long, elegant fingertip and turned one, angling it to face her better. Silence loomed around them as she examined the details in the pictures. Manny and Deshawn waited, as they always did, for her to process what she saw. She would ask her questions and make her comments when she was ready.

Manny studied her face.

*God, she is so beautiful. Even when she is upset with me and trying to ignore me, she is gorgeous.*

He let his eyes linger on her for a few seconds longer until he, himself, could feel the heat coming off of his stare. He broke his eyes from her visage and stacked the papers from the "John Doe Two" file neatly together. He picked them up and tapped them on the desk so that they would meet up evenly with one another. Both Alex and Deshawn regarded him. Manny tapped the papers twice more, then shoved them back into the yellow folder.

"Here." Alex pointed out to Deshawn one of the photos. "See the way the body is? It's pretty much in the exact position as Mr. Stanton was. Even the left arm had been bound, then cut loose. Notice the ligature marks. What is the significance of that?" Alex uttered, more to herself than to either Manny or Deshawn.

Manny and Deshawn watched Alex while she considered her own thoughts and questions, neither offering any suggestions. Alex bit at her lower lip with her two upper front teeth absentmindedly as she thought. Manny found that particular habit of hers endearing and extremely sexy all at once.

"So, we have nothing to go on other than M.O." she finally spoke.

"Correct." Manny replied.

"Still no fingerprints or D.N.A. left behind at the scene that we know of?" Alex asked.

"None." Deshawn offered.

"No hit in AFIS on our vic either?" she asked.

Manny and Deshawn both shook their heads "no".

"Okay, so the question is this… What are we going to do about it?" she asked Manny and Deshawn, expecting them both to answer her.

"Great question. I guess we all need to put our wicked smaht noggins together and figure that out." Deshawn tried out his best Bostonian accent.

Alex snorted. Manny rolled his eyes at Deshawn and sniggered.

*This guy couldn't be serious, could he?*

Manny looked at Alex. Her eyes met his. For a moment he watched as she remembered her frustration with him. It returned to her face wiping away the smile. Manny pushed out his lower lip creating a small pout. When that didn't work, he mouthed the words "I love you" to her. Alex glared at him from across the desk. Deshawn looked at them and then pretended he was studying the photos with fastidious care. After a few seconds of making her point with her hard eyes and stone-faced glare, Manny watched Alex's face soften. The sides of her eyes pinched together as her smile widened enough to crinkle their corners.

*Ah, that's it right there. Perfection,* Manny thought happily. Manny returned her smile and Alex returned to the photos and Deshawn. Manny thought of Alex and her smile. That smile. The very thing that made his heart beat as if he had run the fifty-yard dash. That smile was what had taken his breath away the first time he saw her in college so many years ago. He had pursued her, and she had denied him, but they eventually became close friends. The butterflies her smile could induce in him had never changed though. If anything, they had grown stronger. Alex's voice pulled Manny from his thoughts.

"I have an idea."

# CHAPTER SIX

"Okay, so you'll carry this cell phone and make
sure you keep it close to you. Go into the bar, sit down and
have one drink and wait." Manny instructed.
Sergeant Baker listened, his face intent on every word,
nodding at the appropriate times. His green eyes clear and
understanding. Manny had picked him for his ability to
follow tasks and his calm demeanor. Baker had been with
the department for over ten years. He was seasoned. Manny
knew he could trust him to go to the bar and only have one
drink and wait. A lot of the other guys would have more than
one drink. It was just how it was.
The other officers and detectives of the Unit were gathered
around Manny, Alex and Deshawn. A large white board was
set up with pictures of Mr. Stanton taped to the left side of
the board and "John Doe Two" taped to the right side of the
board. At the top of the board in the center was written in
large block letters "UNSUB" and underneath it was written
the following: female, early to late twenties, long black hair.
Manny was leaning against his desk with his arms crossed,
surveying the room. Deshawn stood across from him on

the other side of the room, watching the troops. Alex stood next to the white board surveying its information quickly to make sure it contained all the pertinent information before she turned to address the crew. Manny watched her scanning the board quickly and efficiently, then nodding her head in appreciation. She turned with quiet resolve to address the team.

"Okay. First of all, thank you for your time. So, we have another serial killer in our midst. Within the last two and a half weeks we have had two bodies of two Caucasian males in their early thirties, both found slain at the Riverdale Inn. Both, as you can see, suffered multiple stab wounds, although according to Dr. Leavy, she believes the actual C.O.D. for both was exsanguination from a horizontal throat slash. Any questions so far?"

Alex looked around the room. A few of the officers looked at one another. Some cleared their throats or shook their heads "no" in acknowledgement. When she was satisfied that everyone was on board, she continued.

"According to our intel, both men were seen at the Lark. Then subsequently leaving with a young woman from The Lark. If you don't know it, it's a local bar a few miles from here. I feel that this particular unsub is very confident that she is completely in the dark. I want to flush her out. I think we can post Sergeant Baker at the bar and wait for her to go to him. He fits her type. He is Caucasian, mid-thirties, and he is relatively handsome."

Alex looked at Baker and winked. This elicited a mass of whoops, whistles, cat calls, and laughter. Alex laughed, and smirked at Manny. He grinned at her and winked. Alex turned back to the group of officers and detectives and waited for them to settle down. After a few minutes the room became still again. Alex finished.

"Alright. Let's wrap this up. We will isolate Sergeant Baker from the others so that the unsub won't feel intimidated." Alex paused again giving anyone time for questions or comments.

No one asked any. Sergeant Baker puffed his chest out slightly at the mention of his name. A few fellow officers chortled his way and he nodded at them with a smirk. One guy snorted. Manny smiled and shook his head. It was sometimes hard to keep things serious in a room full of testosterone. Alex ignored them and continued on.

"We are pretty sure she won't be there tonight, but we aren't positive. Sometimes when serials get going their kills will get closer to one another. To our knowledge this was the unsub's second murder, but we have no way of truly knowing which number it really is, so we have to play it from all angles just to be safe. The first murder seemed to be a crime of passion when we saw the multiple stab wounds. Initially, we thought maybe she was a scorned lover. But then "John Doe Two" showed up with the same pattern of stab wounds. This leads me to believe we have an unsub who is suffering from PTSD and something is triggering her during these murders to then act upon this vicious slashing. Detective Castillo will go over the logistics now." Alex looked at Manny and nodded, all business.

Manny stood from his leaning position and cleared his throat. He walked over to the front of the group and looked at them. They looked to him for further instruction. He appraised them for a split second, proud of the team he had built. They were a good, solid team. They had coalesced well over the last ten years for him. Even the newbies had come in and melded well.

"So, here's the deal. Baker's going in with some new tech we have. It's a remotely activated mobile phone microphone, meaning there's a… Yup, you guessed it, a microphone inside. Spelling," Manny looked over to Spelling, who nodded at Manny respectfully "our resident Brainiac, is an expert in the use of this 'roving bug' tech, as it's called. All Baker has to do is keep it within a few feet of his person. Baker will be positioned at the bar, alone. We will do this nightly until we get a bite. Understood?"

Manny waited. The team nodded. Some murmured affirmations.

"Alpha team will be in position outside The Lark in the van. They are in charge of surveillance. Bravo team will be positioned on the Northeast and Southeast borders of the Riverdale Inn awaiting the signal from Baker."

Everyone nodded.

"Freeman and I will be with Alpha team monitoring communications. Dr. Aguilar will be back here at base waiting to help interview the suspect as soon as an arrest is made. We will be bringing her in unscathed, people. Any questions?"

The officers looked around at each other. Some shrugged. Some shook their heads "no". Some verbalized "no". Sergeant Baker looked around at his fellow officers, his face a mixture of proud regard and admiration. Manny knew exactly how he felt. Manny puffed out his own chest a bit, like a proud father, and smiled.

*Okay, that's enough of that. Let's do this.*

Manny looked at his crew and barked orders.

"Well alright, kiddos, stop standing around then. Get your asses moving."

# CHAPTER SEVEN

"WELL, HANDSOME, DIDN'T I SEE YOU here before? You look familiar" Cindy slurred, spilling her hot, Jameson breath into Baker's nostrils. He pushed his upper lip towards his nose to close the holes off, but it was too late. Her breath was already invading his sense of smell.

*Good Lord almighty,* he thought, *I pray to God this woman does not drive home tonight. Or any other night for that matter.*
"Yeah, I should. I have been here for the last five nights in a row in this same seat." Baker said, trying hard not to laugh.
"Hm, well, you muss' like sumthin' you see then." Cindy slurred again, leaning even further in towards Baker, making a sad attempt to bat her eyelashes at him. Baker resisted the urge to rip Cindy's falsey the rest of the way off her eye— it hung like a dying caterpillar from her eyelid, begging to be rescued. Instead he allowed the chuckle out— he couldn't refrain from both, and he figured that was the lesser of two evils.
"No. Actually, the Missus and I aren't gettin' along, ya know?" Baker turned his head to the side, trying to avoid Cindy's brewery breath. "So, I came here to get away from

the bitch. All bitches, in fact."

Baker smirked at Cindy and her face distorted in inebriated confusion. She backed away from the bar a few inches. Baker could tell she was trying to decide, with her inhibited senses, whether he was joking or not. After a few seconds, Cindy gave Baker a timid giggle and spoke in a less flirty tone.

"Yeah, baby, I hear ya." she said, then turned and walked away.

Baker picked up his cell phone, flipped it open to pretend he was answering a call, and spoke into it.

"This lady wouldn't remember a suspect even if she was sober and it sat on her face." Baker snapped the phone shut and returned it to the tacky bar.

Baker looked around. This was the fifth night in a row he sat in the same spot in the rundown bar. Only a few faces had changed in those four nights. Most stayed the same. He felt like he was in a warped episode of "Cheers". Only this sitcom would be called "Cheers: the Darkside". It was a dismal, outdated bar where the customers never changed and neither did the bartender. Everyone knew each other but minded their business. An old school kind of place where the kind of adages like "snitches get stitches" still applied. It didn't surprise Baker they weren't able to get much info from anyone regarding the last two vics.

Since he had been there, absolutely nothing had changed except for the sports games on the televisions. Even the sticky spot on the bar that was there the very first night he sat down was still there and he was still trying to avoid it. Baker cringed thinking of it. He grabbed the old, tattered cardboard "Bud Light" coaster and covered the tacky wood with it so he wouldn't inadvertently touch it again. When he stopped paying attention to Cindy, she walked away.

*On to the next victim,* Baker thought.

He had to stifle the laugh that was brewing. He pinched his thigh.

*That should do it.*

Baker picked up the cell phone again and had his "fake phone call" with the surveillance van.

"This place sucks, man. Is this chic ever gonna show?"

He sighed. There was no reason to wait for a response. He had no way of receiving one. He wasn't even sure they could hear him. He knew right before he left them that they could because they had done one last test run, but now he wasn't positive. It didn't matter so much to him except recording everything was good for evidence in court. He looked up in time to see the Patriots score against the Jets. The few patrons in the bar exploded with excitement. Baker smiled.

"Ha!"

"You like that, do you?" A sultry, southern voice inquired. Baker started. He turned to see a beautiful girl next to him in a Patriots cap, full lips lined crimson red, and a thick black ponytail hanging down her back. But her eyes— her eyes stopped him dead— crystal clear, green like the shiniest emerald he had ever seen. Baker opened his mouth to speak but he couldn't for a second. She laughed lightly. Baker smiled.

"Sorry, I caught you off guard." she drawled.

"Yes, you did, Miss…?"

"Aeval." she offered her small, pale hand to him.

Baker looked at Raven, looked at her hand then took it into his and shook it gingerly. She smiled brightly, her merlot lips parting to show a set of perfect teeth.

*Wow, she is a beautiful psycho,* he thought.

Baker smiled in return trying to remember to hold back a

little. Dr. Aguilar had told him to try to appear on the timid side.

"David." Baker offered, still holding Raven's hand.

She laughed. It was a low, throaty laugh that didn't just tickle Baker's ears, but parts of him he hadn't felt tickle in some time. He squeezed his knees together in an effort to nullify the feeling.

"Well David, nice to meet you. May I have my hand back?"

"Oh, jeez!" Baker ripped his hand away from her as if she were infected.

There was no need for acting— he had truly embarrassed himself. Somehow, within minutes she had put some kind of spell on him. He could see how the other guys had fallen victim to her so easily. He was acting like an irrational teenage boy sitting next to his first crush. He could feel the flush spreading across his cheeks and knew his pale Irish skin was betraying him. He only prayed the dim lighting in the bar shrouded him in enough darkness that she would not notice.

"Sorry."

"No need to apologize, sugar."

Her green eyes looked right through him. Baker shifted on his barstool trying to get comfortable, but not because of the hard-wooden seat beneath his rear end.  He was surprised at how shy he was feeling.

*No need to pretend with this one,* he thought.

Her thick New Orleans accent was sexy, and it sent little goosebumps down the back of his spine.

*What is happening here? Get a grip.* He castigated himself.

"David, you mind if a girl takes a load off?" Raven pointed to the barstool next to Baker.

"Oh crap, where are my manners? No, not at all. Wow, sorry.

Strike two, huh?"

Baker chuckled as he leaned in and pulled out the barstool next to him so that Raven could sit down. He caught a hint of whatever perfume she was wearing— it was faint, but tantalizing. Baker quickly sat up, pulling himself away from her delicious smell.

"Why, thank you, David. How kind of you."

Raven sat.

She looked at Baker, studying him for a moment.

"I haven't seen you here before." She observed.

"Oh no, you wouldn't have." he answered. "I am a traveling salesman. I am only here in town for the next few days." Baker recited the line, exactly as Alex had instructed him. He saw a flicker of interest flash across Raven's eyes. Alex told Baker she thought the story would benefit them. It would make him a good target, alone, not from the area, unknown to anyone. If the unsub chose Baker, which they felt she would according to his looks and age, the story should cinch the deal.

*Well Dr. Aguilar, looks like you may have been on the money about this one,* Baker thought.

"I see."

Cindy strolled over to the pair with tunnel vision for Baker. Baker noticed Aeval turn her back to Cindy as she approached, feigning interest in the television behind her.

"Hey handsome, you ready for another?" She slurred, apparently forgetting Baker's earlier snarky comment. From the heavy scent of the musky liquor perfume Cindy was wearing, it was obvious that she had imbibed in enough drinks since the incident, to have forgiven Baker his prickly persona.

Cindy's eyes never strayed from Baker's face. It was as if

Raven didn't exist. Baker again turned his head slightly to the side, so he didn't have to swallow Cindy's breath. He was surprised to find his glass empty and wondered for a moment how it had come to be that way. He didn't remember finishing it. Only a small remnant of amber liquid remained at the base, not even enough to wet his lips. Baker turned to Raven.

"Would you like a drink, Aeval?" he asked.

"Sure, thank you, David. I'll take a hurricane." Raven answered Baker, never once looking at Cindy.

Baker nodded and turned to Cindy.

"The lady will have a hurricane, and I will have another Bourbon. Thank you."

Cindy walked away with a huff and grumbling under her breath. Baker looked over to see Raven smiling. It was contagious. He started to smile too.

"Looks like someone doesn't want to do much work tonight." Baker nodded towards Cindy's backside.

Raven laughed.

"She never does." Raven added.

"I see. Seems you know her well. To be honest, I can't say I blame her that much. I mean look at this place. It isn't exactly the Ritz Carlton." Baker laughed.

"Oh, ain't that the truth!" Raven chimed in. "And, no, thankfully I don't know her well. I have only been here twice, but in those two times, she was exactly the same."

Raven rolled her eyes. They laughed together for a moment. Cindy gave them a look as she returned with their drinks. Baker thought it a mixture of jealousy and insecurity. She knew they were talking about her. The bar felt the brunt of Cindy's anger as she slammed them down hard enough to spill some and turned to leave, without a word. Raven and

Baker looked at one another with wide-eyed surprise, which elicited another round of laughter. Once the laughter died down, Baker picked up his glass and raised it.

"Cheers to the beautiful lady next to me."

"Aw, now I will drink to that." Raven raised her glass. They clinked their glasses together and partook of their respective drinks. Baker reminded himself to not drink anymore of his drink. (Only one, Manny had warned.) He returned his spotty glass back to the sticky bar and looked around again at the small crowd of barflies. The crowd, if you could call it that, was thinning out as the night wore on. The fourth quarter of the football game ended minutes ago, leading to a mass exodus of patrons. Although "mass" was a far cry from what it really was when it came to the small number of patrons that infested the bar. When Baker returned his eyes to Raven, she was staring at him.

"Oh, hello there." he grinned.

"Hello."

"Sorry, I was being nosy." he laughed. "How is your drink?"

She raised her eyebrows at her glass and appraised it.

"Definitely not the best hurricane I have ever had."

"Ha-ha! I am sure. Where are you from?"

"New Orleans, sugar. Home of the hurricane." she laughed, her thick accent pouring out of her lips like sweet molasses.

"Alright. That makes a lot of sense." Baker nodded— caught up in the moment, he took another sip of his bourbon. She was near irresistible. He found himself wanting her.

*Knock it off. You are on duty, jackass.*

He pinched his thigh underneath the bar, smiling through the pain. Raven smiled back at him. He itched to move this along, but knew he had to wait for her. This was her show. He had to be patient, but he just wanted to get it over with.

Her aura was beginning to surround him and draw him in. He needed to breathe his own air, not the arousing scent of her perfume with its cloudy promise of sex and pleasure. *You know better than that. It is a ruse. A promise of sex will get your killed.*

Baker choked on his bourbon. Raven looked at him— concern wrinkling her brow slightly. Baker coughed a few times into his elbow. Raven touched his shoulder.

"Are you okay?" She seemed genuinely interested in his well-being.

*Of course, she is interested. You are her next victim.*

Baker held up a hand and nodded as his coughing started to subside. His pale complexion turned a fiery red from the exertion as if he had swallowed a Carolina Reaper pepper whole. His soon to be killer's hand was still on his shoulder and in some twisted way he enjoyed the feeling. A dangerous vibration flowed through her. He could feel it and it translated through to him.

"You sure you're okay?"

"Yeah, yeah." He waved her off politely.

Baker took a big chance. He didn't wait like they instructed him to do.

"Wanna get outta here?"

Baker caught a glimpse of surprise skip across her face before Raven masked it with a devilish smile. A wicked twinkle replaced the startled look in her tart green sour apple eyes. They shimmered in the little light the bar gave off. For a moment, Baker imagined those eyes could light the bar on fire.

"Yes, I do. Let's go."

# CHAPTER EIGHT

Baker sauntered to room six like a Giglio on a mission. He boogied to a beat only he could hear. He held the hotel key proudly after following strict instructions from Aeval. (Pay with cash, give a fake name, don't look back at her behind the fake plant.) Baker was sure she was their suspect, but they had to follow through with the entire sting operation or else they wouldn't have enough evidence to present in court. So, he continued to play the game.

He whistled as he walked, blowing his hot bourbon breath out into the sweltering air. Summer was nearing its end, yet today had been an especially grueling day on the heat index. Ninety-eight degrees with humidity, thick as New England clam chowder— it was about as uncomfortable as you could get in Massachusetts. On a rare occasion it would reach the low hundreds, but that was a heat wave. He flipped the key around his pointer finger, spinning it absentmindedly, as he thought about Raven's scarlet lips and what he would do to them if she were "just another girl".

*No, you are going to be a professional and get the job done.*

He arrived at the door marked number six and stood there regarding it, then looked to his left and his right. Not a soul in sight. He knew she would be along soon because that is what she told him she would do. For one last time, Baker opened his cell phone and mocked a call.

"I'm going in." he said quietly into the speaker, then flipped it shut and pocketed it for the time being.

Baker penetrated the lock with the key, turning it until he heard it click. He pushed the door open and felt the air-conditioned air caress his sweaty face.

*Thank god housekeeping left the A.C. on.*

The room still had the faint hint of stale cigarette smoke even though he knew for a fact this side of the hotel had gone nonsmoking over two years ago. That's what happened when you were an ex-smoker. Your nose became like a bloodhound for the smell of rank cigarette smoke. Baker couldn't stand the smell of it anymore, even though at one point he was smoking upwards of a pack and a half a day.

*Fuck, that is so disgusting.*

There was a soft knock on the door.

*Ah, here she is.*

Baker turned and walked to the door. He peered through the peephole to make sure it was her that stood waiting. It was. He opened the door and welcomed her with a smile. He didn't have to fake or force them anymore, they came naturally, and he hated himself for it.

"Well hello, handsome."

"Well hello yourself, gorgeous."

He moved to the side to let her enter the room. She brushed past him, leaving her signature scent in her wake. Baker sniffed the air, soaking her up.

*God, she smells so good. If it wasn't her looks, it was her smell that killed those poor bastards.*

Baker watched as Raven surveyed the room, laying her large bag on a chair next to the small, circular table that stood near the window of the room. The drapes were closed, hiding them from the outside world.

"Will this do, your highness?"

She raised her eyebrows at him, and for a moment she actually resembled a haughty, dissatisfied queen. Baker smiled and waited to see what his comment had provoked. It was odd. He knew he was dealing with a killer, but he didn't feel threatened or unsafe. He felt as if he were exchanging normal flirtation and banter with an ordinary woman. A young, hot woman, but ordinary, nonetheless.

"I suppose it will have to." She turned her nose up in the air and made a feeble attempt at a horrific British accent.

Baker burst out laughing. Raven joined in. They giggled for a few moments. Baker laid his head back and closed his eyes, he was laughing so hard.

*Ah, that was pretty good.*

He opened his eyes, and she was there, in front of him. Up close. Face to face.

"Oh. Hello." he said, surprised to see her there.

"Hi." she whispered.

"Hi."

Before he knew what was happening, she had her lips on his. Her crimson lips, full and soft on his chapped ones, her tongue dancing in his mouth. Baker was caught off guard.

*Damn it.*

It angered him. He was never blindsided like that. He was a cop. He was supposed to see all angles and never let his guard down. He grabbed her by the arms, his fingers digging into her skin. Always be vigilant. Always be aware. What is worse than being caught off guard? The fact that he liked it. She moaned when he grabbed her and wrapped her arms around him. He liked the way it felt. Her tongue in his mouth. He was kissing her back. Hard and deep. And he liked it. After a few moments, she pulled away.

"I need air." she smiled, breathless.

Her merlot lipstick smeared past the vermillion borders of her lips making her appear as the crazed lunatic they were searching for. Baker didn't care. He wanted her. Desired her body. It had been so long since he had been with anyone. *One little taste.*

"Okay, baby."

"Hey, I got something that'll make you feel so good, *baby*." She cooed.

"Oh, yeah?"

"Yeah." she smiled her clown face smile.

Raven walked over to her bag and rummaged through it. She produced a small plastic baggie with some capsules. Baker knew what they were right away. Molly. But he didn't let on that he knew. He made a face, like a kid in school who was faced with the biggest algebra problem on the planet. She smiled at him.

"Don't worry, sugar. It's a little something to make you feel good. It makes you happy and the sex amazing."

Her voice flowed like silk from her blood-red lips.

*Those poor bastards never had a chance. She could sell a burnt burger patty that was hard as a hockey puck to a starving, toothless, penniless man.*

Thankfully, Baker was beginning to come out of whatever spell she had on him and was starting to remember who and what he was.

"Oh, I don't do drugs." Baker tried to look as timid as he

could without coming off fake.

Raven tried to hide her aggravation, but Baker still caught a glimpse of it.

*Thank god, the drinks and the kiss are wearing off. I need to refocus.*

He had a job to do. Castillo had picked him. Trusted him. He couldn't mess this up. They had a plan, and it had to get to a certain point, which could be dangerous for him, so he needed a clear head. He could see her gears working in her head.

"Okay, sugar, I will take them, too. It's not a biggie. They are great, you'll see." she smiled encouragingly.

Now she looked comical. Not so sexy anymore. Baker was angry for letting himself get swept up with her at all.

*Do what you have to do and get through this. No more bullshit.*

She turned and sauntered over to the area where the mini fridge and microwave were. On top of the microwave she grabbed two Styrofoam cups wrapped in plastic. She ripped the plastic off and threw it in the trash liner then went to the bathroom sink and filled the two cups with water. She returned to Baker and handed him one of the cups.

"I am going to take these pills here, and then I am going to go in that tiny bathroom and freshen up. When I come out, I would love to see you on that bed waiting for me." she demanded in a playful tone, although Baker doubted that she was joking.

Baker flashed his sweetest smile.

"Well, yes, ma'am. As you wish, your highness."

That elicited another giggle from her smeared clown lips.

They tapped their Styrofoam cups together and tossed their pills down, chasing them with water. Baker quickly grabbed his two pills with the tip of his tongue and wiggled them expertly underneath it for safekeeping until he could dispose of them safely without her noticing.

"I'm off to the ladies' room."

"Mhm."

She grabbed her bag and went into the bathroom. Baker knew he had to take off at least his shirt. They had discussed this at the precinct. He hurried to remove his shirt and pants so he could spit the Molly into his pants' pocket. He left his boxers on and with haste, threw his clothes on one of the chairs. He was grateful there was an end table next to the bed. He laid the cellphone on it, then laid himself on the bed and waited as he was instructed.

Within a few moments she came out of the bathroom. She smiled at him, her lips showing only faint remnants of stain resembling that of merlot spilt on white linen someone attempted to scrub away. He feigned excitement to see her. Any previous feelings towards her replaced with the desire to get down to business.

"Ah, I see you are ready."

"More than you know." he replied. "Let's do this."

# CHAPTER NINE

His lips tasted delicious. Raven didn't know why she wanted to kiss him, but she did. A buzzing feeling ran over her skin like the sound she heard late at night running through the powerlines.

*What is happening to me?*

She wasn't sure but she needed to get a grip on herself. She was here on business not pleasure. They were laughing. A lot. He was funny, and she liked it. He laid his head back and belted out a big, booming laugh and before she knew what she was doing she was on him—her lips on his— her tongue tasting his amber poison.

He grabbed her arms and squeezed as if he were going to push her away. Her heart raced, the sudden fear of rejection gripping her. But instead he moaned and pulled her into him, kissing her harder. Her body caught fire. After a few moments of their tongues twisting and turning with one another and their voices harmonizing in moans and groans, she couldn't take anymore. Raven broke free from their lip lock.

"I need air." she gasped.

*I also need to get a fucking grip.*

He looked at her and smiled. She smiled back. He was gorgeous. Fair skinned, green eyes, and freckles on his cheeks and nose. One of his teeth jutted out slightly, but it gave him character, and she liked it. Her belly flipped with excitement; a new feeling like nothing she had ever experienced.

"Okay, baby."

Raven suddenly felt nauseous.

*Oh, David, why? For a moment, I almost forgot. You were doing so well, you almost had me fooled.*

Raven felt a deep pit in her stomach that roiled with nausea once again. "Baby" was what Momma's gentleman callers used to call her. Raven hated it so much. The word incited feelings of fury in Raven.

"I got something that will make you feel so good, *baby.*"

Raven let the word "baby" ooze from her lips.

"Oh, yeah?"

"Yeah." she managed, through gritted teeth.

Raven's stomach started to churn. She turned quickly towards the table and her bag so David wouldn't see her rage building. She walked over to her bag and rifled through it for the Molly. She produced it after a moment and turned to him, smiling again, after taking a few deep, settling breaths. She held the baggie with the Molly capsules in it so that he could see it. He looked at it timorously.

"Don't worry, sugar. It's a little something to make you feel good. It makes you happy and the sex amazing." she coaxed.

He looked at her again with anxious eyes.

*He's scared.*

"Oh, I don't do drugs." he managed to say.

Raven felt the heat of frustration rise in her face, but she squelched it quickly.

*It won't do you any good to lose yourself control at this moment in time, little Blackbird,* Momma's voice told her. *He is sober, bigger, stronger, and untethered. Gain his trust.*

"Okay, sugar, I will take some, too. It's not a biggie. They are great, you'll see." she smiled again.

His face relaxed a little. Raven knew exactly where the Styrofoam cups were, but she turned and pretended to look for them. When she "spotted" them, she walked over to the dark corner. An old, once white, mini fridge stood there, and an even older looking microwave hitched a piggyback on its top. The cups were placed on the microwave and she grabbed two, ripping off the plastic and throwing it away. She filled them with water from the bathroom sink, then returned to Baker and handed him one of the cups.

"I am going to take these two pills here and then I am going to go in that tiny bathroom and freshen up. When I come out, I would love to see you on that bed waiting for me." Raven motioned to the bed with a nod.

He looked at the bed and then back at her with a smile. They simultaneously popped their pills and followed them with a gulp of tap water from their fancy Styrofoam cups after tapping their rims together in a mock "cheers". Raven managed to grab one of her pills with her tongue, but the other slipped down her throat.

*Oh for fuck's sake.*

That had never happened before. She thought she had both pills under her tongue before she shot back her gulp of water. She usually only took one pill, but she knew he would need two. He was sober and he was bigger than the other two had been— denser, full of muscle, in shape. It was going to take more to get him down.

*Oh my god, what in fuck's sake am I going to do with myself
now,* she wondered.

She turned quickly so her back was facing him and waved a
hand up in the air at him.

"I'm off." she managed to say.

"Mhm." he murmured back to her.

Raven snagged her bag and made her way to the small
bathroom. She switched on the light and closed the door.
The exhaust fan hummed loudly next to the bright light in
the ceiling. She hurried to the toilet and spit the remaining
pill into the toilet and flushed it. She thought of sticking
her finger down her throat to make herself vomit, but she
couldn't do it. She was a strong woman in almost every
aspect of life except for some reason the thought of vomiting
or having to vomit made her knees buckle.

Raven walked over to the sink. She scooped some water from
the faucet into her palm and drank it. Her reflection in the
mirror was distorted from the smudges left by the maid's
poor cleaning skills. The blotches on the glass did little to
hide the bright red lipstick ring that had smeared onto her
face from kissing David.

*Oh my god, I look like a crazy person.*

Raven had to swallow the urge to laugh.

*You ARE a crazy person.*

Raven marveled at the way she looked, a quirky smile
forming on her now (thanks to the lipstick) misshapen lips.
Raven wet a washcloth and swiped at her lips. She couldn't
go back out there looking like that. When she was finished
and looking more presentable, she threw the washcloth on
the floor, making a mental note to return before she left to
pick it up and take it with her. She opened the door and
turned off the light.

David was there on the bed, propped up on both pillows looking at her with a smile. Raven felt that same unfamiliar flutter in her belly when she looked at him laid out on the bed. His body was not like the other two men she had brought here. She knew he was muscular and lean, but she was not expecting what she saw before her. His abdominal muscles were clearly visible without him even trying to flex them. His upper arms, both right and left, were tattooed and chiseled, veins popping as if he had just come from the gym. *It is truly going to be a shame to remove this one from the world.* Raven moved towards the table to put her bag down again. She smiled at him. He smiled back. She hoped the Molly would kick in soon or that he might be more open to being bound, because if not, he was not someone she was going to be able to physically overcome. Even though his physique was appealing to the eyes, it was a definite roadblock to a petite thing like her trying to commit murder.

"Ah, I see you are ready."

"More than you know." he replied. "Let's do this."

"I was hoping when I first saw you that you might be like me." she began. She paused waiting for a reaction.

"How so?" he asked.

"Well, I like to play what people call, um, 'sex games', I guess." she offered, cautiously.

Raven waited again for a response. David's eyebrows raised, either from surprise or curiosity, possibly both. After a few seconds, a smile graced his handsome face. Raven again felt a stitch of guilt in her side for having to kill him. But only momentarily. She wasn't sure if she was disappointed or grateful for his next words, but he sealed his fate.

"Yeah, baby, I'm definitely into that shit." he grinned.

Raven could feel her teeth come together so tightly that her masseter muscles seemed as if they might burst from her skin. She clenched her fists together until she could feel her fingernails digging into the pads of her palms. She needed to calm down or else he was going to sense her rage, but she wanted to punch that stupid grin right off of his face.

*I am going to slash your throat, baby…*

"Okay, then lay back and let me take care of you, *baby!*"

Raven went to her bag and pulled out the zip ties, laying them on the table.

She knew she was going to have to give him "a show" before the ties. The Molly hadn't kicked in yet and he hadn't had enough booze at the bar. She knew because she had been watching him from her spot since he had come in. Raven walked over to the alarm clock radio and fiddled with it until she found her rock station. At this point she knew where it was located.

"Would you like a little dance?" she asked.

He looked at her appraisingly.

"Yeah, baby, who wouldn't?"

*I am going to enjoy slitting your throat, baby.*

Raven moved away from the bed to give herself some space to dance. She found the rhythm to the music and started to move, closing her eyes and willing herself away from the dingy hotel room for a few moments in time. As she moved her hips, she slowly pulled at the bottom hem of her Patriots t-shirt, teasing it up her body. She could feel his eyes all over her.

"Yes, baby." he whispered.

*Shut up!*

She turned her back to him, hips undulating back and forth, back and forth. She slowly unbuttoned her pants and pulled down the zipper, then slid them down revealing her backside to him. She heard him gasp. Always a good reaction. She stepped out of her jeans gingerly so she wouldn't trip and still look "sexy" and kicked them to the side. Raven turned to look at her victim.

He lay on the bed in his boxers, and his excitement was evident. His eyes were glued on her. He made no move or attempt to touch her, for which she was glad.

*Maybe he's participated in "sex games" before and knew the rules of Doms and Subs,* she thought.

She couldn't be sure, but it didn't matter. All that mattered was that so far things were going smoothly, and she hoped it would continue because she needed to get the zip ties on him.

"Are you ready to play *baby*?" she purred.

"Oh, yeah, baby." he growled.

Raven walked over to the table and grabbed the zip ties. She returned to the bed and held them up. David looked at the ties but didn't seem shocked.

*Hm, interesting,* she thought.

It didn't matter. It was actually a good thing that he was so calm, wasn't it? Without a word, David handed her his arm. It was Raven's turn to feel timid and slightly thrown off. She was used to some resistance.

*What is going on here? This is strange.*

She recalled the fear and trepidation from her previous victims. The questions. The resistance. This time, nothing. She guessed she should be grateful.

*I guess there is a first for everything. Momma did say men were strange creatures. He didn't even flinch when I mentioned sex games.*

Raven shook off her doubt and worry and took David's arm. She tied it to the bedpost, cinching it tightly. He didn't wince at all, nor did he object to the other one being bound. She was in awe of his trust in her.

*It's not trust. It is lust,* Momma's voice echoed in her head. Raven nodded. She suddenly understood. Momma always made things clearer for her.

*Thank you, Momma.*

He looked up at her and waited patiently, his excitement still showing through his boxers.

*Goddamn, men,* Raven thought. *They are all the same. Pigs.* Raven had to resist the urge to spit on David at that moment. Thankfully he didn't open his mouth and call her "baby".

*I can't believe I was so weak for that moment, thinking and feeling nice things about this piece of shit. How could I be so weak, Momma?* Raven felt sick to her stomach.

She turned and went back to her bag for the black candle. She needed to put some wax on his chest before she sacrificed him. Raven pulled out the black candle and the book of matches. She turned to face David. He looked at her holding the matches and raised his eyebrows again.

"Well now, what have you got there, Miss Aeval?"

"A little pain for your pleasure?"

He chuckled.

"Oh, is that what you call it?"

"Yeah." she giggled. "That's what I call it. Are you game or are you chicken?" she challenged.

"Hell, no. Bring it on." he rooted.

Raven walked over to the bed and held the candle in the crook of her arm while she lit the match. The smell of smoke and sulfur filled her nostrils. She breathed it in— savoring the smell. She lit the blackened wick of the candle and watched it throw off a few small sparks. Raven blew out the match and cast it to the side on the end table, reminding herself to pick it up later before she left. She let the candle burn, watching the flame— mesmerized by its beauty as the wax melted from the heat. David watched, too. For the first time Raven could sense a little apprehension coming off of him now. She, however, was starting to feel good. A warmth was starting to fill her.

*Shit, the Molly. Damn it. I need to hurry.*

Raven looked at David. His eyes widened slightly, but he nodded, and she moved the candle above his chest. She turned it horizontally so that the wax could fall from its tip. Raven made three inverted crosses on David's chest, one on each nipple and one above his belly button. He winced each time she introduced a new stream of hot wax to his bare skin, but he didn't tell her to stop. His fair skin flushed around the cooling wax, and she watched as the ruddiness spread.

"Shit, that's hot!" he finally gasped.

"Yeah, *baby!*" Raven giggled madly. "So hot isn't it, *BABY?!*" She mocked him now. The word "baby" had pushed her over the edge. The Molly should have had her feeling good, but she felt erratic and out of control. She felt furious and vengeful. David's eyes widened with recognition. He could sense her change.

"Aeval?"

"Don't speak, David. It's better that way." she warned.

"Aeval, what's the matter?"

"Nothing is the matter, David, BABY!"

She could hear herself losing it, and she didn't care. She knew she had been losing it for quite some time now. It didn't matter. It hadn't mattered since the day she lost her Momma. She was lost that very second her Momma took her last breath. Her heart ached so much. Nothing could ever or would ever fill that void. It was a black hole. A deep abyss that she continued to fall into, deeper and deeper, no sides on which to grab to stop her fall.

"Aeval, what is it? What are you doing?"

"I'm going to kill you, David, BABY!" she screamed.

# CHAPTER TEN

MANNY WAS POSITIONED OUTSIDE The Lark with Alpha team in the surveillance van. The van was stifling hot, even with the air conditioning circulating air through it. The mass of electrical equipment in the back let off a lot of heat, and the economy van's air conditioner was working hard to keep everything cool. Manny shifted in his seat. He was uncomfortable in the tiny metal chair he had been sitting in for the last three hours, but it was a small price to pay at this point. They had been stuck in this tiny tin can for the last five days waiting for the unsub to show at The Lark, and he was so grateful when they heard her voice over the wire a little over two hours ago.

They listened with quiet intent as Baker and the unsub, who called herself "Aeval", went through the motions at the Riverdale Inn. Manny's Bravo team was positioned on the North and South borders of the Inn waiting for orders to move in, as they were instructed. So far, Baker sounded like he had things under control, except for the kiss. It didn't sound like he was expecting that. Manny had chuckled at that. They also hadn't thought over the whole "Molly" thing, but Manny wasn't concerned about that either. He knew Baker was good.

Manny was grateful this wasn't Baker's first undercover mission. He had been on the Homicide Unit for over ten years and had gone on over a dozen undercover assignments. Before that he had served three tours overseas in the Marines in a Special Ops unit. Baker  was a seasoned field agent. Manny had the utmost confidence in him. However, no expense was spared in keeping a close eye and ear on his safety.

"Hey, Ortiz, can you pass me my coffee cup?" Deshawn asked.

Manny shook his head and scoffed quietly. Ortiz had run out for coffee an hour ago. Deshawn was just now thinking of his coffee. Manny had his done and gone over forty-five minutes ago.

"Man, why do you even bother with coffee?" Manny questioned Deshawn.

"Huh?" Deshawn looked puzzled.

"Dude, I killed mine over forty-five minutes ago." Manny lectured. "You are only now remembering you even had one."

"No, now that is not even true." Deshawn retorted.

"Oh great, I cannot wait to hear this one." Manny joked, looking at Ortiz and Spelling. Ortiz sat upfront in the drivers' seat to watch out front or in case the van needed to make a quick chase, Spelling sat next to Manny working all the communications equipment, and Deshawn sat behind Manny, watching the back. Spelling looked at Manny and nodded but did not smile or laugh. He was of the serious sort. A somewhat nerdy, I.T. techy guy who didn't much like being included in the banter, but participated because Manny was his superior. Ortiz, however, giggled like a schoolgirl who saw Deshawn get pantsed in the hallway after school.

"Okay, Mama Jama, tell me why." Manny smiled.

"I like to wait and let it sit and get more flavor, kind of like when you leave soup overnight and eat it the next day. The flavor is better. Right? Am I right?" He looked back and forth between Manny and Ortiz. He didn't bother looking at Spelling. Spelling was busy punching keys on the laptop and turning dials on the dashboard of some communications device. Plus, it didn't matter, he had put his headphones back on.

Manny and Ortiz looked at each other, then at Deshawn, then back at each other. They both tried, in vain, to keep a straight face. Manny's lips trembled as laughter tried to explode from them. Ortiz's cheeks puffed out as he tried to hold his giggles in. As if a laughter balloon had been popped, Manny and Ortiz both burst at the same time, erupting in laughter. They laughed until tears fell from their eyes. Deshawn joined in. Manny loved that about his partner. He could laugh about anything, even himself.

"Man, Baker would have had a great night if this chic wasn't batshit crazy." Ortiz remarked.

"Yeah, ain't that the truth." Deshawn agreed.

"Man, did you hear her voice? All southern and sexy— a perfect ten." Ortiz raised his hands and outlined an hourglass shape in the air with them.

"How would you know?" Deshawn jested. "You didn't even see her."

They all laughed. At least, everyone but Spelling.

"No, man, I'm not kidding. You know she is. That accent shit is sexy." Ortiz tried to mimic the New Orleans drawl, but his already moderately thick Latino accent prohibited him from fulfilling the tall order.

They all burst out laughing again. Manny thought they all might be getting a little oxygen deprived. They were beginning to act punch drunk. He was starting to think he knew what canned tuna must feel like being stuffed inside of this metal van for so long. His body was stiff from lack of movement. The van quieted down again. He imagined a large hand from above swooping in and peeling the roof off the van, setting them free to scuttle about. The image elicited a farcical laugh from his lips. Everyone turned to look at him. "Oh, um, nothing." he shrugged.

They all turned, one by one, back to their separate jobs. It was a good thing they did because that's when they heard her. Manny stood, whacking his head on the roof of the van, barely noticing the sharp pain that seared through his skull. "Go! Go! Move in!" Manny yelled.

# CHAPTER ELEVEN

RAVEN BLEW OUT THE CANDLE and placed it on the table. She reached into her bag with care and retrieved her hunting knife. She took it out and held it for a moment, rubbing the soft leather sheath. She put it to her nose and smelled it. It smelled almost as good as the day "Auntie" Lalla had given it to her. The leather sheath and the leather gris gris bags had been made by the beautiful Taureg woman who had come to New Orleans from Mali, North Africa, to go to school. Lalla's great aunt lived in the French Quarter for twenty years prior to Lalla coming, so it was planned for Lalla to move there and go to college. Lalla and Momma met each other just a few weeks after Momma made it to New Orleans, alone and pregnant. Lalla and her great aunt took Momma in until Momma got on her feet and made enough money to get a place for herself and Raven. During that time, Momma and Lalla grew very close. So close that Raven grew up knowing Lalla as her "Auntie" Lalla. Lalla and Momma learned some small Hoodoo spells together and worked them for the locals. They made a small name and business for themselves within the community.

Raven could see Lalla's beautiful almond shaped eyes, dark ebony, staring at her as if she were standing right in front of her. Raven remembered watching Lalla preform her Salat, her Muslim prayers, five times a day— at dawn before the sunrise, the early afternoon prayer, a late afternoon prayer, sunset prayer, and the night prayer. Lalla had taught Raven how to pray, but Raven didn't have the heart to tell Lalla that she didn't believe in Allah. She didn't believe in Momma's God either. Raven didn't believe in anything really. She believed people were born, they lived, then they died. She believed in souls and that people's souls could pass on or stay around, lingering or haunting. She also believed souls could be brought back.

"Aeval. Aeval." David called out to her.

She turned to him, even angrier now that he pulled her from her happy memories. She didn't get many of those soothing thoughts or flashbacks anymore and he had just stolen it from her.

*How dare you, you bastard.*

Raven glared at him. She walked slowly over to him with the knife. As she unsheathed it, the blade glinted in the slight glow from the side table lamp. She turned it from side to side, mesmerized by the sparkle the metal cast off its sharp edge. As she approached David his eyes grew wider and wider. His forehead glistened with sweat.

"Ah, what's the matter, *BABY?*" Raven asked him, drawing out the word baby, not pretending anymore to like the word, or him for that matter.

"You know, David, I liked you until you used that word. *BABY!* God, I hate that word, David." Raven continued. She held the hunting knife over Baker's body as she spoke, feeling a growing rage inside of herself. She needed to try and calm down so that she could collect his blood. The way she felt she could easily lose control and do what she did to the other two before she even had a chance to slice his throat and grab any tubes of blood. She stood for a moment willing herself to take a few deep breaths.

Just then a loud boom from behind yanked the breath from her body. She jumped at the noise, then instinctually lowered her body down before turning to see what it was.

"Police! Police! Get down on the ground. Drop your weapon."

"Get down on the ground. Drop your weapon."

"Police! Police! Get down. Get down."

"Drop your weapon now! Drop your weapon!"

Raven was surrounded by wailing demons. Chaos filled her ears, her head, the hotel room. She was inundated by screaming voices barking orders at her. Raven was confused. Her mind was spinning. The room was spinning.

*What is happening? Momma make it stop. Please help me, Momma.*

Suddenly hands were on her. Rough hands were on her. Pulling her. Pushing her.

*Oh God, no. Please no. Not like Momma. Please no.*

Raven's face banged the floor, scraping the carpet. Her cheek burned instantly.

"NO!!" she screamed.

Raven kicked and flailed about, trying to get the demons off of her.

*Why are they doing this to me?*

Raven's mind worked hard to make sense of what was happening, but the harder she tried, the more befuddled she felt. The demons were speaking to her. She could hear their voices, muddled, trying to communicate with her. She could not make out what they were saying.

Then something cold and hard grabbed her wrists and held them tight. *Ouch!*

Somewhere in her mind she recognized what they were, but she could not pull words from her brain to name them. It was as if she were standing in a field full of a very heavy fog, so heavy that it made it difficult to see or hear anything. The fog somehow distorted her memory, her recall. Raven was trapped here in this warped time and space, and she desperately wanted out.

Then, out of nowhere she was weightless.

*What is happening? Am I flying? Am I dead?*

It was as if gravity had been taken from her. She could feel the demon claws on her, but she was not moving of her own accord. Suddenly, her vision cleared, and she was met with flashing lights and fast-moving bodies. Red and blue revolving lights that sat atop squad cars flashed, without sound, and burned her eyes. Uniformed police officers scuttled about here and there doing whatever it was that was bid of them.

Hot, humid air slapped her like a thick, slightly moist sponge in the face. Raven realized she was being carried out of the hotel room, most likely to a squad car or paddy wagon. She took a few deep breaths, steadying herself, and counted to five. After a moment, the door to a squad car opened and she was placed, face down, in the back seat. The seat reeked of astringent and stale vomit. Raven grunted and used her energy to twist and turn until she got herself to where her back was against the seat and her face was up towards the roof of the car.

*How did they know it was me? How had they caught on?*

It didn't matter anymore. Here she was, handcuffed and

locked in a police car waiting to be taken to God knows where for God knows what. But that wasn't even the worst part of all of it. The worst part was now she would never see Momma again. Raven closed her eyes and started to cry.

# RIVERS
# BEND

# CHAPTER ONE

JACK RIVERS SAT IN HIS RECLINER by the fireplace staring at the empty black cavity that some time ago, during the winter months and happy years, used to hold a warm, raging fire. Now, a cold, soot rimmed mouth stood, begging to be fed again. He rocked gently back and forth, more out of boredom and frustration, than for comfort. He was feenin'. He had run out of beer yesterday, and Raven hadn't come home. He considered going to the packy himself to grab some bourbon and beer, but his legs were bothering him, and his head ached from a fall he took a few days ago. He hadn't showered in a few days and the blood was still caked on his scalp, matting down his thick black hair that had grown too long months ago. The hair on his face was also overgrown and unkempt to the point that he had almost forgotten what his face looked like, nor did he care any longer. As of late, more often than not, he sat in his chair and wished to die there.

A loud banging jarred him from his pity party. Jack was startled. He and Raven never received visitors here, not even the obligatory Girl Scouts selling cookies or the occasional

Jehovah's Witness. He wasn't sure if it had to do with the long driveway or the dilapidated state of the house, but either way it worked for him. He had become quite the recluse over the years.

More banging ensued.

"Alright, alright." he tried to yell. Only a hoarse remnant of what was once his voice came from his lips.

*Goddamn it my mouth is dry.*

He felt as if someone had stuffed half a sleeve of Saltine crackers into his mouth and insisted that he force them down without water. He cleared his throat, swallowed what little bit of viscous saliva he had, and tried again.

"Alright, I'm coming."

This time he at least recognized his voice. He stood on shaky, painful legs and waited a moment for them to bear his weight, which wasn't much these days. He had experienced a great deal of muscle atrophy and wasting in the last four months. He knew he was dying, and he didn't care. He welcomed it. He turned and shuffled towards the front door where the banging continued. Had he fixed the doorbell last year, he was sure that would be ringing incessantly as well. He was glad he hadn't. As he drew closer to the door, he could hear someone yelling through the heavy wood.

"Newbury Police, open up!"

*What? The cops?*

"Mr. Jack Rivers, this is the Newbury Police Department, please open the door or we will be forced to open it for you. We have a warrant."

"Okay, okay. Keep your dick in your pants!" Jack yelled, his raspy voice cracking.

He reached for the deadbolt and released it, turning the handle. The large wooden door, the original to the home, creaked when he opened it. Jack laid eyes upon a swarm of uniformed officers, weapons drawn, like scorpions waiting to sting. They all stared at him accusingly. He instinctively put his hands up in the air, momentarily forgetting his lack of balance. He wobbled a bit before he stabilized himself.

"Jack Rivers?" the lead scorpion asked.

"Yeah."

"I am Detective Sullivan. We are here to search the property and to ask you to come with us down to the station to answer some questions." the head scorpion said.

Jack looked at him. He watched his mouth move but he wasn't quite comprehending what he was saying. Jack wondered if it was because he himself didn't speak scorpion language. He wasn't sure. Jack squinted his eyes and stared harder at the scorpion leader trying to concentrate on his arachnid face. His black armored shell and black weapon did not intimidate or scare Jack. It intrigued him. It even impressed him. Jack slowly let his arms fall down as they were tired. Some of the smaller scorpions looked nervous and raised their weapons, tightening them closer to their muscular, arachnid bodies. Jack paid them little attention. He focused on their leader.

"I, I am sorry. Could you please explain?" Jack requested softly.

The leader's jaw twitched. He took a deep breath in and blew it out quickly like he was getting ready to dive off a fifty-foot diving board. He put the safety on his weapon and let it down easy, securing it in his belt's side holster next to his badge. He looked at Jack for a moment as if trying to decide how to approach him. After a time, (Jack felt like it was long enough to have gulped a beer), the scorpion leader spoke slowly and to Jack's surprise, he understood him this time.

"My name is Detective Sullivan. I am here from the Newbury Police Department. These are my men. We are here with a search warrant ordered by Judge Burton about one hour ago. It allows us to rummage, at our will and discretion, through your home. We will also be detaining you at the station for questioning in regard to two murders." Detective Sullivan Scorpion Leader finished.

Jack stood staring at Detective Sullivan, his mouth agape.

*Did he say two murders? What the fuck is going on here?*

Jack managed to close his mouth but not before asking Detective Sullivan what, exactly, he was referring to.

"What the fuck are you talking about, two murders?"

"Mr. Rivers, you're wanted for questioning pertaining to information in regard to two recent murders. That is all I am allowed to discuss with you at this time. My orders are to bring you into the station for questioning." Detective Sullivan replied.

"Am I under arrest?" Jack asked.

"As of right now, no." Detective Sullivan answered.

"Okay, then I guess I will go with you. Tell your goonies they can do their worst. This place is already fucked up." Jack laughed. He was starting to feel the withdrawal shakes coming on.

*Fuck, I shoulda walked. Maybe I woulda missed these punkasses.*

Detective Sullivan looked at him with minute interest, as if he were a tiny ant invading his scorpion domain, more of a nuisance than anything. He motioned towards the walkway. Jack thought for a moment if he needed anything then chuckled out loud.

*A beer and a pack of butts would be nice. I'm sure they don't have those at the station.*

"Please." Jack held up a hand. "Wait a second."

This incited more raising of the scorpion stinger weapons. "Hey, hey," Jack held up his empty hands in defense. "I wanna grab my sweater. I'm cold."

The lead scorpion raised his black gloved hand and motioned his cronies to lower their weapons. They did as they were bid. Jack turned and shuffled into the entryway to grab a light sweater even though the temperature outside was already reaching an uncomfortable eighty-two degrees. He could see the goons were slick with a film of sweat on whatever skin was exposed underneath their armor and clothing.

*Man, what the fuck did they think I had going on here? An arsenal?*

He wrapped the tattered old sweater around his once broad, now bony, shoulders. In his years prior to drug use and severe alcoholism, Jack stood six feet and weighed two hundred pounds of thick, hard muscle. A product of the weight room and good genetics. Now, he was lucky if he weighed a buck twenty, his muscles withered away from autophagy and his spine collapsing on itself. He looked nearly thirty years older than he was. The once sought-after man was a mere ghost of who he once had been, inside and out, and he didn't care in the least. When Mercy died, he died. It was as simple as that. He would have given anything to have taken her place. His only saving grace was the day Raven walked through the front door. She had been the only thing to save him from dying long ago.

"Mr. Rivers. Hello. Mr. Rivers."

Jack looked at Detective Sullivan as if it was the first time he was seeing him.

"Yes?"

"Mr. Rivers, are you ready?" Detective Sullivan asked.

"Oh, um, yeah. Sorry." Jack stuttered apologetically.

Detective Sullivan moved back a step and waved a hand towards the stone walkway as if he were Moses parting the Red Sea. It worked. His goons split ranks and opened a path for the two to walk majestically down the path to the unmarked car that awaited them. Sullivan stayed close on Jack's heels.

*In case I run, I suppose.*

Jack found that amusing considering he could barely walk. His legs were heavy with pain and edema. He was pretty sure his liver was barely functioning at this point. He didn't know for sure as he hadn't seen a doctor since the last time he wound up in the emergency room from an overdose of heroin over five years ago. Raven had locked him in his room and detoxed him when he came home. Torture and compassion in one fell swoop. Jack loved that girl more than life itself.

Jack reached the rear of the unmarked sedan and stopped, waiting. Detective Sullivan came up beside him and opened the rear driver's side door. Jack looked at him and nodded his silent understanding. With a quiet groan he lowered himself into the car, nearly falling into the seat as he neared it. Detective Sullivan reached in to help him, but Jack shooed him away.

"No, no. Stop it." Jack barked hoarsely.

Detective Sullivan pulled his hands away as if Jack had bitten him. Jack chuckled.

"Ha! What's the matter, I got cooties or somethin'?" Jack razzed.

"No, I'm thinking more like rabies." Detective Sullivan jibed back.

Jack tossed his head back and let out a cackle that rivalled that of a movie witch, raspy and high pitched, breaking just at the right moment. The only difference, he thought, was that he lacked the large, crooked nose, the black moles on his face and the magical wherewithal to get himself out of this predicament. As his laughter died down, he began to realize the severity of the implications for which he found himself seated in the unmarked police car. Suddenly the joking seemed out of place and awkward. Jack felt small and feeble in the back of the car with its caged barrier between the front and back seats, and its door with no handles on the insides. Detective Sullivan got into the driver's seat and the car sank slightly with his weight, mirroring Jack's sudden feeling of depression.

*Two murders? How could I possibly be implicated in connection with two murders?*

His mind wandered wildly as Detective Sullivan started the car and pulled out of the long driveway, heading to the Newbury Police Department. Then out of nowhere it dawned on him.

*Oh, Raven, honey, what have you done?*

# CHAPTER TWO



The "interview room" as they called it, was cold and everything was made of metal like a modern-day dungeon. Jack likened it more to an interrogation room than an "interview room". His mind went wild with images of previous detainees being cuffed to chairs or that hook thingy he had been staring at in the middle of the table. He pictured them being beaten bloody, or worse even, for information. Normally, those kinds of images would elicit more devious thoughts in the way of torture methods as a form of entertainment for him, but not today.

Detective Sullivan had been kind enough to offer him some coffee when he brought him in, but it did little to warm him now that he was seated on the metal chair that froze his thin buttocks. The air was kept cold in there, maybe on purpose, to keep detainees awake. He didn't know. He had never been a prisoner. He didn't think he was a prisoner now. Was he? He wasn't quite sure. He picked up the Marlboro Light cigarette he had asked for over three hours ago and placed it between his lips, dragging on it as if it were lit. No joy or pleasure came from doing so, but a sense of relief followed enough that he was able to put it away and wait until he needed it to actually light it. He wasn't sure when he would get the chance to have another.

Jack faced a mirror that covered nearly the entire length of the wall and he tried to avoid looking at himself in it, but he kept coming back to his ghostlike reflection. He was shocked at his image. He had passed a mirror or two in the last few months in his own home but didn't recall seeing himself as he saw himself at that very moment. His normally thick, straight black hair was thin, greasy, and greying. It was matted down, caked with brown blood from where he had fallen, in an unflattering style that needed washed badly. His fair skin usually browned nicely in the summer months, but it had taken on a yellowish hue that had begun to leak into the whites of his once beautiful green eyes. A thin frame had replaced a previously well-built one. It was malnourished and wasting away, leaving sagging skin where muscles once bulged. He felt no remorse for his former self. He had no desire to return to a younger version of himself. In fact, he felt nothing at all.

The door to the dungeon opened and two men walked in. Jack surveyed them quickly. There was a very tall black man who looked more like he should be playing for the Patriots than standing here in this room with him. Leading him was a slightly smaller Hispanic looking man with piercing hazel eyes and strong features. Jack had seen enough cop shows to know what was about to go down. He didn't offer any openers. He sat in silence and waited. The two men, whom he could only assume were detectives on the murder case he knew nothing about, but was dragged in here for, regarded him silently for a few moments. Jack sat patiently, tapping the butt end of his Marlboro Light on the table. After another moment, the smaller one spoke.

*He's in charge,* Jack decided.

"Mr. Rivers, my name is Detective Castillo, and this is my partner Detective Freeman. Do you know why you are here?" Jack looked at Detective Castillo and then Detective Freeman incredulously.

"Do I know why I am here, Detective Castillo? NO! I do NOT know why I am here. All I *know* is that I was sitting in my rocking chair this morning wishing I had a goddamn beer because my Raven never came home, and we are out. Then next thing I know there is a knock, no, correction, a BANG at my goddamn front door. Your cronies came banging at my front door and asked me ever so nicely to come down here and answer some questions about some murders that have happened that I have no goddamn idea about." Jack finished, his face hot and his breath short.

The two detectives looked at him with the same expressions they had when they came in, neither one showing any sign of interest in what Jack had spouted off. Jack didn't know how to take that. He looked past them into the mirror again. His pale, tawny face had taken on an inflamed, reddish tone. It would appear they had made him upset. Jack took a deep, wheezy breath in and let it out. He listened to it waver. He thought, for a split second, that quitting smoking might do him some good, but then he remembered he didn't give a shit.

"Mr. Rivers, you are here because we have arrested your niece, Raven." Detective Castillo looked at Jack expectantly. Three and a half hours ago that news would have shocked Jack. But after having a swarm of uniformed S.W.A.T. show up at his place to search his home and detain him, and then being held in a freezing room all alone for hours, he had plenty of time to think. Jack nodded at Detective Castillo. A dull throbbing was beginning to emanate from behind his left eye, putting enough pressure for him to wish he could remove his eyeball to relieve it.

*A hot poker would do right about now.*

A cynical grin parted his chapped, dehydrated lips before he could stop it.

*Damn it. Now they are going to think I am up to something.* Jack quickly erased it.

"Listen, my *niece* is an adult, and she comes and goes as she pleases. I have no idea what she is up to these days other than that she is a good girl. She takes good care of me. She gets the groceries and buys me my booze. What more could I ask for?" Jack looked at them, waiting for the rebuttal.

"Mr. Rivers, your niece is being charged with two counts of premeditated murder and one count of attempted murder on a police officer. Do you, or did you, have any knowledge of these murders or her plans to commit these murders?" Detective Freeman chimed in.

Jack looked at him. He knew what the detective had said. He heard every word, but it was hard for him to process.

*Murder? Two murders? Premeditated? What the fuck was going on here? Oh, Raven, honey, what have you done?*

Detective Castillo took a file folder and opened it. Jack hadn't noticed it before. Why hadn't he noticed it? Then Detective Castillo closed the folder and laid it on the metal table where Jack was seated. The detective pulled out the only other metal chair in the room that sat adjacent to Jack. The chair's feet scraped on the concrete floor, screaming in opposition to being moved. Jack cringed, but neither Castillo or Freeman seemed to notice Jack or the sound.

Castillo sat down across from Jack and studied him for

a while; as if bored, he picked up the folder again and opened it. He shuffled some papers around, then he picked something up, laying the folder aside. Jack could tell Castillo was holding some kind of 5x7 photos in his hand, but of what he did not know. He didn't want to know either, but he was pretty sure he was about to find out. Castillo began to methodically place each photo neatly in a row of six, then another row of six, then another—all so that they were right side up for Jack to see— until there was a total of twenty-four photos laid out neatly on the table. Only, they weren't "neat". They were messy. They were bloody and gory. They were vicious and vile. It appeared to Jack to be two different men but somehow the same. Jack's stomach pitched; the acid that had built up inside it the last few days burned its way up his esophageal tract. He swallowed it back down with a sip of equally acidic black coffee, cleared his throat, and spoke.

"You're saying my Raven did this?" he asked quietly.

"We are." Castillo declared.

Jack shook his head and sighed. His chest hurt. He knew it wasn't just the heartburn. It was the heartbreak. The pain he had been trying to run from all these years. The hurt he had been trying to drug and drink away returned.

"Mr. Rivers, is there anything, anything at all you can tell us about Raven that would give us a clue as to why she might have done this? What might have 'set her off' so to speak? Did you know about the blood samples?" Castillo questioned.

"Huh?" Jack looked up at Castillo.

*Blood samples, what is he talking about?*

"Yes, we found a mini fridge in Raven's bedroom that contained a few vacuum tubes of blood samples. We will have them tested but we are going to assume for now that they will probably match at least one of our victims because, when we arrested her, she had the equipment with her to draw more blood samples. We have not interviewed her yet. We wanted to talk to you first and see if there is anything you can give us or help us with. See if there is maybe any information that we can use to get her to talk to us and tell us her side of the story." Castillo solicited.

"Why should I tell you anything that will get Raven in trouble?" Jack looked defiant.

Castillo stared at him. Jack could see Castillo truly felt sorry for him.

"Listen, Mr. Rivers, I can tell your niece is very sick. I want, *we* want to help her. We already have enough evidence on her to convict her. What we are looking for is some information, from you, to help us understand her. I have a friend here who is going to help me talk with Raven. Her name is Dr. Alexandra Aguilar, Alex. She is a psychologist. She believes Raven suffered something very traumatic and it has caused her to respond this way." Castillo explained.

Jack took a shuddering breath in.

*Man, you have no idea. I have to tell them. I have to.*

"Your niece…"

"My daughter!" Jack interrupted.

"Excuse me?" Castillo choked.

"My daughter." Jack repeated.

"But we asked her who we should call, and she said you, her Uncle Jack." Detective Freeman almost sounded wounded.

"Yeah, I know." Jack uttered.

He lowered his head for a moment in shame but knew if Raven was going to get any help at all, he was going to have to tell them the truth. From the beginning.

"That's what she believes. The truth was too… "Jack paused

searching for the word. In his mind it was beautiful. In Mercy's mind it had been love. To their parents' it was a sin in their eyes and in the eyes of God. To the world it was considered incest, punishable by law. "Taboo." he finished. Castillo and Freeman were quiet. They both looked at him intently, waiting for the rest of the story. Jack felt like a washing machine on the wash cycle, all the colors and fabrics of emotion being twisted and tossed inside him. He and Mercy had never told anyone their secret. This was the first time he had ever told their story out loud to anyone. He didn't know if he felt relief or embarrassment. He supposed he should feel both. He was hoping to feel relief the most, but he didn't feel the whole "weight off your shoulders" feeling everyone always described. Instead, he just felt sad and more exhausted than he ever had in his entire life. Jack fingered the Marlboro Light, flipping it between his fingers like a tiny baton. He figured now was as a good time to have it as any.

"Hey, can I get a light so I can finish this story?" he asked. Detective Freeman reached in his jeans pocket and produced a lighter. He bent down and held it in his hand close to Jack's face. Jack put the cigarette butt in his mouth letting it hang there loosely and waited for the detective to ignite the lighter. When he did, Jack could feel a little warmth emanating from the small flame. He leaned into the tiny fire with his cigarette and puffed on it a few times to get the thing started, watching as a few small plumes of smoke rose from the tip. He inhaled the first drag deeply, enjoying the way the smoke burned his throat and lungs. After a time, he spoke again.

"Mercy, Raven's Momma, and I were twins. Fraternal twins. Our parents were very strict Irish Catholics. We would go to church every Sunday, to the first Mass at 7:30 a.m., right on the dot, without fail. The community saw our family as the perfect Irish Catholic family of four. Dad worked at the law firm uptown and mom stayed home. Mom came from old money, so they were more than well off. Let's just say, we never went without. Mercy and I went to St. Bernadette's half a mile down the road from the house."

Jack paused to drag on his cigarette. As he spoke again, puffs of white smoke came out of his nostrils and mouth with the first few words.

"What nobody knew was that good old dad was an abusive alcoholic, and he would beat mom for stupid shit like not having the fridge full of beer, or like if dinner wasn't hot on the table when he got home from work. His fists found me a lot when he was done with mom. You never knew what you were going to walk in to. Good old dad was famous for banging mom up for forgetting to give him his morning paper when he left for work or for burning the toast at breakfast. He was no dummy though; he would hit us everywhere but our faces. Even when he was so shitfaced that he would piss himself on the couch— he would still be clear minded enough to know not to hit our faces."

(Another pause, another drag, more smoke puffs).

"He also never laid a hand on Mercy for some reason. Dear old mom held a hell of a grudge about that one, I'll tell ya. She wouldn't make a peep to Pops, but she would beat the living shit out of Mercy for looking at her sideways. Mom needed someone to take the stink out on, you know. Plus, I'm pretty sure she actually hated Mercy."

Jack dragged on the burning cigarette and, along with the smoke, he blinked away the image of a small, bloody-nosed Mercy, sitting dazed on the kitchen floor. It was a few seconds after Mom had hit her with a closed fist for asking for more milk. Mercy wasn't more than five or six then. Jack could never bring himself to hit his mother because he had sworn to never be like his father.

*Goddamn them both.*

Jack blinked again as the cigarette smoke and the tears burned his eyes. He was grateful. It helped him blurr the memory.

"So, as you can imagine, Mercy and I started trying to stay away from that shit as much as possible either by staying outside in our treehouse or by staying up in either my room or hers." Jack paused again, only this time out of fear and chagrin. He took a deep breath in and blew it out to steady himself.

"The first time Mercy and I kissed we were probably about ten. We were two kids playing house. We didn't know any better. I was the dad; she was the mom. It was innocent, really. We didn't even know what the hell we were doing." Jack laughed, nervously.

He paused for a moment to clear his throat. The detectives continued to observe him, neither one saying anything to him or one another. Jack didn't know what he had been expecting their reaction to be anyways. Their jaws weren't hanging wide open. They weren't pointing at him and laughing like he was some kind of sideshow circus act, so he continued.

"Then it happened again. We kind of just started *playing house* a lot more as we got older. It was a great escape for us from the abusive house we lived in. Then, one thing led to another. Before you know it, we were inseparable, even more than before as twins. We fell *in love* with each other. We tried to hide it. We hid it until Mercy came up pregnant. She told our parents she had gotten pregnant by a boy at school, and they wanted her to have it and give it up for adoption. Our dad tried to beat the baby outta her when she first told him. Strict Irish Catholics and an unwed pregnancy don't mix, right? That shit was not going to look good at the church. I had to get in the middle of it. That's the first he ever hit her, and I ever hit my father back. I socked him right in the jaw and knocked him down. He was a big, surly guy, but he went down and stayed down for a time. I think more because he was shocked than anything. But the next day he nearly beat me to death. He put me in the hospital with a severe concussion, four broken ribs and a bruised spleen."

Jack looked at the burning cigarette in his hand. The smoke rose into the air, twisting into the shape of a DNA helix cloud until it dissipated into nothingness.

*Kind of like us humans. Ashes to ashes, dust to dust.*

He placed it to his lips and took another long, deep drag. He inhaled and held the chemical heat as long as he could in his aging lungs. He blew out a plume of smoke into the air, wishing he could send with it all his demons.

"Go on, Mr. Rivers." Detective Castillo requested gently.

*His eyes are kind,* Jack measured up Detective Castillo.

"So, I'm sure you can guess, Mercy was upset. She wasn't giving up our baby. So, the night I got out of the hospital, she came into my room so we could talk about what we were going to do about it. We were sixteen at the time and both of us were shell shocked but knew we had to do something. Well, being in my room late at night had never been an issue before because our father was an alcoholic, remember, and drank himself into a sleeping stupor every night by seven thirty p.m. Our mother took sleeping pills, among other things, every night to fall asleep and take away the pain from the bruises he liked to leave on her. That is how we got away with what we did for so long. Well, I don't know if it was because of Mercy's news or the stress of everything, or what. But for some reason our mother was not sleeping, and she was apparently spying on us instead. So, she heard us talking about what we were going to do about *our baby* and *our relationship*. Well, that woman burst into my room like a banshee from the burning depths of hell, screaming and swinging her arms at Mercy. She slapped Mercy right across the face before I could stop her. It was a shit show."

Jack stopped to take another drag. His mouth was dry. He felt like he had a handful of cotton balls stuck in each cheek. He picked up the paper cup and swished the little bit of black coffee around.

*Yup, a little left. Just enough to wet the hole.*

He took a swig, not caring that it had turned into iced coffee by then. After the inside of his mouth didn't feel as dry, he looked at his cigarette. It was done.

*How sad.*

He pulled the lid off the cup and threw the smoking stub into the tiny bit of cold, black liquid that remained in the bottom of the cup. He watched, entranced, as the liquid ran it over, dampening out the lit stub. Jack enjoyed the hissing sound it made as it died. He licked his chapped lips absentmindedly.

"Mr. Rivers?" Detective Freeman nudged.

Jack looked up at Detective Freeman with cloudy eyes, confused for a second.

*Oh yes, where was I?*

"Sorry. So, I detained my mother, not so nicely. Mercy packed her shit, stole some money from Pops and hit the road. She didn't even tell me where she was going. All I know is that she was determined to keep that baby."

"Mr. Rivers, what happened to Mercy?" Detective Freeman asked, his eyes glued upon Jack.

"Mercy wound up down in New Orleans. She started sending letters to a high school friend of ours who would give them to me. That's how we kept in touch. She met a woman named Lalla, and they did some hoodoo shit. Little stuff. But Mercy, she grew up having things. Ya know? So, we always had things. Good ol' dad would make sure Ma would buy herself, and us, shit after he beat on her, you know. I guess you'd call it retail therapy. Well, anyways, Mercy… she started selling her body. I begged her not to, but she insisted she was being safe about it. It pissed me off and hurt me. Most of all it scared me, especially because I knew Raven was there. I knew that Mercy would never let anything happen to Raven, but there was always that fear in the back of my mind. That 'what if?' kind of thought. That went on for years. Raven grew and so did Mercy's clientele." Jack snorted in disgust.

He was so tired. He was upset. Angry that he was sitting in that frigid room, in that cold chair, reliving bitter memories.

"Mr. Rivers, do you need a break?" Detective Castillo asked.

*There are those kind eyes again. He truly seems like he cares. So, few do anymore.*

Jack sighed. His whole body ached, but mostly his heart. He wanted to sleep. A lot.

*Preferably go to sleep and not wake up,* he thought.

"No, I want to get this over with so you can help my Raven." he sighed again.

This was all too much.

"One day, when Raven was home, apparently one of Mercy's clients got extra rough with her. Um, like murderously rough. Raven was out back on the tire swing and heard the commotion. She ran in to find the man pounding on Mercy's face. So, she grabbed a kitchen knife and started stabbing him." Jack finished.

Detective Castillo and Detective Freeman looked at each other and nodded to one another. If Jack hadn't been paying close attention it would have gone unnoticed.

"So, Raven killed the man. Mercy died from blunt force trauma to her head. He must have hit her in the temple just right, they said. The report said she was covered with bruises, sustained multiple broken bones, and she had internal bleeding." Jack paused, the tears wetting his face. He reached up and swiped them away with his sleeve. "Raven held her while she died. She bled in her brain, they said."

The two detectives sat, silent and polite, and waited for Jack to continue when he was able. Jack sucked in a deep, quivering breath.

"After that Raven came to live with me. She went to school, then to college, and now she works in the hospital as a phlebotomist." Jack pushed out the rest of the story as fast as his tongue would allow, wanting to be rid of it forever.

"Yes, phlebotomy." Castillo perked up a bit. "Can you tell us why you think Raven is collecting blood samples?" he asked.

Jack stopped thinking whatever he had been thinking. What had he been thinking? At that moment he couldn't even remember. He had to replay what Detective Castillo said in his mind twice before he could answer him.

*That's a great question buddy, you got me.*

"Listen, I know a lot about Raven Rivers, Detective Castillo, but that is one you're gonna have to ask her yourself."

# CHAPTER THREE

ALEX STOOD BEHIND THE TWO-WAY MIRROR observing
Jack Rivers. He was the poster child for alcoholism at its
finest. She wished desperately that she could help him. His
skin was sallow and hung off his bones, like a white sheet
stained yellow from sweat, left dangling on a rope line in
the sun to dry. He looked like he hadn't showered in days,
probably more. His hair was an oil slick of disheveled tresses
and his clothes were just as tousled. Alex watched his hand
tremble when he brought his cigarette to his mouth; his thin
lips were chapped and ashen. She believed Jack Rivers might
be reaching the end of his life or was at least trying to get to
the finish line as fast as he could crawl there.

She could hear the interview thanks to the small speakers
that were attached to the hidden cameras in the interview
room. Jack's raspy voice wove a tale of remorse, regret,
embarrassment and love lost. She couldn't imagine growing
up in chaos, restriction and abuse like Jack and Mercy—
abused by their alcoholic father and unprotected by their
codependent mother. She could understand how they wound
up turning to one another, no matter how twisted it may

have seemed that it became sexual. They sought solace in one another. They were seeking safety, refuge and acceptance. But most of all they desired love— the most basic need for the most basic emotion, required by every human being for survival.

Alex thought back to a study in school that had been conducted on twenty infants to determine if humans could thrive only on basic physiological needs without affection. The babies were kept in a sterile housing facility and had caregivers. But the caregivers were instructed to only do the basic things needed to care for the babies such as change their diapers, feed them, bathe them, and change their clothing. They were strictly prohibited from touching the babies any longer than what was necessary to complete the tasks given, and they were explicitly forbidden to talk to, or make eye contact with, the babies. After four months of the ongoing experiment, it had to be halted as half of the twenty babies had perished, not from infection or illness, but from failure to thrive. It was determined that, even though their basic physiological needs were being met, the lack of attention— touch, talk, love— caused them to just "give up" and die. It had taken her a long time to write her paper on that study, as she struggled with the thought that someone could even subject those tiny creatures to such torture. The only saving grace for her was the thought that at least they were tiny creatures that she prayed had very little concept of what was happening. What happened when a child was older and understood what it was to need love? What would that do to a child? She had seen the different outcomes of the effects it has on someone when they are given the "wrong kind of love" as a child in her practice as a clinician, and even more so since helping Manny and Deshawn with their cases.

She thought of the Rivers' household as Jack had described it. The kids, Mercy and Jack, growing up in the dark halls of that large Victorian with its abusive hands, blind eyes and deaf ears— all of those secret rooms and yet nowhere to hide. She felt small and afraid *for* them, but most of all her heart ached, especially for Mercy. Sixteen, on the run, pregnant with your twin brother's baby; cast out of your own life. How does one survive that?

*Mercy did. At least for a while,* Alex thought.

She could hear Manny and Deshawn wrapping it up with Jack Rivers. They were thanking him for his help but also letting him know he had to stick around in case there were any new developments. He nodded and told them he understood. Jack asked them to keep the news of Raven's paternity to themselves. They promised that, at least for now, they would keep it confidential, unless something came up warranting the need to divulge the information. Jack seemed satisfied with that arrangement. They allowed him to go under the pretense that he would remain housebound, or at least not leave town, until the case was finished.

Alex watched as Jack rose from the metal chair, his stick legs barely supporting him. He held the back of the chair and the top of the table for support, his skeleton arms trembling from the exertion. She shook her head, sad that at the young age of thirty-eight this man looked like he was in his mid to late sixties, aged by years of drugs, alcohol and the haunting nightmares of the skeletons in his closets. She could understand it. Jack had been raised with an iron fist dictated by alcohol and a codependent mother who laid down and took it. He had fallen in love with his twin— a forbidden love ripped from his grasp— then suffered the loss of that love again when she was brutally murdered.

The trio exited the interview room, leaving an empty chair—Jack's momentary throne of truth— for Alex to fill with her own visions of abuse and pain.

The door to the observation room opened behind her, jolting Alex from her cloud of illusion. She turned to see Manny there, bewildered and angry. He nodded to the female officer, Guzmán, who had accompanied Alex inside the observation room during Jack's interview. Even though Alex was considered an integral part of the team, she was still not allowed to be alone in certain police procedures, including interviews. Officer Guzmán returned Manny's nod, then smiled politely at Alex before she quietly took her leave. Alex knew, before Manny even spoke, that he was angry at what had happened to Jack and Mercy. She knew Manny struggled with believing that all people were inherently good and that this would just be another blow to his already sinking ship of faith in humanity. She saw him trying to hide his growing anger and resentment towards the job that had once been his calling. She knew he was struggling, like she was, to make sense of a job that once seemed to be the only thing that mattered.

Alex went to him and wrapped her arms around him holding him tightly. Manny embraced her as if she were a buoy and he was caught in an undertow, fighting for his life. She kissed the curve of his jaw right below his ear, feeling the tension leave it as her lips touched his skin. He sighed heavily. She wished she could take away his stress and anxiety.

"Dime, mi amor, tell me what has got you wound up so tightly?" she breathed against his ear.

Alex pulled away from Manny enough so that she could look into his eyes. His dark hazel eyes brewed torment. She gently turned his head so that they would be face to face. They had known each other long enough now that at times they could look at one another and communicate without words. Alex locked eyes with Manny. She held his gaze with hers and willed him to feel her. As they stood together—eyes fastened on one another, bodies touching— she could feel his body softening. The stormy clouds in his eyes threatened tears. "No, mi amor, no llores. Please, don't cry." Alex's heart ached to see him this way.

She pulled him to her, like a protective mother holds her child. What hurt the most was that she knew he was not sad. No, he was affronted. She knew Jack's story was lighter fluid for the raging bonfire that was Manny's belief system: that most of humanity was, if left to its own devices, inherently evil. Alex had tried for many years to dissuade him.

"What about us? You and I?" she had challenged him many times.

He had refuted her argument saying they were a product of their environment. They had been "raised right" by "good people".

"But, if given the opportunity, most people would do bad if they knew they could get away with it. Even murder." he had insisted.

Alex recalled his words as they held one another. Sometimes she wondered if he was right. After the murders they had investigated over the years. After what she had gone through. After hearing Jack's story and seeing what Raven had become because of what she had been "subjected to". Maybe Manny was right. Maybe every human was born with the capacity to become something evil; an evil seed inside each and every one of them. Maybe their environment was the garden for that seed— to either die off and fade away or be fed and watered in— with the potential to grow into something very dark and monstrous.

"Manny, please. Let it go."

He looked at her, the hazel storm now a tsunami.

"I don't know if I can do this anymore."

Alex looked at his jaw muscles as they danced under his taut skin, spasming from clenching and unclenching his teeth together. It wasn't often that Manny got upset. He was usually an even keeled man. But when he did, he became someone she hardly recognized. His body was taut against hers.

"I understand." she said. "I felt the same way the other day at the office." she admitted.

Manny looked at her, surprised.

"You?"

"Yes, me." she confessed.

He shook his head, confused.

"I don't believe you." He argued.

*Oh, my love, so stubborn.*

"Yes, Manny. I am not the same. Not since…" Alex paused to catch her breath and, even more so, to gather her nerve to push the words out. "since it all happened. I know you are not either. It changed us both." Alex whispered.

It was harder than she thought to speak the words. She nearly aspirated them, but she needed to say them, not just for him but for herself. Her heart was pounding in her chest as if she had sprinted to catch up with him. Manny's crinkled brow slowly disappeared; the smooth, chestnut skin returning to normal. He touched her face with a tender hand.

"You are so beautiful. Do you know that?"

Alex smiled.

"I want to protect you, always." he whispered.

"I know."

Manny gently took her face with both of his hands and pulled her forehead to his lips. He kissed her forehead tenderly, letting his lips linger for a second longer than usual. Alex's entire body ignited with excitement. She felt a moment of shame as it wasn't the right time for her to be feeling those desires. She couldn't help herself. He did that to her. Manny must have felt the same because an almost inaudible moan brushed her ears. Alex pretended not to hear it.

"I suppose the next step is to go interview Raven?" she knew the answer before she uttered the question.

"Yes, mi amor. But I have an idea."

"Yes? What is it?"

"How would you like to interview her with me?"

Alex felt her mouth fall open but couldn't catch it and she didn't care.

*What?*

"What? Manny that is against protocol." she argued.

"It is for you to interview her *alone*. You can interview her if I am there with you aiding in the interview. Listen, we feel a female interviewer can reach her best. We also feel that, as a psychologist, you have an advantage over us. For us it makes sense. Does it make sense to you?"

"Yes, of course." Alex beamed.

Manny looked at her and laughed.

"What?" she insisted.

"You."

"What about me?"

*Why is he laughing at me?*

"You look like a cat who caught a mouse and is hiding it in her mouth. All smiles." he said, beaming.

"Oh. Well, it is rather exciting. My first precinct interview." she admitted.

"Yes, I know." Manny agreed.

"Okay, good. I am glad you understand."

"Of course, I do. I was there once too, remember." he smiled.

"Okay, well then, let's do this."

# CHAPTER FOUR

RAVEN SHIVERED IN THE COLD OF THE STEEL GREY ROOM.
She felt as if the world was closing in on her. Her mind
raced. Never in her wildest imagination did she picture being
caught. Sure, it had always been a tiny glitch in the back of
her mind that on occasion she would have to reset; but to be
sitting here awaiting her fate was a bit of a blow.

*I got too cocky,* she thought. *Or was I too complacent?*

Raven huffed and rolled her eyes, thoroughly disgusted with
herself. She tried to dig her fingernails into the tabletop, but
they bent against the unyielding metal.

*Ouch.*

She winced a little at the pain, but tried it again, nonetheless.
The same result occurred.

*Well, fuck me sideways.*

She looked around the room for at least the hundredth time.
The room was small, and even though she knew it was kept
cold, the air was stifling. Two small, black bubbles hung
from opposite corners of the ceiling, each with a single red,
flashing light. She counted a three second interval between
flashes. They were like two black bug eyes staring at her and

she wanted to smash them with her feet. The walls were painted a dull grey. Her chair was cold metal. The door keeping her locked in was metal. Everything was metal. Grey and metal.

*How cold and impersonal.*

The door opened. A beautiful woman with almond colored skin and piercing blue-green eyes walked in followed by a slightly taller man with similar colored skin and darker hazel eyes. He was not bad looking himself. She could see his muscular build under his dress shirt and his well-fitting suit pants revealed strong, thick legs.

*Yummy, I could have used some of his life force for sure,* she thought fiendishly.

Raven eyed them both carefully. She made no attempt to greet them. She was in the wolf's den with the enemy and her hackles were up. The beautiful woman smiled kindly at her, but Raven held her ground. Then the woman spoke. "Hello, Raven, my name is Dr. Alexandra Aguilar, but you can call me Alex. I am a clinical psychologist. This…" she pointed towards the handsome man "is Detective Castillo. We are here to ask you a few questions. How are you?" she smiled again, warm and inviting.

Suddenly Raven wanted to speak to her. This "Alex" somehow felt familiar to her, but Raven couldn't place it. She felt the urge to return Alex's smile, but she didn't. Not yet. Raven needed to find out what angle this woman was coming from. Whose side was she on? Raven glared at Alex. It angered Raven that she felt an instant feeling of trust towards this woman she had never met. Raven pinched her lips together tightly signaling her refusal to speak, as if her mouth had been bound by invisible tape. Alex looked at her for a moment then glanced up at Detective Castillo. He looked at

Alex and nodded. Alex turned her attention back to Raven. Raven held Alex's gaze, focusing not on Alex, but trying to see through Alex. She wished her no harm, yet she did not want to speak with Alex for fear of incriminating herself. After staring "through" her for a moment, she realized where the familiar feeling was emanating from. Alex somehow reminded her of Lalla.

*Oh, my sweet Lalla, how I miss you.*

"Raven, honey, it's okay. I am here to help you as much as I can."

"Ha!" Raven shouted.

That was enough. Raven didn't believe anyone wanted to help her. Quite the opposite actually. Everyone was out to get her. They had been out to get her and her mother since the day Momma ran from home. Raven knew it deep down in her soul.

"Nobody wants to *help* anyone, Dr. Aguilar. They only wanna hurt each other. It's the way of the world."

Raven watched as Alex's smile wavered. Something clouded over her startlingly bright eyes, dimming them momentarily. A small twinge of guilt nagged at Raven's gut, but it was fleeting.

*No one cared when Momma's smile faded. Some days she had hardly even smiled.*

Raven knew her Momma had suffered— it was always there, in her eyes. The eyes told everything about a person. It was said the eyes were the "windows to the soul", but Raven thought that was bullshit. Raven believed that the eyes were the *gateway* to the soul— the only way in and out. There were many ways to tell a lie, but Raven knew the soul was incapable of doing so.

Momma would always put on a brave smile for Raven, but

as Raven grew, she also grew to know a forced smile versus a genuine one. Alex's was genuine, and for that, Raven felt remorse, but she had to stick to her guns.

"Raven, honey, we know about your mom."

Raven felt a sudden, immense pain in her chest. She sucked in a breath and grabbed at her breast. It felt like someone had shoved their fist right through her sternum, reached in and grabbed her throbbing heart— ripping it out while it pulsed and bled, to squeeze it until it beat no more.

"Momma. Oh, sweet Momma." she whispered, grasping at her chest trying desperately to remove the vice grip that held her.

Her voice was tiny, that of a small child. Raven didn't even recognize the voice that spoke for her. Her head began to spin.

*Why? Why is Alex talking about Momma?*

"We know what that bad man did to your poor Momma, Raven." Alex continued.

*Oh God, Momma. Why? Why did that bad man hurt you, Momma?*

"We know you had to protect her."

*Yes, I did. I protected her. But I was too late. Tell her, tell Alex. I can't, I can't tell her. I can't trust anyone. They are all out to get me.*

"Raven, we know how painful that must have been for you to see your Momma like that, honey. How bad it hurt. How you only wanted to make him stop."

Raven could see it. The flashes of memory, like strobe lights with images in each ray of light, being forced into her mind. It hurt so badly. It hurt her head, her heart, her soul. She could see it all flashing behind her eyes. The tire swing and the sunny, hot day. The kitchen, Momma singing, her coloring pages. The raggedy old mutt. The bad man beating Momma, his massive body hovering over her. She could hear Momma's cries for help. Momma's blood.

*Oh, God, the blood.*

Red smeared on Momma's beautiful face. Raven's breath grew shallow. It was getting harder for her to breathe.

*Oh, Momma, your eyes. They are fat and closed shut, black and blue and purple.*

Thud-Thud-Thud.

*Make him stop, please make him stop. Make him stop, please make him stop.*

Raven grabbed at her ears. She covered them tightly and squeezed her eyes shut. Her stomach churned as much as her mind. She couldn't take it anymore. Raven stood from her metal chair. It flew back and banged the cement floor; the crash of the metal reverberated in the small room. Raven couldn't hear it over Momma's cries.

"Make it stop, please make it stop." Raven screamed, pulling at her hair.

Dr. Aguilar and Detective Castillo looked at each other with shock and confusion, but Raven could not see them. She could not see anything. All she could see was red. It was just like that day, like the day her own blood was in her eyes and the whole world was red.

*Make it stop, baby, please make it stop.*

Raven scratched at her face and her eyes. She wanted to rip her eyes and ears from her body. It was the only way to make it stop. Her nails pierced the tender skin of her eyelid and her cheeks, sending streaks of stinging pain. She could feel hands on her. Someone pulled her hands away from her, taking what little control she had left away from her.

*No, don't, please. Stop. Let me go!*

Raven let out a blood curdling scream and the world stopped.

# CHAPTER FIVE

ALEX TOOK A DEEP BREATH IN AND EXHALED before she
pushed open the door to the interview room.
*This is it. My first real interview. No pressure.*
She almost laughed hysterically from her anxiety and had
to catch herself as she walked into the room. Thankfully
Manny was with her in case anything went South. She
couldn't understand why she was so nervous. She had been
a practicing psychologist for over ten years, but for some
reason, the idea of being face to face with Raven Rivers was
daunting.
Alex smiled at the girl sitting at the table. Technically she
was a woman, but there in that steel ice box that served as
an "interview room", Raven presented more like a young
girl than a woman. Her long, straight black hair had been
tousled in the arrest, leaving it straggly and unkempt looking.
Alex imagined the coal black smudges that encircled Raven's
bloodshot eyes and made her look racoon-like, had once
been expertly painted on black eyeliner that enhanced her
green eyes perfectly. The same beautiful, blood engorged eyes
that glared back at Alex now.

*Ouch.*

Alex continued to smile at Raven. She imagined Raven felt scared and trapped. It was a tricky business dealing with a trapped animal. You never knew what direction they might take. Would they submit to you, belly up? Or would they rip your face off? Alex only knew she had to tread carefully and approach with caution.

 "Hello, Raven, my name is Dr. Alexandra Aguilar, but you can call me Alex. I am a clinical psychologist. This…" Alex paused and pointed towards Manny "is Detective Castillo. We are here to ask you a few questions. How are you?" Alex tried with a smile again. It did nothing but seem to rile Raven up. Alex watched anger flash across Raven's eyes and a stubborn determination set in. Raven's lips, once full and thick, formed a thin line barely visible as if they were on some magical drawstring and someone had cinched them shut.

*Oh, this one is going to be tough.*

Alex smiled again but smaller this time. She felt like a balloon that Raven had unknotted. She watched, helpless, as Raven let out her air right before her eyes— deflating her bit by bit, until she withered into a spineless blob.

*No, I am not flattened yet, little one.*

Alex thought she had caught a glimpse of something subtle; a slight change in Raven's demeanor. Raven's stony facade weakened a bit.

*I hope I am not imagining that.*

Alex took in a breath in an attempt to inflate herself again. "Raven, honey, it's okay. I am here to help you as much as I can."

Big mistake. Whatever Alex thought she had seen was gone in an instant. Anger broke through Raven's face. It was as if

Alex slapped her.

"Ha!" she sneered. "Nobody wants to *help* anyone, Dr. Aguilar. They only wanna hurt each other. It's the way of the world."

Raven hissed like a cornered cat. Alex felt her lips falter, retreating from the smile she had planted on her face. Raven's words echoed in her head.

*Nobody wants to help anyone. They only wanna hurt each other.* She sounded so much like Manny. How many others felt this way? How many had given up on humanity? A flashback of a time being bound, cold and scared in a dark trunk of a car clawed its way into Alex's mind. She pushed it out as quickly as it had come in.

*Yes, some wanted to hurt, but some wanted to help. I want to help.*

Alex dug in her heels and tried again.

"Raven, honey, we know about your mom."

Alex watched Raven's face change from a mask of rage to sorrow in an instant.

"Momma. Oh, sweet Momma." Raven whimpered.

The young woman that sat before her changed forms like a magical creature from tales that Abuela used to read to Alex as a child. Like a shapeshifter, Raven morphed from young woman to little girl right before Alex's eyes. As much as Alex hated to, she knew she had to use it to her advantage and push a little more.

"We know what that bad man did to your poor Momma, Raven." Alex continued.

Raven's eyes brimmed with tears. Her lower lip puffed out in a childish pout. Alex knew she was getting to her. It killed Alex to be goading her, but she knew she had to get her to talk and this was the best angle she could think of. Alex knew

Raven's trauma was her driving force. All Alex needed was Raven to tell them what she had been doing with the blood. 'We know you had to protect her."
Alex studied Raven closely. Raven's mind worked furiously. Her lips moved as if she were trying to speak, but nothing came out. A slow stream of tears wet Raven's cheeks, smearing them with black mascara. Her lips quivered and her body began to shake with silent sobs. Alex's heart ached for her. She wanted to grab her and hug her; to hold her and tell her it was going to be alright. But she could not; she had to finish this.
"Raven, we know how painful that must have been for you to see your Momma like that, honey. How bad it hurt. How you wanted to make him stop."
Raven sobbed audibly. She closed her eyes. Alex watched as Raven clenched and unclenched her fists rhythmically. Alex's heart raced.
*Oh God, poor baby. She has been through so much. Such pain.*
Alex knew Raven was reliving all of it in her mind. Alex knew because that's how it happened for her. The memories never went away. They slept in the dark recesses of the mind, waiting to be awoken. A word, a scent, a sound— anything would stir it from its slumber, and she would have to relive it— all over again. Trauma was like that. Even though it was done, it had a way of repeating itself, over and again. Nighttime was the worst; trapped in dreamland with no way to escape. At least during the day, you could remind yourself you were awake and banish the monsters from your mind.
Alex was pulled from her thoughts when Raven moved to grab at her ears. She covered them tightly and squeezed her eyes shut. Alex watched Raven's face go from pale to ashen. Raven stood from her metal chair unexpectedly. The force

caused the chair to fly back and bang against the cement floor. The crash echoed in Alex's ears but didn't even phase Raven.

"Make it stop, please make it stop." Raven cried out.

Alex could tell Raven wasn't talking about the sound of the crashing chair. Alex and Manny looked at one another. Without speaking, they communicated their concern, but neither one wanted to make a move yet, in case Raven came around and revealed something.

Alex watched in horror as Raven suddenly began to scratch at herself, her long nails marking her face with bloody warpaint. Alex cried out for Raven to stop, but Raven could not hear her because at that moment Raven emitted a scream that could have only come from the very depths of her tortured soul. It stopped Alex in her tracks.

*Dios mío, what have I done?*

# CHAPTER SIX

MANNY HELD ALEX CLOSE TO HIM. He could feel her body still shaking. He rubbed her back to soothe her, although he knew it would do little to ease her. Alex was going to blame herself for what occurred in the interview room with Raven— even though they both agreed as to the tactics they were going to use to get her to talk before even entering the room. She had been against it at first, believing Raven to be too unstable.

*Boy had she been right. Man, I hope she doesn't hold that over me.*

"Alex." he whispered.

"Manny, please. Don't. I can't."

*Okay, well, that answers that.*

Manny felt his stomach leap into his chest. He knew she blamed herself, blamed him, blamed the process. But it had to be done. No matter how you spun it, Raven was still a murderer. She had to be treated as such and that is exactly what they had done. Anger slipped into his frustrated mind, slithering through his thoughts. Why should he feel guilty for pushing a murderous scum to the brink of insanity? It was obvious she was already there, wasn't it?  He put his hands gently on Alex's arms and moved her so that he could look at her. She looked up at him, her eyes filled with sadness and frustration.

"Listen Alex, I know you are blaming yourself. Well, you can't. It was *our* idea, remember? Mostly mine. So, if you want to blame anyone, blame me." he paused waiting for a response, knowing none would follow. After the silence threatened to swallow him whole, he spoke. "Deshawn called and said they have Raven over at the hospital and she is sedated, but able to speak. I think we should bring Jack over there and see if he can get her to talk."

He watched Alex considering it. When she still didn't say anything, he decided he would.

"I have Jack's file right over here, we can give him a call."

He walked over to his desk and shuffled some papers around, trying to ignore the searing heat he felt burning on the back of his neck from Alex's scowl. He spotted the file and grabbed it. Then put it back down.

"On second thought, it might not be a good idea for them to see each other."

He turned back around to see Alex frowning.

"Hey, what's the matter?"

Alex didn't respond. She stood there; the scowl frozen on her face.

*Is she thinking or brooding?*

"Earth to Alex."

She did not smile. Then, after a moment of brooding she spoke.

"Listen, Manny." Alex warned, in a voice Manny had ever heard before. "I already screwed up once. No, correction, WE already screwed up once! This is our chance to set this straight. At the hospital with Raven, we cannot screw up again."

Manny could hear an urgency in Alex's voice. Her eyes were ablaze with determination. He knew he could not let her down. Manny grasped Alex's hands in his and held them tightly.

"Alex, honey, we will not screw this up." he promised.

He watched her eyes searching his face, as if he held the most precious answer in the world to her most perplexing question. After what seemed an eternity, he could see the resolve settle over her. Her shoulders relaxed and her hands no longer felt like frozen cinder blocks in his. He squeezed them gently to let her know he was on her side. Thankfully, she returned his squeeze.

*Okay, we are good.* Manny sighed in relief.

"Alright, let's grab a car and head over to the hospital, okay?" Manny urged.

Alex nodded. Without a word she grabbed her purse and waited as Manny retrieved his badge from the top drawer of his desk. He cupped her elbow gently with his hand and guided her down the aisle of scattered desks and police officers. They walked silently to the elevator together, each deep in their own thoughts and neither having the energy to open up the forum for discussion. It had been such a long few months; between Benson and now Raven. Manny's body and mind ached to the point he couldn't decide which hurt worse. He snuck peeks out of the corner of his eye at Alex while he stood next to her in the elevator. She looked as tired as he felt. Her face was slightly drawn and the dark circles under her eyes tattled on her for not sleeping. Manny grabbed Alex's hand and held it. She looked at him and smiled. Manny smiled back. They held hands until the elevator hit the ground floor and came to a stop.

The elevator chimed and, after a brief lag, the doors opened. Alex released Manny's hand and stepped out. Manny followed. The main hall wasn't too busy, thankfully. Manny could see Officer Davis at the front desk trying to console an older gentleman who looked somewhat distraught. Officer Davis pointed to another uniformed officer and the elderly man looked at the other officer and nodded. After a moment, the elderly gentleman patted Officer Davis on the hand then walked towards the other uniformed officer.

Manny touched Alex on the small of her back, nudging her towards the desk where Officer Davis stood, and followed behind her. Officer Davis turned to face them and smiled. Manny liked Officer Davis. He was always in a good mood. Manny had never seen him angry or cranky. Officer Davis always had a smile for everyone it seemed. Manny returned the smile.

"Hey Davis, we are going to need a car."

"You got it, Detective Castillo."

Davis walked over to the key box with a spring in his step and retrieved a pair of keys for Manny. He returned, whistling happily, and handed Manny a pair of keys.

The keys jingled, producing beautiful twinkling notes, to accompany Davis' cheerfully whistled tune. Manny couldn't help but continue to smile. Officer Davis' mood was contagious. Manny glanced at Alex to see her smiling as well. Davis grabbed the "key" logbook and neatly wrote Manny's name, badge number and the date then handed the pen and the book to Manny for his signature. Manny signed it. Davis took the pen and book back, exchanging them for the keys and another genuine smile.

"The keys to your chariot, Sir…" then looked at Alex "and

madame."

Davis bowed, holding one hand to his belly and flipping the other into the air a few times. He twisted his hand at the wrist circling it rapidly— a perfect flurry of extravagant revolutions resembling a whirling ballerina amidst a pirouette. Manny watched in admiration and curiosity. *How does one learn to twist their hand like that? I wonder if he is double jointed,* he thought.

Manny heard Alex chuckle. He glanced to see a beautiful smile gracing Alex's face for the first time in a while, and he basked in it. But, as quickly as it had come, it was gone. It faded from her face as the weight of reality sank back in. He could see the glee that had brightened her eyes suddenly replaced by something unsettlingly dark. It dampened the light that had been there only seconds ago, like a candle that had burned to the end of its wick. What remained smoldered behind her eyes.

"You ready?" he asked, softly.

Alex looked at him as if she were seeing him for the first time, her eyes focusing on him from somewhere far away. Manny could only imagine what ghosts had been hovering about in her mind when he interrupted. The guilt for jarring her was tangible, but he did not want her getting lost in whatever darkness was trying to pull her under. Alex straightened her blouse and cleared her throat. She attempted a weak smile.

"Yes, of course." she lied.

Manny nodded and made a weak attempt at mimicking Davis' theatrical move, motioning Alex towards the elevators. Alex giggled and turned, seemingly grateful for the distraction. He followed close behind, catching the faint hint of her perfume on the breeze she left from her movement.

He inhaled it, reveling in the feelings of love it stirred within him. She was the only woman that had ever been able to make his belly feel as if there were tiny fireflies fluttering around inside, struggling to find their way out.

"Manny?"

He heard Alex's voice calling.

"Hmm?" he answered.

He looked up to see her in the elevator attempting to hold the heavy, automatic doors open. Manny ran towards her and the elevator as it dinged angrily at whatever was in its way. Alex was tall and lean, strong for her weight, but the force of the heavy, metal doors was causing her to strain to keep them open.

"Jesus, Alex, sorry." he apologized as he reached her.

His movement into the area of the elevator door's sensor made them jump away from Alex, nearly knocking her off balance. Manny grabbed her by the shoulders to steady her.

"Whoa!" Alex yelped.

"Steady now."

"I wasn't even expecting that." Alex laughed. "It happened so fast. I feel like I usually have more time before the doors close like that." she tried to explain.

Manny chuckled with her to ease her embarrassment.

"I know. I don't know why this one seems to close faster than others. I swear someone upstairs rigged it that way for shits and giggles and put a hidden camera in here. They probably sit upstairs in their office and watch people struggle with it all the time just to laugh about it. Entertainment for the masses that sit on their asses." Manny laughed and pushed the button for the parking garage level.

Alex burst out laughing. Manny felt warm inside as if he had been injected with contrast dye before a CT scan— it

was sudden, warmth filled him from head to toe. He loved
when he could make her laugh that real belly laugh. It was
unbridled and beautiful like Alex herself, and he relished
every second of it. Alex's eyes shifted. Her laughter faded, and
her smile softened. Manny knew she could feel the love he
felt for her. Alex walked over to him and touched his stubbly
face. He wished he had shaved that morning so he could
feel the soft skin of her palm without the quills of his five
o'clock shadow blocking it. He grabbed her hand and held
it to his face. Manny closed his eyes and breathed her in. He
loved her smell, her touch— even her temper tantrums and
stubbornness.

Manny leaned down and kissed Alex, his lips finding hers
easily. She responded, sending chills down his spine.

*God, I wish we weren't in this damn elevator,* he thought.

His body tingled with longing. Alex's tongue found his and
sent a tidal wave of pleasure through him. He pressed his
body against hers and moaned just as the elevator belled,
announcing their arrival to the parking garage. Alex broke
the embrace and turned towards the doors leaving Manny
feeling breathless. He blinked a few times trying to wake
himself from what felt like a dream every time their lips met.
He had waited so long to get the chance to be with her, to
hold her, to kiss her. Now that he had her, it always felt as
if it was still some sort of fantasy— a fleeting moment that
could be snatched from him at any given second.

"Here." Manny pointed towards a black, unmarked sedan
that sat in the parking space painted with the number seven.

"Lucky number seven." Alex walked around to the front
passenger's side door. "Good! We are going to need some
luck."

Manny looked at her and wished he could ease the anxiety

he heard resonating in her voice. He came around quickly in front of her to unlock her door and open it for her. She smiled gratefully at him with tired eyes. Manny planted a gentle kiss on her crinkled brow before she ducked down into the car.

*If I could only take it all away.*

He closed the door and walked to the driver's side. He slid into his seat and checked on Alex to make sure she was all set before putting the keys into the ignition. She nodded at him like a novice copilot, unsure of the controls or the flight pattern, but confident in her pilot. Manny smiled and turned the keys in the ignition to start the car. It rattled a bit as it came to life.

*Damn exhaust shield,* Manny thought. *Would it kill them to do a little maintenance on these freaking things?*

Manny put the car in drive and with fire in his eyes, he turned to Alex.

"Ok, Mamacita, let's go see Miss Rivers."

# CHAPTER SEVEN

MANNY AND ALEX WALKED DOWN THE BUSY HALLWAY
of Newbury Hospital that led to the nurses' station in the
E.D. It resembled a modern-day war camp— beds littered
their path, each filled with various ailing patients. Some were
more alert than others, every single one with their own story
of woe to tell. There were patients sleeping, crying, yelling
or begging for pain medication. A few would quietly open
a curious eye or throw a glare at Manny and Alex as they
passed.

 Manny flashed his badge at the cantankerous charge nurse
that sat behind the computer at the nurses' station, stone
faced and unimpressed. She made no gesture that she even
saw Manny and Alex standing there for a few seconds, much
less his badge and its shiny metal facade. She continued to
type on her keyboard furiously, her fingers moving gracefully
like a soloist performing the rondo portion of a piano
concerto, her face rigid with concentration.

"Nurse Axelrod excuse me. I'm sorry, but North five is asking
for pain meds again." a voice came from beside Manny.

A young woman in purple scrubs and frazzled hair looked

at Nurse Axelrod with steady eyes and awaited a response. Manny looked down to see her badge hanging from her scrub top: Nurse Meagan. Nurse Meagan couldn't have been more than twenty-six, but Manny saw her experience went far beyond those few years. She exuded it. She stood tall, chin high, and confidence was her aura. Manny liked her instantly.

The clicking of the keyboard ceased, and Nurse Axelrod turned a pair of agitated eyes on Nurse Meagan, who stood not so patiently waiting. Manny could see a small, brown stain on Nurse Axelrod's white coat, just beneath her embroidered name, either from coffee or soda.

*That could say a lot about a person once you knew a few details about them,* he thought to himself. *Or it could just be a stain,* he could hear Alex chastising him in his mind.

Manny smiled, unable to help himself.

"I will send over a message to Dr. Girardi. She has already had Oxycodone. If it isn't managing it, I guess we can try Fentanyl. But it isn't going to last as long. Go check on North hall seven. He was complaining of needing to urinate but feeling dizzy. Maybe one of the C.N.A.s can assist." Axelrod barked.

Without a word, Nurse Meagan turned and quickly strode away. Manny listened to the clickity-clack of her clogs, and thought it sounded a lot like a clock ticking.

*Time, time ticking away. We are always on borrowed time, aren't we?*

"Can I help you?" Nurse Axelrod asked, sounding like she'd rather not.

"Yes, I am Detective Castillo, and this is Dr. Aguilar." Manny nodded at Alex "We are here to interview a suspect that is currently being treated here. A uniformed officer should be with her, guarding her. Her name is…"

"Raven Rivers." Axelrod finished for him.

"Yes." Manny replied, not even remotely surprised she knew who he was referring to.

"We have her in a private suite in the obs section. Your uniformed officer is outside the door, yes. She nearly scratched her eyeballs out, you know. The self-inflicted lacerations to her face are deep so we cleaned her up and dressed the wounds. She has been sedated, but as you know, we couldn't give her anything too strong. So, she will be able to talk." Axelrod reported.

"Why couldn't you give her anything too strong?" Alex asked, confused with Axelrod's statement.

Axelrod looked at Alex and then Manny, her eyes wide with surprise. It was the first emotion she had shown besides irritation. A cynical look slowly crept over Axelrod's face, twisting it into an even uglier version of its previous one. Manny wondered how a woman with such a disposition had climbed to the level of charge nurse. She was wrought with jaded disdain for the world. Manny could feel it oozing from her skin.

"Hmph, you don't know, do you?" Axelrod grinned, baring a row of overlapped teeth, yellowed and stained from years of smoking.

She looked like a child who was going to get the chance to tattle on a sibling. Manny got a nasty taste in his mouth for her at once.

"No, why don't you enlighten us." Alex spoke quietly through tight lips.

Manny knew that tone. Apparently, Alex did not like Axelrod either.

*Hmm, must be contagious,* Manny thought.

"Your *suspect…*" Axelrod hissed "is five months pregnant with a little girl."

Manny felt his mouth try to fall open. He snapped it shut.

*Pregnant?*

He turned to look at Alex and saw the same shock on her face that he felt. She looked at him, bewildered. Manny placed his hand gently against Alex's back to ease her, then looked at Axelrod.

"So, obs?" he asked.

"Yeah, obs." Axelrod looked at Manny as if he had three sets of eyes. "Obs as in observation, where we keep patients overnight to make sure they are okay. It's also a locked facility. Keyless entry only. You need an encrypted keycard to get on the floor." Axelrod showed them both her "keycard" like a car salesman showing off the most spectacular feature on the latest model Mercedes, as if Alex and Manny were supposed to be impressed.

After a moment, Axelrod let go of the keycard she had pulled out from her lanyard she had it attached to in order to show them. It whipped back against her ample bosom snapping so loud that it should have elicited at least a small wince. But the stone-faced charge nurse looked as if she had tripled up on her Botox; her face frozen in a nasty smirk. Manny found himself wishing it had smacked her in her chubby face. After a few seconds, her head slowly peered up from behind the desk and, she looked around the floor with steely eyes, like a hyena searching for its dinner. Manny could see exactly when Axelrod's hungry eyes locked onto their prey.

"Parker." she barked.

Manny watched as "Parker" reacted as if someone had poured ice water down her back. She stopped mid stride and inhaled deeply enough to thrust her chest out, her lips pursed together, when seconds prior they had been split with a smile. Manny got the feeling that the general consensus on the floor was that Nurse Axelrod was not well liked. He could understand. The five or so minutes he and Alex had been around her was uncomfortable, to say the least. With her rough exterior and matching tone, it was hard to imagine anyone being fond of her on a professional level, much less a personal one.

Nurse Parker, a petite, pixie-haired blonde with muddy green eyes, walked timidly over to the nurse's station. Her clogs made more of a hesitant shuffling noise, unlike the confident clickity-clack of nurse Meagan's— which was evident when you looked into her capricious eyes. Nurse Parker was shy and wary of Nurse Axelrod. Parker's slumped shoulders, slightly bowed head and the way she averted her eyes told Manny all he needed to know about their relationship.

"Parker, bring these two over to obs three. Then report back to me. I need you to go to North six. Jensen needs help on a lift for a bedpan." Axelrod sneered.

That "cat just ate a canary" smile was on Axelrod's lips again. Manny felt the urge to tell her off. Nurse Parker looked at Manny briefly and motioned for him and Alex to follow her. She shuffled down the hall, negotiating her way past stretchers and staff yelling orders, her head slightly down. Manny would have followed her anywhere at that point just to get away from Axelrod and her vicious aura that seeped spite and illusions of grandeur. Manny imagined her as a chubby child being picked on in the schoolyard, vowing to get revenge someday.

Nurse Parker stopped suddenly at a set of doors marked "Staff Only Locked Facility Observation Unit" and grabbed at her keycard that was attached to a lanyard similar to

Axelrod's. She waved it in front of a black box that was mounted on the wall to the right of the doors and moved back a few steps. A low buzzing sound discharged from the box. A loud buzz came from the doors, then clicking sounds as the doors opened slowly like two guardian soldiers creating passage for their king and queen. Nurse Parker let her sacred keycard return gently to her body and motioned again for Manny and Alex to follow her.

The trio entered an area that looked similar to the one they had left minus the mass of bodies and jumble of stretchers. It was clean and quiet, save for the rhythmic ear-piercing beeps transmitting from the heart monitors that were attached to bodies housed in private rooms, each with a different affliction, important enough to earn them a reservation in the "obs suite". Nurse Parker shuffled along the shiny white floor, its waxy shell reflecting the fluorescent lights from above, and stopped short of the uniformed police officer outside of observation suite three. Manny did not recognize the young officer who stood guard in front of the shaded double glass doors, but the officer's reaction told a different story. He smiled and nodded as Manny and Alex approached. Manny thought he looked no more than eighteen with his freckled face and traces of acne.

"Detective Castillo how are you Sir?" the officer inquired. Manny looked quickly at the officer's name badge. *O'Connor.* The name tugged at Manny's memory bank door, but the kid's face was unfamiliar to him. Manny's look of confusion must have been obvious to the young cop. His smile grew, bouncing his freckles further up on his cheeks and nose, making him look more like twelve than eighteen. That's when the kid removed his hat revealing a crown of burnt russet hair cut high and tight. There was no mistaking that signature hair and from whom it descended. O'Connor now rang a bell.

"Aw, Liam O'Connor's kid!" Manny smiled, and shook O'Connor's hand vigorously.

"Yes sir!"

Officer Sean O'Connor returned Manny's shake with a strong grip and a hearty laugh that echoed Liam O'Connor's from years ago. Liam O'Connor had been Manny's first Sergeant when Manny was a newbie, a virgin who hadn't even popped his cherry on the streets yet. They had worked together for four years, becoming close friends until Liam was shot down in a robbery gone bad. Liam hadn't even been on duty when it happened, just in the wrong place at the wrong time. Although, had he survived, Liam would have told everyone differently. He would have said "I was in the right place, at the right time." Liam O'Connor had believed in that kind of stuff— fate, "timing is everything", "soulmates". Manny shook his head as he thought back.

"You're thinking of him, aren't you?" Officer O'Connor asked, still smiling.

"Yeah, I was, kid." Manny smiled. "I sure was."

"Hi, I am Alex."

Alex held her hand out to Officer O'Connor. O'Connor smiled at Alex and Manny kicked himself for not recognizing him right away. He looked so much like Liam it was as if Liam had spit him out himself.

*Damn it.* Manny chided himself silently. *All those years working so closely with someone, becoming his friend, meeting his family. Then not knowing his son when he was standing right in front of you with a damn name badge on for Christ's sake?* Manny wished he had been able to handle that differently, but now all he could hope for was that Sean didn't take any of it personally. Manny looked at Alex.

"Officer O'Connor… Sean," Manny emphasized Sean's name so the kid would know he remembered. "is the son of an old friend of mine." Manny turned back to Sean. "I can't believe I didn't know you were on the force, kid."

Sean's smile was full of pride. It made his freckles jump even higher than before and his large ears bounce up as if they were tied to invisible strings maneuvered by an invisible puppeteer. It was bittersweet to see Sean in a uniform. Manny last saw him standing next to his crying mother at his father's graveside. At that time, he was a wide-eyed preteen with a mess of fiery red hair and long, lanky limbs that were outgrowing his wardrobe. Manny remembered Sean tried hard that day to stay strong for his mother. But at the end of the service when the rifles shot off their three volleys, Sean had jumped with each shot. As TAPS started to play, Sean had finally broken down and cried. The soldier that walked over to Sean and Mrs. O'Connor to present them with the flag had looked at Mrs. O'Connor for her approval before handing the flag to Sean because he was crying so hard. But when Sean looked up at the soldier with the folded flag in his hand, Sean's body stopped shaking and he stood tall. Manny remembered seeing something change on Sean's face then. Sean took the flag gingerly from the soldier's hands and hugged it close to his chest. Manny didn't see Sean cry the rest of that day, not even as they lowered his father's casket into the ground.

"Plus, I know dad would have wanted me to follow in his footsteps." Sean was saying.

Manny blinked and tried to focus back on grown up Sean's face. Manny wasn't sure how much Sean had already said or how much he had missed while he was away in his memories with little Sean. Manny smiled at Sean to let him know he was listening.

*Clearly, I am not good at that either,* Manny thought.

Manny caught Alex looking at him with her clinical eyes.

*Shit, she is analyzing me,* he thought.

Normally he would tell her to knock it off, but at that moment he was too weary to care. He was only interested in getting through the next few hours so they could hopefully close the case and get it ready for the courts to take over.

"Well, Sean, it has certainly been great seeing you. I know your father would be proud. I'm sure you can guess why we are here." Manny began.

"Yes, sir." Officer O'Connor responded.

"Anything to report?" Manny returned to all business.

"No, sir. Suspect has been relatively quiet. She is cuffed to the bed more for protection from herself, but she has been good since arriving as far as I know." O'Connor stated.

Manny nodded.

Sean smiled.

"Why don't you take a walk. We are going to head in and conduct an interview. You look like you could use a bite to eat." Manny urged.

Sean nodded his appreciation.

"It sure was nice seeing you, Detective Castillo. I will tell mom you said hello." Sean smiled.

"Yes, please do that." Manny agreed and patted O'Connor lightly on the shoulder before he turned and headed towards the hallway marked "Cafeteria".

Officer O'Connor walked like a young man on a mission. Manny nodded his approval before turning to Alex. He could feel her eyes on him. For the first time since he had met her, he did not want to answer her questions. Not yet.

"Manny?"

*Oh, man.*

"Si, mi amor." Manny turned to face her.

"It's okay, we don't have to talk about it now, but we will." she warned.

He noticed again that Alex looked as tired as he felt. Manny felt a jolt of frustration for them both. They should be home making love, not here in this hospital with its ear-piercing beeps and cranky charge nurses. He knew she wanted to know about Liam, but now was not the time. She was right, they would talk about it later. Manny was not one to "talk about things". Alex knew that, but she tried to get him to talk about things with her sometimes anyway. She told him it was good to "talk and get things off your chest". Manny understood and accepted it for the most part. He loved her for it, although he still believed seeing a shrink was for the weak.

He brushed her cheek lightly with his fingers. Alex closed her eyes and leaned into the caress. Manny's body tingled. Alex opened her eyes and looked into his. He held her gaze. He was still amazed at the amount of love he felt for the woman in front of him, and the physical and emotional feelings she was able to elicit from him.

"Well," she sighed "should we get this over with so we can go home?"

"That, mi amor, is the best thing you have said all day."

# CHAPTER EIGHT

THE ROOM WAS DARK except for the little light cast by the monitor with its Christmas light reds and greens flashing in conjunction with the annoying beeping sound of the heart rate monitor. Alex noticed right away the distinct *blub-blub-blub* of a different heart rate monitor set at a slightly quieter volume but audible nonetheless... a rhythmic beat pounding in the background, strong and fast.

*Blub-Blub-Blub.*

For a moment, Alex was overwhelmed with emotion at the sounds of the tiny pulse. The thought of a miniature human inside of another, alive and thriving, made Alex feel sentimental.

*What is wrong with me?*

Alex swallowed the bulge in her throat and walked over to the hospital bed where the small lump of blankets and wires that was Raven Rivers lay.

Alex reached the edge of the hospital bed with Manny by her side. Raven lay still with the covers pulled up to her chin. Alex sucked in a surprised breath when she saw the bandages covering one of Raven's eyes and both of her cheeks. Raven had lost it and started clawing at her face in the interview room, but it was such chaos Alex didn't know what kind of damage was done. By the looks of things, she had done more harm than Alex thought. Alex felt a plunge of sadness for Raven. The girl had been through so much from birth to now. Alex knew her pain and her sorrow to some extent. She wished she knew why some people became killers like Raven and some went on to search for killers, like herself.

"Raven." Alex whispered.

Raven didn't move. The steady beeps and *blub-blub-blubs* continued in the background. Manny put a reassuring hand on Alex's back. She took a deep breath in and tried again. She reached down and nudged Raven with a gentle, but sturdy, hand.

"Raven. Raven, it's Alex. I need to speak with you."

Raven stirred under the blankets. She moaned; a frustrated sound muffled by blankets, bandages and movement. Alex gave her a moment to adjust. When she didn't sit up and come to, Alex motioned to Manny to turn on the overhead light. Manny nodded and walked over to the wall. He flipped the switch and an explosion of blinding light descended upon the three of them. Raven hissed like a vampire whose skin sizzled from being exposed to sunlight.

"Raven! We need to talk." Alex raised her voice.

Raven growled; a vicious, feral sound that crawled its way up deep from the pit of her bowels.

"I'm sorry, but we aren't going anywhere until you speak with us." Alex stood her ground.

"Raven, we have enough evidence to convict you of two murders and an attempt on the life of an officer. If you'd like, we can go ahead and prosecute. Or we can listen to you and get your side of the story. It may help you… and your baby girl." Alex softened her voice a bit when she spoke of the baby, trying to play to Raven's emotions.

The blankets erupted like a volcano and the heart rate monitor exploded, the beeping nearly doubling its pace instantaneously. An invisible force ripped Raven up from the bed into a sitting position. She glared at Alex with one green and red eye, the colors matching that of the Christmas theme in the room. Alex could see that most of the capillaries had ruptured, spilling blood into the white of the eye, surrounding the green iris in a pool of bright, frightening red. Most of Raven's face was covered in bandages, but Alex imagined it was also bright with red, like her eye. Her small, pale hands gripped the bed rails, the skin pulled taut, blanching from the grip. Alex found herself wondering if the pressure would be enough to cut off the blood to the I.V. needle that was in Raven's right hand.

"My *baby*?" Raven sneered. "You know nothing of *my baby*!"

Alex stepped back from the bed and bumped into Manny. He did not move but gently held her there, a hand on the back of each of Alex's arms to steady her. Alex was grateful for him. Her rock, always. Alex took a breath and stepped forward again.

*I am in control here. Not Raven.*

"Well, then why don't you enlighten me?"

"Ha, why should I? You contemptuous bitch!" Raven mocked.

Raven's hands let loose their grip, and she held her belly protectively. She looked away from Manny and Alex, dismissing them. Alex had to figure out a way to get to her. The baby was obviously a trigger, but Alex had to try a different angle. Her chest tightened with anxiety.

*I can't mess up again.*

A memory blew into her ear. A whisper of a time when she was a little girl on the sidewalk holding her scraped knee and crying after having fallen in her new roller skates for the fourth time. Abuela knelt down beside her, and with a gentle fingertip, tilted Alex's head up until their eyes met.

"Levántate, mija, get up and try again." Abuela had said. Alex remembered shaking her head violently back and forth "no".

"Por qué, mija, why not?"

"Because, Abuela, I am afraid. What if I fall again?" Alex had whispered, fearfully.

"Pero, mi amor, como sabrás, si no lo intentas? How will you know if you do not try?" Abuela coaxed.

Abuela had kissed her forehead, kissed her knee, then told her to get up and try it again. Alex did. She tried again. She fell again, many times that day. But she had also learned to skate by the end of it and hadn't broken any bones; only suffered a few minor scrapes and bruises.

Alex took a deep breath.

*Ok, girl, Abuela was right. Get up and try again. How will you know if you don't try?*

"I'm sorry, you are right. We don't KNOW anything about your baby girl. Why don't you tell us? I mean… What about your baby girl, Raven? Don't you get it? We are trying to help you *save* your baby girl." Alex urged.

Raven started to laugh hysterically. Alex felt the heat of confusion and frustration flood her body from head to toe. She looked back at Manny to see if he was feeling the same. Manny looked at her and, with one raised eyebrow and a shrug, confirmed Alex's feelings. Why was Raven acting so nonchalantly about her unborn daughter? It was as if she didn't care what became of her.

*Maybe she doesn't care.*

The more time Alex spent with Raven, the more obvious it was to Alex that Raven was definitely mentally ill, but to what extent she was not sure. Alex needed more time with her. She needed to get Raven talking. Talking about something. Talking about everything. She didn't seem to have any emotion or empathy for her victims. The only emotion Raven showed was toward her mother, and each was intense and extreme. All other emotions were either void or lackluster.

"Okay, so you don't want to talk about your daughter, then tell us about the blood. Why were you taking blood from the victims?" Alex probed, all softness and sensitivity gone from her voice. She was all business now.

Silence.

"The blood, Raven. What were you doing with the blood?" Alex pushed.

Silence.

"Raven, I am sure your mother wouldn't have wanted…"

Raven turned on Alex like a wild animal trapped in a corner.

"My Momma? Don't you DARE talk about my MOMMA!" she howled.

The heart rate monitor beeped wildly again. The double doors opened, and Raven's nurse popped her head in and looked at Manny and Alex. Manny flashed his badge at her and shooed her away. The nurse frowned at him.

"Uh uh." she said, unimpressed "If her heart rate doesn't come down, I'm going to ask you two to leave."

She came into the room to assess Raven's vitals and demeanor. Raven turned on her, red faced and angry.

"Don't touch me, bitch!" Raven sneered at her.

"Listen, honey, I'm not the bad guy. I am here to help you, so calm down." the nurse said soothingly.

"You don't wanna help! No one wants to help. Everyone is bad!" Raven whispered.

"No, honey, I do want to help. I want to help you feel better. Let me just give you a little something here." the nurse responded sweetly to Raven.

Raven looked up at the nurse with one cautious eye and gritted her teeth. She laid back on the bed looking tired and defeated. The nurse uncapped the valve on the I.V. line, wiped it with an alcohol swab and flushed it with saline. Then she inserted the tip of a syringe into the I.V. valve and plunged all of its contents, of what Alex could only guess was another dose of light sedative safe for the baby, into the line. She recapped the needle and the I.V. valve and disposed of the needle into the red biohazard box that was mounted on the wall. She did this expertly and in record time, like a seasoned pit crew member of Dale Earnhardt's NASCAR team. She checked Raven's vitals once more before giving Alex and Manny a glowering look.

"Please," she said, without any hint of benevolence, "do *not* make me come in here again!".

She left with such a quickness that a detectable breeze came from her movement.

Alex looked at Manny with the eyes of an admonished child. Manny returned the favor. Then as if someone ordered them to, they both turned their eyes upon Raven. The beeping of the heart monitor had settled to a calm rhythm of seventy-eight beats per minute. In the background, the baby's heartbeat, although faster than Raven's, had calmed down as well. Raven was still, other than the rise and fall of the blankets when she took a breath. Raven's hands lay still on the bed, her pinkie fingers touching the rails. Even if she wanted to lift them, the handcuffs prevented her from bringing her hands much higher than a few inches off the bed. She stared up at the ceiling with her good eye.

*I wonder what the other one looks like,* Alex thought morbidly. Alex hesitantly peered down at Raven's hands again, but this time with a more observant eye. There she saw what she was hoping not to see, but expecting, nonetheless. Raven's now short, jagged fingernails were dirty; caked with dark brown blood, dried to a crust, underneath and around each nail. The hospital staff had obviously clipped them once she got there as a safety measure. Alex knew Raven had gone to town on her own face, but to what extent she wasn't sure. The dried blood on her once long nails and bandages on her face were a good indication that she had harmed herself pretty badly.

*Why?*

Alex felt sad for Raven. Raven had lost her mother like Alex had, and Alex knew that kind of pain. It was enough to drive someone mad. It was enough pain to make someone want to scratch their face or rip their eyes out. Alex's heart hurt.

*I have to try one last time.*

"Raven, I'm sorry about your Momma. I lost my momma, too."

She stopped and waited. Raven showed no sign of having heard her. She continued to stare up at the ceiling with her one good eye, unmoving, other than to blink every once in a while. Then after what seemed like an eternity to Alex, a quiet voice spoke from the hospital bed.

"It won't be long until I see Momma again." Raven admitted, grinning.

Raven spoke so quietly, Alex almost missed it. Alex leaned towards Raven so she could hear her better, confused by what she said. Alex hoped she wasn't suicidal with a baby in her womb.

*She must be delusional. The sedative wasn't that strong.*

"Raven, killing yourself won't bring back…"

"Ha, ha!" Raven howled. "You think I'm gonna kill myself? Now why would I wanna go and do sumthin' like that, darlin'?" Raven sneered.

Raven's hysteria brought out her New Orleans accent thick as Creole Jambalaya. Alex wished it was as warm. The chill froze Alex in her spot next to the bed, sending shivers down her spine. Raven turned her accusing eye upon Alex. The scrutiny made Alex feel as if she was under a microscope.

"How else would you be seeing your mother soon?" Manny spoke up beside Alex.

Alex watched Raven's focus shifted from her to Manny. The scraping sound of metal against metal as the handcuffs banged and shifted along the bedrails, grated on Alex's ears. When Alex looked down, she could see Raven's hands curled into balls of inflamed red and blanched white, a latticed pattern of rage. A gritted toothed smile spread Raven's barely visible lips, hooded in bandages and arrogance.

"Y'all surely are stupid for detectives." Raven cackled.

Raven clicked her tongue in a *tisk-tisk-tisk* sound like a reproachful teacher ashamed of her poorly performing students. She shook her head back and forth—her cyclops eye moving slowly between Alex and Manny— dissecting their faces.

"Raven, we are here to help." Alex attempted.

"Help? Help me what? Unless you can get me more blood then there is nothing anyone can do for me now." Then, as an afterthought she added "I have to hope what I had was enough." more to herself than to either one of them. "Isn't that right, Momma?" Raven whispered and rubbed her belly, ignoring Alex and Manny.

Alex cocked her head to the side like a puppy alerted to the sound of the bacon flavored beggin' strips being opened.

*What did she say? Did she call her baby Momma?*

Alex shook her head of the ridiculous thought that had hijacked her mind like a terrorist.

*No way. It was a term of endearment. She wasn't actually calling the baby "Momma". It was more like "mama".*

 Alex held an internal debate in her mind— two voices, both belonging to herself, deliberated— one argued that Raven was calling the baby "Momma" (as in "her real Momma") and the other debated that Raven was purely using the Hispanic term of affection *"mama"* for her unborn daughter. Before Alex could decide which of her two inner voices was correct, Manny had decided for her.

"Your little *mama* won't have a chance to know her momma if you don't help us out, Raven. Your baby will be thrown into the foster system while you serve out a couple of consecutive life sentences in prison. Your tiny *mama* will never know you, Raven." he warned.

Raven began to utter beneath her breath a jumble of words that Alex could not make out. Alex squinted her eyes as if seeing Raven more clearly would help her hear her better. A cadence of a language she was not familiar with began to become loud enough for Alex's ears, and Raven continued to chant it in a fervent intonation. It reminded Alex of an old, ancient Indian Shaman performing a spirit ritual of some sort. Alex looked at Manny for some sort of guidance or idea of what was happening, but he only looked back at her with a curious stare.

Suddenly the room was quiet. After a few moments, Raven

spoke causing both Alex and Manny to jump.

"Lalla taught me to chant those words. Her words. In her language. She was raised Muslim growing up in Africa until she moved to New Orleans. Then she learned about the hoodoo. She and Momma started doing it to make some money at first, but Lalla got deeper into black magic. Momma didn't wanna mess with that voodoo stuff. She wore her taurine stone to ward it off. But Lalla, she was not afraid. She had somethin' inside her, deep down. Told me growin' up she knew."

Raven paused looking at the wall as if she could see the past written there like a movie script for her to recite.

"She said Muslim may have been in her blood, but it wasn't in her soul, and she didn't believe in her Allah anymore. Lalla told me she believed in light souls and dark souls, like angels and demons. Told me 'it is that cut and dry, lil' blackbird'. Lalla went and learnt herself some black magic, y'all. Even the darkest kind. The blood spells." Raven drew out the last part so much at the end that Alex had a difficult time deciphering what she said, her twang thick as mud.

Alex looked at Raven's face and saw the shimmer of a tear pooled in the corner of her eye. The woman lying in the hospital bed, bandaged and restrained, had lost two mothers that she loved deeply at such a young and vulnerable age. Alex pieced together a clinical assessment of Raven. Raven suffered from severe Post Traumatic Stress Disorder from seeing her Momma being beaten. To cause further damage, Raven was the one who held her mother in her arms as her Momma drew her last breath. Then she was ripped away from Lalla, the only other "family" Raven knew growing up and moved here to an "uncle" she barely knew.

Alex no longer saw a woman before her, but a young, fragile

child. A child born to a teenaged mother who had suffered her own PTSD. Years of parental abuse, sexual intercourse with her twin brother who got her pregnant, family history of mental disease. Raven was practically guaranteed to be predestined to have some form of mental illness diagnosis based on familial history. But then, to be thereafter subjected to the trauma Raven was exposed to, probability became destiny chiseled in stone by the hand of God.

*Dios mío, pobrecita... my God, poor thing.*

"She taught me too, ya know." Raven turned her eye to Alex.

"I'm sorry," Alex cleared her throat. "What?"

"Lalla." Raven spoke a little louder, then waited to make sure Alex was paying attention to her this time.

"Oh yes, I'm sorry." Alex apologized again. "Please, go on."

"Lalla. She showed me some black magic. When Momma was doing her treats with her gentlemen callers, Lalla would show me some black magic stuff. Mostly to protect me. But also, in case I needed anything when I was a bit older." Raven's voice trailed off, growing quieter with each spoken word.

Alex wasn't sure if Raven was deep in memories or if the sedative was taking hold of her. She stood quiet, hoping Raven would continue as long as she was uninterrupted. She wasn't sure what had finally gotten through to Raven so that she would speak to them. Maybe it was Manny, and what he said about the baby going to foster care. Alex hoped Manny would stay quiet, but she was too nervous to look his way to signal him for fear it might throw Raven off her recount of events. Alex thought she had already almost messed it up when she interrupted Raven a few minutes ago.

"I need that black magic, ya know." The strength returning to Raven's voice again.

Insistent even.

*That's your cue.*

"I know, Raven. I get it. You do need it." Alex cajoled.

"I do!"

"We know. It's okay. We understand."

"She is in me, Alex. I stole the life force and drank it. I spoke the forbidden words, the blood magic spell, and now she will be reborn."

The clink and screech of the handcuffs on the metal bed rails as Raven tried to raise her hands when she said "reborn", like an enthusiastic Preacher baptizing one of the congregation, seemed loud enough to perforate Alex's eardrums. Raven's voice was laced with mania and it rose excitedly with each word. Her one eye grew wide and wild. It was all Alex could do to stay still and play along. She knew she had to figure out what Raven was talking about, and they were on the cusp, so close.

*You're almost there.*

"Who will be reborn, Raven?" Alex asked.

Raven looked at Alex as if she had answered wrong to the easiest question in the universe. Alex regretted asking the moment the words fell from her lips. For a split second, Alex was afraid Raven would withdraw and not answer her question. Raven glowered at Alex.

"*Who?*" Raven drew out the word in obvious awe of Alex's ignorance.

"My Momma, you idiot! My momma! My momma will be reborn. I drank the blood and said the words. Them black magic words of the blood spell, and now she's coming, y'all. She's coming! She's growin' in my belly and she is gonna be born again!"

Raven's voice was shrill with hysteria. Her laughter filled

the room and covered Alex's skin with goosebumps. Raven repeated herself without pause. The nurse ran in and, with a glaring eye and angry voice, told Alex and Manny to leave. Alex felt Manny's hand on her elbow ushering her gently out the door. On their way out, Alex's ears were filled with the same obstreperous chant.

"My momma is coming. My momma is coming."

# CHAPTER NINE

ALEX AND MANNY SAT ACROSS FROM JACK RIVERS in the cold conference room, the fluorescents abuzz and casting eerie light upon Jack, jaundicing his already sallow face. Alex thought Jack appeared to have lost even more weight in the few days since she last set eyes on him. His gaunt frame looked more haggard, bordering on emaciated, and his skin hung on his bones like melting cheese. His black hair, once slick with oil, had become dry and brittle. It was long enough to be braided, or at least pulled back, but he let it fall into his eyes, maybe to hide his face. He was also sporting the same long beard, but now it was one that made him appear an avid ZZ Top fan.

Jack pushed back his hair and looked at them with eyes that had seen too much. Alex saw now where Raven got her unique jade green eyes. Unlike her bright, gem colored ones, her uncle's were murky and watered down.  Jack tapped his wrinkled hands on the table, either out of nervousness or tobacco withdrawals— most likely both, Alex guessed. Alex looked at Jack's hands, his face, his skin, his yellowing eyes. *Jack Rivers is dying of liver disease, maybe even liver cancer,* she thought sadly.

Even though Jack had done some deplorable things, she still would never wish that on him. She thought of Abuela, her grandmother who passed, not so long ago it seemed, from ovarian cancer. Alex clenched her teeth, fighting hard to keep the tears from spilling from her eyes. Abuela had been her best friend. The memory of Abuela's antics spread a warmth across Alex's chest. Her grandmother lived a good life, well into her early eighties. Jack? He was only thirty-eight. He hadn't even had a chance to live even half his life yet. After hearing how he had lived the beginning act, Alex could guess he was ready to draw the curtain and exit stage left. Looking at him now, it appeared he wasn't too far off from the final curtain call. It still amazed Alex what drugs, alcohol and a history of abuse and trauma could do to someone's body and mind.

*Shit, what it could do to their souls.*

Almost as if he could read her mind, Manny placed a hand on her leg underneath the table and squeezed gently. Alex took a deep breath. Even after all the years of being friends, and now lovers, Manny never ceased to surprise her with his ability to know when she needed him most.

"So." Jack interrupted Alex's thoughts. "What happened? And, more importantly… what is going to happen next?"

Alex looked at Manny for approval. They had already discussed how this would go down. She just needed his nod for the go ahead.

Manny nodded.

*Alrighty then.*

Alex took a deep breath and began what she had rehearsed. "Mr. Rivers, we had Raven sectioned for her safety and evaluation. We went to the hospital to see her two days ago."

"Jack. Please call me Jack." Jack smiled, but there was no warmth within it. "Mr. Rivers was my dear old dad."

"Ok, *Jack*." Alex complied. "We saw Raven on Tuesday and spoke with the nurses on staff. I have a report in front of me here from the Psychiatric doctor that interviewed Raven on Friday." Alex tapped on a file folder marked "R. Rivers" that sat on the table in front of her. Alex paused and waited for Jack. He looked at her, his wrinkled hands tapping on the table again. When Alex was satisfied that he was ready to continue, she did.

"Raven had some pretty bad self-inflicted facial wounds. When we arrived she was bandaged. The hospitalist said Raven sustained a small laceration to her cornea from clawing at her eye with her fingernails. It's pretty rare, he said. I guess usually abrasions are common, but due to the length and sharpness of her nails and the force at which she dug into her eye, she was able to penetrate the cornea. Both eyes have subconjunctival hemorrhages, but the doctor says they are pretty benign compared with the laceration." Alex paused when she saw Jack cringing.

He looked at her as if she were speaking a different language. "I've gotta be honest, doc. It sounds horrible, but I have no freaking idea what you are saying."

Alex let out a small chuckle.

"It's okay, Jack. Unless you went to school for medical terminology, I guess you wouldn't. Sorry. All it means is that Raven has a pretty deep scratch in her eye that, if it doesn't heal, may require some surgery. Also, she has some pretty bad bleeding into the whites of her eyes, so her eyes aren't really white right now, they are bright red; but it is not dangerous."

Jack winced.

"Are you okay, Jack?" she asked.

"Yeah, sure." he sighed. "Is she gonna still be able to see?"
"Yes, we believe that is the case. The hospitalist said he put
her on topical antibiotics and hopes she doesn't need any
surgery on the eye. He is watching her for the next few days."
Jack nodded.
"Okay, well that would be good if she doesn't need the
surgery, so let's hope that cream works." Jack continued to
tap the table.
"Jack, would you like a cigarette?" Manny asked.
Jack looked up from his drumming hands with excited eyes.
"Yes! Man, I would love one. I, uh, I haven't been out, as I'm
sure you know..." Jack issued an embarrassed laugh.
"No problem."
Manny stood from the table and walked to the door. He
opened it, poked his head out briefly, then returned to the
table and sat down.
"It'll be a minute." Manny smiled.
"Wow, okay, great. Thanks." Jack smiled, splitting his lower
lip open and drawing a thin line of bright red blood from his
severely chapped lips.
Silence filled the room and hung over them like a thick mist
on a humid day, heavy and uncomfortable. Alex dreaded
the rest of the conversation. She was sure Jack could feel her
anxiously tip toe around it.
A knock on the conference room door made them all jump.
"Ha, I knew that was coming and still jumped." Manny
laughed.
Alex and Jack both guffawed, more for the pleasantry of it
than for the true humor of the situation. Everyone was on
edge and the angst was veritable.
"Yeah, come in." Manny answered the knock.
The door opened and a plain clothes officer walked in,

holding a pack of Marlboro Light cigarettes. She handed them to Manny with an almost imperceptible nod, then turned and left the room, letting the door shut softly behind her. Manny slid the box of butts across the table to Jack. A shaky hand reached for it, and a pair of grateful eyes looked up at Manny.

"Thank you, Detective. I haven't had one in a few days, and I am feenin' like you wouldn't believe. You wouldn't happen to have a Bud Light on hand, would you?" Jack teased.

"No, Jack. Unfortunately, we do not." Manny snickered.

"Ah, yes. Ha, well it was certainly worth a try, wasn't it?"

"It was." Manny chuckled again. "No worries. Listen, after this if you'd like, I can arrange for an officer to bring you to the store to grab some things for your house."

"Wow, that would be great. Thank you very much." Jack's voice quaked slightly.

Jack's smile waivered, then vanished completely. She recognized the look. It was the look that came when one remembered the good stuff is fleeting, and the bad stuff always follows. He was waiting for the bad. Alex felt an underlying sadness for him. The emotional attachment she had to this family was undeniable to her.

*Maybe it's because I feel like they didn't have a chance from the beginning.*

Alex knew that people could be born with mental illness, but a lot of how they turned out had to do with one's environment. Of course, there was the whole "nature versus nurture" debate. This particular family had been through the ringer of all ringers as far as the alleged mental and physical abuse went. Although studies had shown that not everyone came out of an abusive home a killer or a drug addict, someone with a familial history of mental illness and abuse like Jack described, did have a higher probability of showing some form of violent or antisocial behavior. Jack, Mercy and Raven had all been born into less than favorable conditions for a positive outcome.

*It isn't fair.*

"I know you have some bad news for me. I mean, *more* bad news." Jack sighed. "Right? Like, why else would you be being so nice to me? My kid killed people, for fuck's sake." Jack's voice quivered, on the verge of tears.

He took the pack of Marlboro Lights and flipped them over so that he was holding them by the bottom edge, then banged the top end into the palm of his other hand a few times to "pack them". The sound reverberated in the quiet conference room. With trembling hands (that Alex now believed to be a constant tremor and not just from alcohol withdrawal), Jack unwrapped the plastic off the cigarette pack. He removed a butt and stuck it between teeth yellowed from years of smoking. Jack produced a worn book of matches from his pocket that looked like it hadn't seen the light of day in months but had instead seen the inside of the washing machine a few times. The book's outer flap was tattered, and whatever name had once graced its face had been nearly smudged completely away. Alex would have bet a few dollars that he wasn't going to get any of those matches to light.

Jack pulled the first comb off of the strip and flipped the book around, then ran the tip of the match against the striker. Nothing. He tried again. Nothing. Jack discarded the dud and picked off another comb from the book. He ran that one against the striker. Nothing. Again, he tried. Nothing. Jack grunted. Alex looked at Manny and shrugged. Manny smiled. Alex could tell Manny was trying not to giggle. Alex kicked him gently under the table. This was not a time or place to be laughing.

Agitated, Jack sighed and tried once more. *Poof.* The match flamed up and lit, glowing a bright yellow orange. The smell of sulfur and heat-filled smoke impregnated the air. Jack took a deep drag of the cigarette, closing his eyes as he did, savoring the moment.

Jack blew out a puff of smoke and looked at Alex and Manny expectantly.

"Okay, shoot." he said.

"Jack," Alex began, "Raven is being held at the E.M.H.U., the Emergency Mental Health Unit at the hospital. We sectioned her, like I said, for her safety and for others' safety, but now the Psychiatric Team has decided that it is best for her to be transferred to Buena Vista Heights, which is a hospital that specializes in psychiatric care. She will remain there until her court date."

Jack sat, quietly listening. Alex's stomach churned. She knew she had to tell Jack about the baby, but she wasn't sure how to, and worse, she wasn't sure if he could take it. Jack wasn't in any condition to take care of a baby, but the thought of having her given over to the child welfare system would probably kill him. Alex rubbed the file folder in front of her for comfort while she considered, for the hundredth time, how to tell Jack about what Raven had admitted to them at the hospital. Jack interrupted Alex's thoughts.

"Go ahead and say it, Dr. Aguilar. I can see your gears working. What else is on your mind?"

"Okay, Jack" Alex inhaled deeply "Raven is five months pregnant with a baby girl."

Jack's eyes grew wide and his cigarette almost dropped from his mouth. He grabbed at it clumsily, fumbling with it and nearly burning his fingers. Reminiscent of his last visit with Alex and Manny, he removed the lid to his cold coffee and dropped the burning butt into the remaining liquid until it sizzled out. He looked up at Alex with confused eyes.

"Pregnant?" he asked.

"Yes, five months along." Alex repeated.

Jack looked down at his lap silently. Alex wondered what Jack was thinking and was about to ask when he looked up briefly to grab at the pack of cigarettes. Alex saw a tear fall down Jack's scraggy cheek. He didn't bother to wipe it away. Alex felt guilty for having to tell him, but she didn't know why. She just knew she felt it, deep inside.

"Jack? Are you okay?" she asked.

"I can't believe she's pregnant." Jack imparted.

"You obviously didn't know." Alex said.

"No, I didn't." he answered angrily.

"Sorry, Jack."

"No." Jack practically screamed. "It isn't possible."

Jack shook his head back and forth and muttered to himself again. He looked confused and upset. Alex looked at Manny. Manny looked at her and shrugged again. Jack became fidgety and seemed more agitated.

*You are of no help this very second, Jack. What is wrong with you? Why are you so upset?*

"She can't be pregnant." Jack finally said, more to himself than to Alex or Manny, shaking his head in disbelief. "It isn't possible."

"Jack?" Alex pushed.

Jack looked directly at Alex with scared eyes.

"She can't be pregnant. I had a vasectomy. They told me I couldn't have any more kids. How the fuck is this possible? If she is, it isn't mine. She must be fucking someone else." Jack's eyes were wild with fear and anger.

Alex felt a surge of fury, disgust and sadness balling up inside her belly. Alex could not speak. The threat of vomit spilling from her mouth was too strong. Thankfully Manny was there for her. Her saving grace, always.

"Jack, are you saying that you have been having sexual intercourse with Raven?" Manny demanded, all business, all previous kindness gone from his tone.

Jack looked at Manny. Alex could see the cloud of shock begin to clear from his eyes and the reality of what he had just admitted to setting in. His face settled with acceptance and he looked at them both with a sigh.

"Yeah, I guess that's what I said, isn't it." he admitted, reluctantly.

Jack opened the Marlboro Lights and lit another, inhaling deeply. He blew out a large puff of white smoke into the air above them and looked at Manny.

"Yes, I was sleeping with my daughter. Disgusting, I know. No, I didn't think she could get pregnant because I had a vasectomy fifteen years ago. I never wanted to have any more children with anyone. Not after what happened with Mercy." Jack paused and sucked in a big breath, dragging off the cigarette like it was his last, and blew it out into the air. *Maybe it is.*

The sound disgusted Alex. Jack disgusted Alex.

"I don't know why I slept with Raven. Maybe because in some way she reminded me of Mercy. Maybe because she reminded me what it felt like to be needed again— at least what it felt like to have someone around who cared for me. She needed me. I needed her. I guess we were both lonely and in a vulnerable state after Mercy died."

Alex had to swallow as her mouth filled with saliva and bile

and her head filled with images she pushed quickly away.
All the guilt and sadness she had felt for Jack Rivers before
disappeared with the puff of smoke he inhaled into his lungs.
All she felt for him now was disdain.

*What kind of person slept with their twin sister and their own
daughter?*

"Jack, you do realize incest with a minor is a felony?" Manny
asked.

"Yes, sir." Then as if it would make some sort of difference
Jack looked at Alex. "We haven't slept together in about
four months. I haven't had it in me. As I'm sure you can
tell, I haven't been feeling quite healthy lately. I doubt she
is sleeping with anyone else though. Raven is very… loyal."
Jack replied, his voice devoid of remorse.

Alex's had a thought.

"Jack, did you know about the murders?" she asked.

Jack looked at her, surprise on his face.

"No!" he insisted.

"Did you know Raven was taking blood from her victims
and drinking it?" Alex continued, her voice rising.

"Huh?" Jack asked, a look trapped somewhere between
confusion and disgust on his face.

"Yes," Alex persisted, drawing pleasure from his shock. "she
was drinking it and using Black Magic blood spells." Alex
stood, pointing an accusatory finger at Jack and knocking her
chair backwards. It slammed against the floor. The banging
sound rang through their ears. It didn't stop her. "She
believes her baby, *your baby*, is Mercy reincarnated." Alex
sneered.

Jack's mouth fell open. This time the burning cigarette butt
did fall, right into his lap. He made no motion to show he
noticed. After a second, he jumped and uttered a few curse

words while he fumbled around for the lit butt. He found it and tamped it out on the table.

"What?" he squawked.

Alex reveled in his dismay. Manny stood and put a hand on Alex's shoulder. Jack's eyes moved from Alex to Manny and back to Alex, searching for a sign of, what? Possibly deceit?

*You could only be so lucky.*

Alex felt something inside her. Something dark, almost sinister. She didn't like it, but she couldn't push it out. The distaste had morphed into a new, darker feeling and it made her uneasy. Yet she was unable to stop feeling it. What was it? She had felt it once before, not so long ago. Yes, that was it. Hate. She found herself feeling hatred towards Jack Rivers. She had felt it towards Bobby Benson, Jr. after he kidnapped her and raped her months ago. Now, similarly, she felt it towards Jack. Her body was shaking.

*Why? Why do I hate him?*

Manny wrapped a gentle hand around Alex's wrist and turned her to face him.

"Alex, why don't you go for a walk." Manny held her gently. Alex turned astonished eyes on Manny. His expression stopped her in her tracks.

*He thinks I've lost it.*

Her body stiffened as the fury flowed through her like molten lava. She glared at Manny. Manny's face changed. The wrinkled brow faded and instead he looked as if he was suddenly lost; his eyes searching for the way home.

*Oh no, what have I done? Manny?*

Alex's body softened. She nodded and turned towards the door without looking back at Jack again. She was afraid if she did, she would say something she might regret. Manny opened the door and ushered her through to Officer Guzmán who was standing guard outside.

"Guzmán, can you take Dr. Aguilar to grab a coffee, please?" Manny requested.

Officer Guzmán nodded obediently.

Alex looked at Manny. His eyes were tired. Dark, puffy half-moons had formed beneath them. She felt guilty for losing her professionalism. She didn't even know how it had happened; it just did. She stopped and reached for his arm. He smiled at her.

"Manny, I..." Alex began.

"No te preocupes, corazón, I understand."

"Oh, Manny, I'm sorry." Alex felt a deep pit in her stomach.

"No te preocupes. Don't worry. We will talk about it later. I need to get back in there and place Jack under arrest."

Alex nodded. Manny leaned in and kissed her gently on her forehead. He smelled so good still, even after hours at the precinct, and being exposed to Jack River's cigarette smoke. Alex breathed him in. Manny squeezed her hand.

"Don't worry." Manny reassured her again. "I will see you soon. I will come get you as soon as I am done. I promise." Manny touched Alex's lips with his thumb, then headed back into the conference room, the door shutting behind him with a decisive click. Alex looked at the door for a few moments, until she heard Guzmán clear her throat.

"Oh, yes, sorry." Alex apologized. "I bet you're itching for a coffee, aren't you, Officer Guzmán?"

Alex managed a half smile for the officer. Officer Guzmán returned a warm smile and motioned to the hallway.

"Shall we?" Guzmán asked.

"Yes, let's." Alex said, and the two walked side by side down the hallway, eventually disappearing into the crowded entryway of the precinct.

# CHAPTER TEN

MANNY HATED LEAVING ALEX DISTRAUGHT, but he had
to finish with Jack. Alex had lost it, and Manny couldn't let
her remain in the room and risk Jack shutting down. Manny
needed to see if he could get Jack to give him any more
information voluntarily.

"Sorry about that, Jack. I am sure that the news was a little
disarming."

Jack looked up at Manny from the table, his bloodshot eyes
glistening with fresh tears. Manny wondered what a man like
Jack, obviously lacking in the moral compass department,
would have to cry about.

"Yeah, I'm… I'm… I don't… I don't know what to say." Jack
paused, searching for words.

"Well, I guess it isn't every day that a man gets told he is
going to be a father again when he thought it wasn't possible,
right?"

Manny tried to get back in with Jack for the moment. Jack
emitted a sound that could have been interpreted as either a
sob or a laugh, and if Manny had to guess, he would venture
to say it was a combination of both. Manny watched the

man sitting across from him. A man was only a few years older than Manny who, by his looks could easily have been Manny's father. A man who was abused by his own father, ignored by his mother, impregnated his sister, and then did the same to his daughter. A man that, at one time, was once handsome and, according to the family records, had been well off financially. So why would this man, who outwardly seemed to have it all, squander everything away on drugs and alcohol?

*To forget the things he had done and numb the pain of those things.*

Manny understood Alex's outburst. It was abhorrent what Jack did. How could she not be sickened by him? Manny certainly was. It was difficult for Manny to even be in the same room with Jack without wanting to sock him in his skeleton face.

"Jack, how long have you been sleeping with...?"

Jack's head snapped up. His eyes glared at Manny.

*Damn, I just lost him.*

"I'm not sure that's any of your business, Detective." Jack hissed through gritted teeth.

"Actually, it is, Jack. It is my business." Manny had enough. He didn't want to lose Jack, but he was done playing games. It was time Jack Rivers knew who he was dealing with. "We can either discuss it now, or we can discuss it at the trial. Either way, we *are* going to talk about it. Your choice, I guess."

Jack sat, lips pursed tightly. Manny waited patiently. Jack ran his scrawny hands through his brittle hair and grunted. Manny half expected to see chunks of hair come out in Jack's fingers. Manny disliked him more and more every minute that passed. It was all he could do to keep himself from grabbing him by his dirty, slipshod collar, throwing him on the floor, and beating him to a bloody pulp. Manny wasn't prone to violence, but when it came to scum like Jack, he would make an exception.

Jack sighed again and laid his sunken eyes on Manny.

"Since about a year after she came to live with me," Jack admitted.

Manny had to resist the urge to climb over the table and slam Jack's face into the conference table. He was glad Alex had left.

"She was just a goddamn child, Jack." Manny groaned.

A burning feeling hit the back of Manny's throat, and he swallowed it down hoping the bile would stay away. The detestation he felt for Jack at that moment was causing such a nauseating feeling, Manny was afraid he might spew his Italian grinder all over the conference room table. It rolled around in his stomach like a world class MMA fighter in the last round, kicking and punching his gastric mucosa for the win.

*Hot peppers and vinegar were a bad idea today.*

Jack glared at Manny with his yellowed eyes like a dirty coyote. Manny would love to bring Jack out to the desert, shoot him between his lurid eyes and leave him for the vultures to tear him apart limb by limb.

*This piece of shit doesn't deserve to walk another step.*

"You're telling me she didn't tell you she was pregnant?" Manny provoked.

Jack looked at Manny as if he had taken the last cookie right out of his hand, licked it, and handed it back to him. Shocked through and through.

"No!" he yelled. "She did not tell me she was pregnant! I am not supposed to be able to GET anyone pregnant!"

Jack's face was candy apple red, and his breath came in short spurts. Manny didn't care. Jack was done getting special treatment of any kind; he was just another pedophile in Manny's book. Manny opened his mouth to say something when a familiar look came over Jack's face. Manny had seen it before. It was the face they all made when they realized they had been duped, and they didn't have to say anything more to Manny without being read their rights or without a lawyer present. It was almost always the same. First it was a wide eyed and stupid look, but then anger and a "dig your heels in" kind of determination followed. And that was exactly the look Jack had plastered on his meagre face.

"I want to speak to my lawyer!" Jack said through thin, craggy lips.

Manny smiled.

"Of course, you do. No problem, Jack."

Manny walked over to the door and opened it, poking his head out and speaking quietly as he had earlier to lay purchase on Jack's pack of cigarettes. Manny returned and sat across from Jack without a word. He kept the overzealous smile plastered to his face. Manny knew if he let it waver, his lips would release a host of unprofessional profanities and accusations, like a swarm of hornets into Jack Rivers' face. Although nothing would give him more pleasure, Manny couldn't risk getting in trouble with the Chief over a scumbag like Rivers. He sat, and he waited, smiling like he just got a lollipop at the bank.

A knock came and the door opened. Manny didn't move. He knew it was coming. Jack, however, jumped in surprise. Two uniformed officers waltzed in. Manny recognized them as Jones and Masterson; the two rookies that had responded to the call at Alex's house the night Bobby Benson had killed her cat, hanging it from her shower curtain rod. Manny gritted his teeth at the memory. He nodded to Jones and Masterson. They nodded in return.

"Jack, these are Officers Jones and Masterson. They are here to take you to booking. There you will be fingerprinted and processed. You are under arrest for the rape of a child under the age of sixteen in accordance with chapter 265 section 22A. You have the right to remain silent. Anything you say can and will be used against you in a court of law. You have the right to an attorney and have one present while you are being questioned. If you cannot afford one, one will be appointed to represent you before any questioning, if you wish. You can decide at any time to exercise these rights and not answer any questions or make any statements."

Jack sat quietly, staring at Manny with flat eyes. Manny was expecting an argument. Fiery eyes. Yelling. But Jack sat there in silence, holding his pack of cigarettes and looking at Manny.

*He's looking through me.*

"Jack, do you understand each of these rights as I have explained them to you?" Manny asked.

Jack looked at Manny but didn't move.

"Jack?" Manny asked.

Jack nodded.

"Jack, I need you to verbally say yes or no." Manny insisted.

"Yeah." Jack answered, flatly.

"Having these rights in mind, do you wish to talk to me now, or say anything else?" Manny asked.

Silence. Staring.

"Jack?" Manny called Jack's name again, frustration heating his feet.

A small smile began to separate Jack's lips. As the smile grew larger and wilder, the previous crack that had since scabbed over opened up again, letting loose a small pool of bright red blood. A droplet fell down Jack's chin and crawled slowly toward its tip. Sickly Jack now looked like Crazy Jack.

"Well now, isn't that funny, Detective? Seeing as how I already spilled my guts to you." Jack laughed, although Manny felt zero humor behind the tone.

Manny looked at Officer Jones and nodded the go ahead.

"Mr. Rivers, if you would please stand." Officer Jones requested politely.

Jack made no indication that he heard Jones, nor any attempt to rise. He continued to glare at Manny from across the table. Manny felt nothing from the darts that flew at him out of Jack's eyes. He couldn't wait to see Jack behind bars. Now Raven's acts of violence made more sense to him.

*Poor kid.*

"Jack, do yourself a favor and play nice with the officers." Manny cautioned.

Jack squinted his eyes at Manny, but after a brief showdown of stubborn opposition, he stood. Officer Masterson removed a pair of long plastic zip ties from his belt loop.

"Mr. Rivers, please step out from your chair and place your hands out in front of you." Masterson instructed.

Jack did as he was told without taking his eyes off Manny. Manny enjoyed the grimace on Jack's face when Masterson pinched Jack's skin into the zip tie on his right wrist as he cinched it. The way Jack cried out "OUCH!" was gratifying, almost comforting; like a bowl of Abuela's homemade sopa de pollo y tortilla, chicken tortilla soup made for the soul.

"Jack, you will be going to a cell where you will be held until you have a hearing." Manny informed him.

Jack broke his gaze from Manny to look down at his tethered

wrists. A funny thought popped into Manny's head like a Mexican Prairie Dog poking its head up from beneath the hardened dirt, making its presence known. A chuckle escaped his lips before he could contain it. Jack's head jerked up.

"It's ironic you know, seeing you like that with your wrists bound. Did you know… well, no, you wouldn't have known would you?" Manny paused, thinking.

Manny scratched his head as if he were pondering something. Jack raised his eyebrows as he waited for Manny to finish. When Manny remained quiet, Jack lost his patience.

"What?" he almost screeched. "What wouldn't I have known?"

Manny eyed Jack for a moment.

"You wouldn't have known how Raven bound her victims' wrists, now would you?" Manny goaded. "No, Jack, you wouldn't know that because you didn't know about the murders, right? That's what you said, isn't it?" Manny poked. Jack opened his mouth to speak, then seemed to think otherwise, and snapped it shut. He looked at Officer Jones and Officer Masterson and asked them if he could bring his cigarettes. Masterson agreed and pocketed them. Jones grabbed the tattered flannel shirt that draped the back of Jack's chair, fitted to the chair better than it did Jack.

"I just find it very interesting that your daughter, whom you *forced* to be your *lover*, was binding her victims' wrists with zip ties. The same thing you are now cuffed with. Hmph." Manny scoffed. "Ironic isn't it?"

Manny clicked his tongue and shook his head. He looked at Jones and Masterson.

"Get him out of my sight."

# CHAPTER ELEVEN

ALEX SAT AT MANNY'S DESK WITH HER COFFEE and sipped at it, although she did not taste it. She was upset with herself for losing her cool with Jack, but she couldn't help it. It was like those silly science projects kids did of the volcanoes in school when they added the baking soda. It had all bubbled up inside and exploded out of her. The thought of him sleeping with not only his *twin sister* but then *his daughter*. She had worked with a lot of mentally ill people, but Jack Rivers was a blue-ribbon winner. At least now she had a little more insight into why Raven had turned out the way she did.

The shrill ring of the phone on Manny's desk broke through Alex's self-deprecation. She stared at it while it rang but did not answer it. It stopped ringing eventually. Alex found herself wondering who was on the other line. Just then the phone rang again, making her jump. Alex watched it again, counting. It rang thirteen times.

*Hmm, maybe it is important.*

Finally, it stopped. She took a breath and sat back in Manny's chair. It wasn't as comfortable as her chair at the office. It was a basic office chair with plastic arms and metal feet without rollers. The seat was padded as was the lumbar support, but it was no competition for her leather captain's chair that sat stoically behind her large cherry wood desk. Just the thought of her comfortable chair made Alex yawn. Manny's phone rang again, scaring Alex's yawn away.

*Damn it. That scared the crap out of me. Even worse, that hurt. What the heck is so important?*

Alex let the phone ring again. This time it rang sixteen times. She decided that if it rang again, she would answer it. She didn't feel completely comfortable answering his phone. She was sure she could take a message for him, but it was his phone, his desk, his territory. She would rather leave it be.

"Hey there, 'perty lady." a familiar voice from behind her spoke, attempting a hideous southern accent.

Alex smiled. She knew the voice, even with the horrible Yosemite Sam accent. She turned to see Deshawn standing there, his large hands on his hips, looking down at her with his grandiose smile. Alex felt a warm spot in her heart for the big jokester.

"Hey there, yourself."

"Whatchya doing up here?" Deshawn asked, walking around to his desk so that he was facing her.

"Waiting for Manny. He is down in the conference room with Jack Rivers." Alex said, trying not to make eye contact with him.

"Well now, ya went and got yourself kicked out, didn't you?" he asked gently.

The boil of frustration could be felt in Alex's chest and face, but she looked at Deshawn and saw he meant no malice. As always, his face was kind and understanding. Her anger dissipated instantly.

"Yes." she sighed, resigned at her own foolishness.

"Don't sweat it. I've lost it before." he stood and walked towards her. "More than once that's for sure."

"D, the point is I shouldn't have *lost* it. I'm a professional. A trained psychologist. I am supposed to keep my cool at all times, under *all* circumstances."

"Alex," Deshawn said, leaning on Manny's desk so he could look down into her face, "no one is perfect. We are human beings. We are not infallible."

He put a warm hand on Alex's shoulder, letting it sit there for a moment before he squeezed gently. She let her hand find his and returned the squeeze. Their friendship had grown tight in the last few months and she cherished it.

"Alright, enough of this mushy stuff. I gotta go find your man and help him out. You know, do the 'ol partner stuff." Deshawn chuckled.

Alex smiled at Deshawn. He was a great partner and friend to Manny. She appreciated him more than he knew. He had a good heart and soul. She cherished his loyalty.

"Okay, D. Tell him I said don't be too long if he can help it. I am going to go ahead and make my way home. I am exhausted. If he needs me, he knows how to get hold of me." Deshawn nodded.

"No problema, senyorita. I'll tell 'em. Be careful headin' home to the ranch and sleep well there, 'perty lady." Yosemite Sam Deshawn said in his atrocious southern accent again.

Alex giggled and watched Deshawn head down the hall.

She stood to leave and caught sight of a yellow pad of sticky notes. She grabbed one and drew a heart on it. She stuck it on the frame Manny had sitting on his desk that held the photo taken of the two of them at a carnival, when they were still just "friends", a few months prior to Bobby Benson, Jr.

She stared at the picture for a moment, noticing the way
their eyes laughed as much as their mouths in the photo. She
found herself longing to feel that carefree again, if even for
just a moment.

*Someday. It will come again. It will just take time.*

Alex kissed her pointer finger and touched it gently to
Manny's face in the photo. She knew if anyone could help
her to feel that way again it would be him. Alex grabbed
her briefcase and traced the same steps Deshawn took only
moments ago then turned the opposite way at the end of the
hall and headed towards the exit to go home.

Manny sat slumped down on the bench outside the
conference room, feeling defeated and tremendously tired.
Only one thing kept him going at that second. He looked up
and peeped Deshawn coming down the hallway.

*Ah, and there it is.*

"Well, don't you look like a ball of joy." Deshawn chortled.

"Yeah, more like a blob." Manny laughed. "While you were
out galivanting around town, I was here dealing with some
pretty fucked up shit." Manny defended.

"Galivanting for *you!* And, so I don't forget, Alex went home.
She asked me to tell you." Deshawn stated.

"I know, I know you were, and I completely appreciate it.
I do. It's been a shitty day, buddy." Manny paused. "Yeah,
thanks, I kind of figured she would get sick of waiting
around."

"Well, hopefully, this," Deshawn reached into his jeans
pocket and produced a small, black box. "will make things
better."

Deshawn handed the velvet box to Manny with his signature smile, full of teeth and silliness. Manny smiled at him, grateful for him. Just holding the box did make Manny feel immediately better. It also made him feel slightly nervous. Not nervous for himself. He knew one thousand percent that he had zero doubt. Manny opened the box enough to peer inside to make sure its contents were exactly as he had requested.

*It's perfect.*

"So, what is the plan, Stan?" Deshawn inquired.

"Well, my friend, I will be making..."

Manny's cell phone rang. He dug for it in his pocket and flipped it open on the second ring.

"Castillo."

There was a long silence as Manny listened to the caller on the other end. A few "mhm's" and "yeses" broke the silence here and there. Deshawn stood by, patiently waiting for the call to end. Two female cadets walked by, looked at Manny and Deshawn and nodded, straight faced. Once they were a few feet past, they put their heads together, whispered something, and began to giggle not so inconspicuously. Manny hung up the phone in time to notice. He rolled his eyes and looked at Deshawn.

"More fans, I see."

"You don't know that." Deshawn argued halfheartedly.

"The hell I don't." Manny snickered.

Deshawn looked at Manny with a sheepish grin. Deshawn knew a lot of the women in the precinct "liked" him, but he chose to pretend he didn't. Manny chose to point it out to him and tease him about it every chance he could. Manny thought it funny the way Deshawn got embarrassed by it. It was endearing, to say the least, to see a two hundred plus pound, six-foot three man turn bashful. This time, it was Deshawn's turn to roll his eyes. He shook his head as if to shake off the whole discussion. Deshawn was as loyal a husband as he was a partner, through and through.

"What's up?" he asked, pointing to Manny's phone and changing the subject.

Manny sighed.

"That was Davis. He said that Jones and Masterson are done booking and fingerprinting Rivers. He's being housed in a holding cell until his arraignment in the morning. He chose to decline his phone call. Judge Nicholson will set bail in the morning, and we will go from there. Raven's arraignment is in three days, barring any changes in her stability. As of today, the hospitalist and hospital psychiatrist feel she will be stable enough by then. She will be escorted from the hospital with strict one-on-one observation and go before Judge Burton. You will need to plan on being there, as will Alex and I." Manny rubbed his temples.

"Oh, is that all?" Deshawn said sarcastically. "No wonder that call only took a second."

"Actually no, but nothing important, just some admin shit. Some manila envelope came in for me that I need you to remind me to grab later." Manny shrugged. "But right now, I have to call and make some dinner reservations at La Trattoria or we will *never* get a table there." Manny pinched his nose when he said "La Trattoria" so that he would sound nasally.

Manny became an imitator of what he liked to call the "overtly rich" whenever he spoke of La Trattoria. He found it to be "Snooty Booty" (his own personal label). But Alex loved it there, and he could not argue that the food was delicious. To Manny, it was a place for high society folks and tourists, (with more money than God), to gather and order small plates of fancy food for gargantuan prices. Deshawn looked at Manny. Manny had his nose pinched with his thumb and two fingers. Deshawn guffawed at how Manny's pinkie finger stuck out as if he were having "teatime" at one such "Snooty Booty" restaurant as La Trattoria.

"Man, you sure are somethin' else, you know that?" Deshawn laughed.

"Pardon me, sir." Manny said, in his best high society voice. Manny and Deshawn burst out laughing.

"Dude, we... are so... stupid." Deshawn said between giggles and trying to catch his breath.

"Hey, hey now! Speak for yourself!" Manny castigated playfully.

They laughed a few seconds more, then quieted, trying to recapture their breaths. Once they had settled completely, Manny looked at Deshawn and clapped him softly on the back.

"Alright, buddy, I've got to head home. I have kept Alex waiting long enough."

"Yeah, I hear ya. Muriel is gonna kill me. This is the third night this week she's had to give the kids their baths."

Deshawn put his head down, shaking it back and forth, but not before Manny caught the grin on his face.

"Oh, I'm sure you're all broken up about it."

"For sure, man."

"Mhm. Well, I hope you at least make it home to put them to bed."

Deshawn's head popped up.

"Hell, yes!" Deshawn said, all joking gone from his demeanor. "Now that, that is definitely something I never wanna miss."

Manny looked at Deshawn.
*I can only imagine, my friend.*

# CHAPTER TWELVE

Judge Burton was positioned atop her throne of justice in her black cloak, wielding her gavel like a magical scepter. She faced her courtroom of subjects with tight curls in her short hair and her bright pink, tightly pursed lips to match the recently tightened skin on her face. Manny wondered how old the old judge was really was. Appearance placed her in her late fifties, but documented service dates put her in her late seventies. Since Manny had known her, she hadn't changed. That is how he knew she had a highly skilled plastic surgeon on her payroll.

Manny was in the first row directly behind Raven Rivers and her court appointed lawyer, Attorney Andy Friedberg. Manny knew Freidburg. He was a run of the mill court appointed lawyer. He did the basic work that needed to be done and got paid by the state. His record was about "Even Steven". Manny knew he was going to plead insanity for Raven. Any lawyer in their right mind would do the same. Anyone who spent more than fifteen minutes speaking to Raven about her family could clearly tell she had a few screws loose.

Raven sat with her head down. Her face still brandished the bandages from her self-induced wounds. Her wrists and ankles were bound with shackles as a safety measure, although to look at her petite body in the oversized hospital scrubs, imposing was not the first word to come to mind. Andy Friedberg fidgeted next to her, his paperwork making a shuffling sound as he tapped his left foot on the floor to the beat of a song no one else could hear. The quiet in the courtroom around them resounded the noises of Andy Friedberg's restless footsie jitterbug.

*Bang! Bang! Bang!*

"Order in the court!" Judge Burton demanded.

Judge Burton's harsh voice echoed almost as loudly as her gavel in the vast room of empty chairs. The only bodies present for the preliminary hearings were the District Attorney Marty Ross, who was prosecuting the case, and his assistant, the defense attorney, (who was still squirming in his chair), Raven, the hospital psychiatrist, Manny, Alex and Deshawn. The quiet buzz of whispers between D.A. Ross and his assistant died down with a stern look from Queen Justice— her surgically enhanced face hushing the room to an uncomfortable silence. Even Manny felt a sense of tension under the glaring eye of Judge Burton— like the unease one feels while sitting outside of the Principal's office waiting to be called in, but not being quite sure for what. He felt a warm hand grasp his and squeeze gently. Manny looked over to see Alex looking at him, not Judge Burton. If Alex felt ill at ease, she didn't show it. Manny returned the tender squeeze and gave her a grateful smile.

Judge Burton began her opening statement to the barren courtroom. Manny watched as Raven made no indication that she was aware anyone was speaking. She sat like a statue, motionless. D.A. Ross began his opening statement to Judge Burton, presenting the charges the state was bringing against Raven along with the evidence it had to substantiate the allegations. Manny listened to D.A. Ross as he recounted the murders of Leo Stanton and William "Billy" Watson. Images of their bodies flashed through Manny's head as D.A. Ross spoke.

Judge Burton quietly listened.

After almost forty minutes of information, it was Attorney Friedberg's turn to speak. Manny watched as Friedberg stood, awkwardly, on pencil thin legs.

"Your honor, if it pleases the court, may I approach the bench?" Friedberg asked.

Judge Burton raised an eyebrow quizzically but nodded. Friedberg reminded Manny of a stork with his long, skinny legs, his round midsection, and the strange way he moved. A long, pointy nose, beak-like in appearance, served as a shelf for thick silver framed glasses, poised at the halfway mark. He was balding on the top of his head, but thick black curls encircled the rest of his head in a horseshoe shape. In an effort to hide his balding rooftop, he had grown out some of his hair and attempted a haphazard combover. This only managed to add to his already birdlike appearance, as it created a "plumage" effect atop his scalp.

Queen Justice and Birdman conversed for a moment, then Judge Burton raised her head and addressed her sparse courtroom of subjects.

"Attorney Friedberg has requested to meet in chambers to review some information with us, on record of course. He feels the information too traumatic to be discussed in front of the defendant at this time due to her delicate state of mind. I know this is not customary, but I will allow it as this is a preliminary hearing. I would ask only the defense, prosecution, and hospital psychiatrist be present. The rest of you will remain here with the bailiff until we return."

Judge Burton banged her gavel once, then stood decisively and turned, with a flourish of her black robe, towards her chambers. Manny looked at Alex and Deshawn to see if they were as confused as he was. Their wide eyes confirmed his assumption. They all watched as the requested bodies headed toward the judicial chambers. Manny glanced at Raven to see that she still had not moved. It was as if she was catatonic. He wondered if she was sedated still. The bailiff moved closer to Raven as the group headed toward Judge Burton's chambers.

Manny reached into his pocket and touched the velvet box, making sure it was still there. It was safe and sound. He had been keeping it on his person for the last four days, and when he couldn't physically keep it on his body, he had hidden it somewhere safe. He couldn't chance Alex finding it. The velvety texture soothed him momentarily. Manny struggled a bit to keep from smiling as he thought of the night ahead of him and the plans he had made. He glanced over to find Alex staring at him.

"Are you okay?" she whispered.

"Yes, why?" he whispered back.

"You have a funny look on your face." Alex's eyes moved over his face, analyzing him.

Manny checked himself before he answered.

*You better chill, hermano, before she thinks something is going on.*

"I'm fine, sweetie." he smiled, reassuringly.

Alex stared at him for a few more seconds then relaxed. She sat back against the wooden bench and let out a small sigh.

Manny was satisfied that Alex was pacified for the time being, so he turned his attention to Deshawn. Deshawn sat to the right of Alex on the bench, slumped down with his long legs stretched out in front of him, his head back, and his eyes closed.

*Man, he can make himself comfy anywhere. Not a care in the world.*

From behind them, Manny heard the creak of the large wooden courtroom doors. He turned to see who was entering as it was supposed to be a closed hearing. He recognized Officer Díaz right away and nodded as he approached them. Manny stood and walked towards Officer Díaz.

"Hey, Díaz, what's up?"

"Hi, Detective, sorry to bother you, but I was instructed to inform you right away." Díaz had the face of the bearer of bad news.

Manny stiffened preparing for hear what was written on Diaz's face.

"Go ahead." he ordered.

"CSI Dickerson requested you at the scene of a homicide." Diaz announced.

Manny sucked in a breath.

*Can't this damn town catch a break?*

"Any info with that request, Díaz?" Manny asked.

Díaz cringed a little, making Manny more intrigued and afraid of the answer all at once.

"I guess a body was found at a warehouse just over the line in Ashertown, and the vic is apparently completely burned almost beyond recognition." Díaz cringed.

It was Manny's turn to flinch a little.

"Okay, hang tight at the door." Manny instructed.

Díaz nodded and turned to walk toward the large oak doors

that Manny had dared to think, for the moment, kept them safe from the outside world.

*Apparently not,* Manny thought.

Manny walked back to Alex and Deshawn. They were both looking at him curiously.

*Alex must have roused the sleeping giant,* Manny thought.

He would have thought the image that ran through his mind of Alex as a female version of Jack, climbing her beanstalk into the clouds, to find a larger than life Deshawn snoring away on a massive sized wooden bench funny, had he not just been given the information from Díaz.

"What's the matter?" Alex asked.

"Um, I actually have some bad news."

"What's up, partner?" Deshawn asked.

"We've got ourselves another homicide."

Deshawn and Alex both looked at Manny as if he'd told them Christmas was cancelled— shock, surprise and frustration all fighting to fill the emotional spaces of their visages. Deshawn was the first to speak.

"Okay, buddy, what do we got?"

"The body is… completely scorched."

# CHAPTER THIRTEEN

MANNY AND DESHAWN SAT IN SILENCE on the way back to the precinct. The vibration of the Mustang was not the slightest bit soothing after what they had witnessed. In their combined years of service, Manny and Deshawn had each seen their fair share of burns, but neither had visualized anything like this. Deshawn had, for the first time ever, vomited at the crime scene. Normally, Manny would have made fun of him but he had barely been able to hold his own stomach bile in; opening his mouth to tease Deshawn would have been a mistake.

The air conditioner blew cold air on their sweat soaked skin, cooling them both. Manny was grateful for it. He was also glad that he had been able to convince Alex to stay at the courthouse to represent them while they went to the scene. There was no way she would have been able to tolerate the carnage that was now permanently embedded in each of their minds.

With anyone else, the long silence would be strained and uncomfortable, but not with Deshawn. Manny always felt at ease with him; they were too close as partners and friends to ever feel ill at ease with one another— even when the silence was heavy with the burdens of their jobs or private lives. Deshawn had his head laid back against the seat. He was looking out the passenger side window, but Manny would bet money Deshawn wasn't seeing anything they passed by.

"That was intense." Manny finally spoke.

"Hell, yeah, it was." Deshawn chimed in. "Never seen anything like it."

He sucked in a deep breath and pushed it out, wishing all the images of the scorched body would go with it.

Deshawn grunted and rubbed his temples.

"The smell. I don't think I will be able to get the smell out of my nostrils." Deshawn's voice held a tinge of dread. He sniffled as if to drive home his point.

"Yeah," Manny agreed. "It was like an acrid, burnt up barbecue, and I'm not trying to be funny either. That's what it smelled like. Like someone left the pork roast in way too long."

"Yup, that's about right."

Deshawn rubbed his temples again. Manny could tell he was stressed. Temple rubbing was Deshawn's tell, and at that moment, Deshawn couldn't bluff his way to a winning hand. Manny was glad they weren't in a poker game where their lives were at stake because they would definitely die. Manny turned the Mustang into the parking garage and found his usual spot. He threw it into park and killed the engine, then leaned back and blew out another long, exasperated breath. He reached into his pocket, found the velvety box and touched it for comfort. It was the only thing keeping his mind stable and calm the last few days.

"Well, let's head on in and start going through what little information we have. We can at least initiate our report while we are waiting for Leavy to complete the autopsy. I've got to make a call over to Trooper Cutty of the F&EIS Unit to see what kind of residue the canines picked up at the crime scene." Manny advised.

"I'm telling you one thing my friend," Deshawn warned "that is one autopsy you ain't dragging me to no matter what you say!"

"Ha!" Manny chortled.

"Oh yeah, you yuck it up all you want, but I am dead serious! I am not gonna see or smell that again. I'm gonna be lucky if I can sleep tonight. I'll tell you one more thing. Jim Beam and I are gonna have a little one-on-one time tonight before bed. Then after that, Muriel is just gonna have to have a little ménage à trois whether she wants to or not."

Manny burst out laughing and slapped the steering wheel.

"Well, my advice is be careful. She may wind up falling in love with Jim."

Deshawn glared at Manny, then they both roared.

Humor was their twisted way of dealing with the gore and violence of the job. For them, it worked, at least most of the time. Manny smacked Deshawn's leg.

"Let's go, D."

They both begrudgingly opened their doors and exited the car. The chirp of the car alarm reflected off the parking garage walls behind them as they walked towards the elevator.

Manny touched the small, black box in his pocket again. It was becoming a habit at this point. He wondered what he was going to do once it was no longer there for him to touch. He glanced at his watch, as the elevator groaned upwards toward the ground level, to see how much time he had before his dinner reservations.

*I still have two hours. Good, that's enough time.*

The ring of the elevator brought Manny out of his thoughts. Deshawn looked at him expectantly.

"What?" Manny asked.

"You gonna move, or do I have to move you?" Deshawn laughed.

"Shit, yeah. Sorry." Manny laughed.

Manny exited the elevator with Deshawn on his heels.

"You're nervous." Deshawn observed from behind him.

"Nah." Manny denied.

"Ha! Manny you are a horrible liar. Come on, man, it's me you're talking to." Deshawn guffawed.

Manny sighed. They walked towards the precinct's front entryway where, surprisingly, only a few civilians loitered around the desk.

"Yeah, I know, I know. Yeah, okay, I am a little nervous I guess." Manny admitted.

Officer Davis turned his head and locked eyes with Manny as they approached the desk. Davis nodded at Manny and then his face changed as if he remembered something important. He held up a hand to the other officer that was speaking to him, muttered something to her, then quickly walked towards Manny and Deshawn.

*Yup, he remembered something,* Manny thought.

"Detective Castillo, I'm glad you're here. I have been trying to get this to you since the other day, but I didn't want to leave it on your desk or just give it to anyone else. Remember I told you an envelope had been delivered here to you?" Davis said.

Manny searched his memory for the information Davis was spouting but could not recall what he was talking about. His confusion must have been visible on his face because Officer Davis looked slightly frustrated.

"I called you the other day to tell you a few things, and one of them was that a manila envelope with your name on it had been delivered here. It has been sitting on my desk since then. Would you like it now?" Davis asked.

"Oh yeah, shit! Sorry Davis, it has been a long few days. Crazy few days. Yeah, yeah, I remember now. Sure, hand it over. Thanks for keeping it for me." Manny said.

Officer Davis walked to his desk, grabbed the envelope sitting at the top left corner and brought it back to Manny. Davis handed it to him, for the first time ever, without a smile.

*Wow, all business,* Manny thought, surprised.

Manny felt bad for getting Davis miffed at him. He wasn't sure why Davis would be agitated, but it was obvious he was.

"Thanks, Davis." Manny nodded his appreciation.

"Sure thing, Detective." he replied, flatly.

Manny turned to Deshawn and nodded towards the stairs. They began climbing, what seemed an unusually daunting four flights together, avoiding the occasional descending body here and there.

"I have to call Alex as soon as we get into the office." Manny remembered as they were almost to their floor.

"Yeah, I know. I wonder what Judge Burton had to say."

"Yes, I am wondering the same thing."

The homicide unit was thrumming as usual. Uniforms and plain clothes alike moved about from desks, to computers, to phones.

"Home sweet home." Deshawn smiled at Manny.

Manny returned the favor. Manny's cell phone rang. He threw the envelope down on his desk and fumbled for the phone in his coat pocket, flipping it open on the third ring.

"Castillo."

"Manny." Alex called.

It was so good to hear her voice. Manny's body relaxed instantly.

"Mi amor. ¿Cómo estás? How are you, my love?" he asked.

"I'm okay. How are you, is the question?" She asked, urgency in her voice.

"I am fine, corazón."

"Tell me. Tell me about the body." Alex insisted.

"You first." Manny said. "Tell me what happened with Judge Burton and Raven."

He could feel the sigh come through the phone line. Alex's frustration at him for not sharing the information with her about the new victim right away was tangible, but he needed to know what happened at the courthouse first.

*Sometimes she can be so stubborn.! Mierda!*

"Friedberg entered an insanity plea and told Burton that Raven isn't fit for trial. He also apparently divulged her entire past history of trauma, including the information regarding the incest and pregnancy, as part of the defense. Judge Burton bought it. Apparently, D.A. Ross knew only about the past history. Looks like Friedberg will probably win this case."

"Well, rightly so." Manny sighed. "Let's face it, the poor girl truly is guilty by reason of insanity."

"I would agree with you. There was a motion filed against Jack Rivers by D.A. Ross and the court for chapter 272, section 17 and chapter 265, section 23. He is going away for the rest of his life, which won't be much longer, from the looks of him."

"Yeah, he didn't look too good, did he?" Manny said, solemnly.

"No, honey, he didn't. But I can't say I feel badly, if I'm being totally honest." Alex admitted.

"It's okay, Alex. I know how you feel."

He could hear the guilt in her voice. He knew it was painful for her to lose the sense of faith that everyone was good. It was the one thing she had truly believed in for so long.

"Is it?" she asked, her voice trembling with doubt.

"It is." Manny insisted. "It truly is. You are human, like the rest of us. Although, I will tell you, you are much better than the rest of us." Manny paused for a moment. "And Raven?"

"They are moving her to Buena Vista. Private room. Keeping her sedated for now. She will stay there until the baby is born at which point it will be put up for adoption. Judge Burton has ordered intensive therapy. A trial may be set once the baby is born, depending on the psychoanalysis written by Buena Vista. That is if Raven ever seems stable enough to even stand trial."

"Sounds like a plan."

"Now, your turn." Alex prodded.

*! La persistente! Always the persistent one,* Manny thought.

"Well, the body was just over the line in Ashertown in an old, abandoned warehouse. A small bomb was ignited. Trooper Cutty was there investigating with the Fire and Explosion Unit. They will have a report regarding what type of explosive was used shortly, I hope. Dickerson and Leavy say the vic has probably been there around a week or so. There was hardly anything left to it. I say "it" because we aren't completely sure of the sex yet, mostly everything was down to bone." Manny cringed, the memory and the smell so fresh not only in his mind but in his nostrils.

"Dios mío" Alex breathed into the phone.

"Yeah, I know. I feel like it's all I can smell. It's almost like…" Manny trailed off.

Silence smothered the conversation.

After a moment, Alex spoke.

"Manny?"

"Yes?" he hesitated.

"It's almost like what?" Alex nudged.

Saliva inundated Manny's mouth. He swallowed, closed his eyes and willed himself to finish his sentence.

"It's almost like... I can taste it."

# CHAPTER FOURTEEN

Alex held the phone to her ear, but her hand grew weak when Manny's voice came across the line. Like an incantation to invoke paralysis, his words turned her body into an immobile living carcass. Guilt for having stayed behind and knowing he would have to live this new nightmare alone tugged at her. But the relief of escaping it unscathed for the moment trumped the shame. She already suffered night terrors; she didn't need a new boogie man haunting her sleep.

*I am selfish.*

Suddenly, she felt worse.

"Oh, my love, I'm so sorry." she uttered.

"No, don't be. It is what it is. Part of the job, I guess. Right?" Manny said.

Alex could hear his feeble attempt to make light of the situation. She decided to let him have his way for now and let the subject go. She generally tried to get Manny to talk about things with her. He liked to keep things pent up and act like nothing was wrong, which went completely against everything Alex was ever taught in school. Manny would try to tell her kindly not to use her "psychological expertise" on him, but she couldn't help herself when she knew deep down it wasn't good for him to keep it all inside.

*Now only if I could practice what I preach.*

"... and then we can meet. Okay?" Manny was saying.

"Oh, honey, I'm sorry I got distracted. Can you please repeat that?" Alex apologized.

"Ha, it's okay." Manny chuckled. "I said I have a few things to wrap up here, but I should be done within the hour or so and then we can meet, okay?"

*Meet? What is he talking about?*

Alex wasn't sure if Manny was talking about meeting at home, or if she was missing something. The silence on the line must have clued him in that she had no idea what he was talking about.

"You forgot, didn't you?" he asked, unable to hide the hurt in his voice.

Now the guilt Alex felt earlier could not have been trumped by anything; it was the high card. She rapidly searched through the file folders in her mind but could not come up with an answer quickly enough.

*Don't bother, you know you can't bullshit a bullshitter. The truth is always the best option.*

"Yes, mi amor, I am so, so sorry. I did. I forgot." she admitted with some reluctance.

"It's okay. It has been quite a week."

"Yes, it has."

"Let me refresh your beautiful mind. I made dinner reservations for us at La Trattoria."

She could hear his tired smile. Alex smiled at his thoughtfulness. She knew Manny wasn't the biggest fan of the place, but he knew she loved it there. The familiar tingle she felt when Manny did something loving, or thoughtful, or sexy, covered her skin with goosebumps and filled her insides with warmth.

"Shit, I'm so sorry! How could I forget?" Alex exclaimed. "I cannot wait!"

Manny laughed.

Alex laughed.

"Well then, I guess I had better get my butt home to get cleaned up and presentable."

"Well, I would say you look great with what you have on, but I know you will argue with me. So, if you would like to get ready and change while I finish up here, then I will meet you at La Trattoria?"

"Okay, sounds like a plan to me."

"Perfect. I cannot wait to see you and, I'm not gonna lie, I am also a little excited to see a bottle of chianti."

"Now *that* sounds like an even *better* plan." Alex laughed.

Manny hung up the phone and looked at Deshawn. He was smiling; the devious grin of a child up to no good.

"What?" Manny asked.

"Are you excited yet?" Deshawn asked.

Manny looked at Deshawn and subconsciously put his hand in his pocket to check on the precious box, its delicate texture soft against his fingertips. He rubbed it gently for a moment as he contemplated Deshawn's question.

"Yes. I am excited and nervous." he admitted. "I'm glad I have an emergency change of clothes in the locker room, man. I can't imagine what these clothes might smell like because all I can smell in my nose is some shitty, burnt carne asada."

Manny twisted his face in disgust.

"Damn, you ain't jokin'." Deshawn nodded. "Don't be nervous, though. I have a good feeling everything is going to go smoothly." He smiled his brilliant, toothy grin.

Manny beamed. Deshawn's smile was contagious. It could not be warded off, fought off, nor denied. It had to be obeyed. It demanded a return smile, and it always got one. Manny laid his cell phone on the desk and noticed the envelope.

*Shit, I totally forgot about this damn thing already. I'm losing it.* The manila envelope was a standard nine by twelve, with no return address, no stamp or markings from the postal service, and no address underneath Manny's name. It only had "Attn: Detective Emmanuel Castillo" printed in small, black sharpie ink right in the middle of it. Manny didn't remember getting any calls from anyone regarding any information being sent over from somewhere, but that didn't mean much. He received a lot of correspondence at the precinct this way.

"What's in there?" Deshawn asked.

"No idea, actually." Manny laughed.

"Well, open 'er up so we can find out." Deshawn coaxed.

"Man, you are nosy." Manny shook his head.

"Um, yeah, why do you think I make such a great detective?" Deshawn laughed heartily.

Manny snorted.

The envelope was sealed shut. Manny grabbed his metal mail opener and stuck it between the small opening at the edge of the lip that held it shut. With one single movement, Manny ran the opener through the adhered paper, listening to the ripping sound it made as the thick paper yielded to the metal. When the opener reached the other corner of the envelope, the mouth gaped open sending a cascade of black and white photos upon Manny's desk.

"What the...?" Manny exclaimed, surprised at the pile of photos on the desktop.

Deshawn popped out of his chair like a Jack-in-the-Box at the end of its song, springing to life and scaring the shit out of Manny. He was at Manny's side before Manny could catch his breath and say anything else.

"What the...?" Deshawn parroted.

They both stared down at the photos sprawled out on Manny's desk. Some pictures were right side up, some upside down or sideways. Some of the pictures had fallen so only the backside was visible, blank white matte staring up at them. Yet what they could see was all recognizable.

"Holy shit!" Manny whispered, reaching down to spread the photos out to display them better.

There were over twenty or more pictures, all in black and white— pictures of Manny, Alex, and Deshawn. Some of the pictures had them together, some had them alone.

"These look like surveillance photos. All taken with a professional grade camera." Deshawn said "Like, by someone who knows what they are doing."

Deshawn flipped one of the photos over that had landed upside down and dropped it as if it had Ebola on it.

"What the fuck?" Manny exclaimed "How is this possible?"

The photo was of the burn victim they had seen not more than a few hours ago. Manny felt his stomach lurch. His mind raced. Cold sweat beads tickled his skin as they crept down his forehead. His heart was beating hard enough he could hear it in his head.

"This is fucking crazy!" Deshawn stared.

"You're telling me." Manny retorted.

"Someone has been following us, D. Following us and taking photos of us. And, I'm gonna go out on a limb here and state the obvious. Whoever did this is our unsub for our John Doe-Jane Doe."

Manny's voice was little more than a whisper. His body vibrated with anger and fear. He could hear Deshawn's breath, shallow and fast. Manny turned to look at him. Manny wasn't the only one sweating. Deshawn reached past him and flipped another photo over. Whatever Deshawn saw made him look like he had seen a ghost. Manny reached out to steady him, but without a word, Deshawn stumbled backwards, caught himself, then ran.

*What in God's name?*

Manny turned back to his desk to see if he could figure out what had triggered Deshawn to bolt from the unit without saying anything. It didn't take long. He locked eyes on a beautiful photo of Muriel, Justice and Reagan at the park playing and laughing; innocent and totally oblivious of their stalker. Manny's heart sank.

*Damn it, D. Hold on, I'm coming, buddy.*

# ABOUT THE AUTHOR

Author of recently released thriller, "Smothered", Jo Light is a California native transplanted to Massachusetts in her teenage years. She found solace in reading her favorite fiction authors including Stephen King and Dean Koontz. It soon became a passion and desire to write, which she dreamed of doing since high school.

However, Jo became a Registered Dental Hygienist (after serving in the Armed Forces) and a busy single mother of two children.

Finally, after many years, she was able to rekindle that passion to start writing again. Jo is currently working on the third book of this series which she hopes to release by the beginning of next year.